THE UNUSUAL POSSESSION
OF ALASTAIR STUBB

The unusual Possession *of* Alastair Stubb

DAVID JOHN GRIFFIN

Publications

urbanepublications.com

First published in Great Britain in 2015 by Urbane Publications Ltd
Suite 3, Brown Europe House, 33/34 Gleamingwood Drive,
Chatham, Kent ME5 8RZ
Copyright © David John Griffin, 2015

A CIP catalogue record for this book is available from the British Library.
ISBN 978-1-910692-34-9
EPUB 978-1-910692-35-6
MOBI 978-1-910692-37-0

Cover design by David John Griffin
Text design & typeset by Julie Martin

Printed and bound by CPI Group (UK) Ltd, Croydon, CR0 4YY

urbanepublications.com

FSC

The publisher supports the Forest Stewardship Council® (FSC®), the leading international forest-certification organisation.
This book is made from acid-free paper from an FSC®-certified provider. FSC is the only
forest-certification scheme supported by the leading environmental organisations, including Greenpeace.

To my wife Susan, my sister Maria,
and my friend Mike

Contents

1	RELEASE	1
2	THE MANOR HOUSE	9
3	THE POCKET WATCH	16
4	RAVISHMENT	23
5	CONFRONTATION	28
6	AN ARGUMENT	33
7	THE MEETING	38
8	DECISION	42
9	RAT POISON	52
10	THE NOTES	55
11	ARSENIC	59
12	THE PARTY	65
13	HYPNOSIS	72
14	THE PERPETRATION	76
15	A DEATH	85
16	THE DEAL	90
17	SPECTRE	96
18	THE MISSING BODY	106
19	THE ASTONISHMENT	114
20	FIRE	119
21	AFTERMATH	131

Thirteen Years Later

22	THIMRIDDY FAIR	137
23	THE QUESTION	143
24	A FIGHT	152
25	MR BADGER	159
26	SHOCKING NEWS	161
27	FOG	169
28	QUEENIE	173
29	THE BREAKDOWN	178
30	A DREAM	183
31	POSSESSION	188
32	THE NURSE	192
33	DEPARTURE	198
34	ABERGAIL	203
35	PUMP AND GRISTLE	205
36	THE CONFECTIONERY SHOP	209
37	THE CANAL	212
38	THE PISTOL	224
39	DISCOVERY	228
40	MOLESTATION	232
41	AN ARREST	239
42	INSECTS	248
43	THE BUTCHER	257
44	THE CHASE	269
45	THE CHURCH	273
46	CRYPTS	277
47	FINALE	283

CHAPTER 1

Release

Eleanor Stubb, trapped in a wakeful delirium and speaking strangely, had been taken to The Grinding Sanatorium for the Delusional. For Eleanor, the doctors and nurses were phantom jailers. Only insects inhabiting dark places were real, all other living creatures seen as dream imaginings, coloured shadows cast onto an equally shadowy world.

But after twelve months of confinement, there were less quizzical expressions and shaking heads from those who kept her under lock and key.

'I admit, no longer will I be known as The Queen nor talk with insects. The magnificent castle has vanished, along with my numerous servants,' Eleanor had said.

This had been a turning point, a change in her fortunes. By simply telling untruths, as she considered them to be, their interrogations lessened. Most of the vapour shadows became solid and real again. Sometimes even, the staff allowed the window shutters in her room to be closed during the day, for her to commune with candlelight in the mysterious darkness, to seek the hiding place of her beloved offspring Alastair. And when Eleanor had convinced the medical staff of her recovery they decided she could leave the musty sanatorium.

Today, a nurse had thrown back those wooden shutters from the room's bay windows. The bright morning sun danced within, highlighting irrelevance – the handle of her hairbrush was glinting, as well as the basin tap by the dressing table.

A breeze, drifting lightly through the open windows, brushed the warmth from her poised face. Eleanor was excited at the prospect of going home with her husband William; convinced she would find, at last, her dear son Alastair.

Her refined lips smiled back from an oval mirror. The straight, mahogany hair tied in a coiled bun, those wide eyes, a white-skinned face unblemished by makeup, and an attractive demeanour, all belonged to that young woman from the other side. Each time the visitor from the opposite dimension stood in a reflected replica of Eleanor's own surroundings, she tried to convince Eleanor they were the same woman. Yet the more this stranger pleasantly smiled from behind the mirror's smooth surface, the more Eleanor became perplexed. How could there be any connection with this unknown person; why should there be any true relationship with the duplicate's imitation realm?

Eleanor had often contemplated the elegance of this opposite. But when encouraged by the reflection to compare further she always turned away, often adjusting her double's bodice or sleeve by adjusting her own. She could never appreciate her beauty and sensual disposition, unknowingly sending waves of charm and enticement to men of all types. They desired her, easily captivated and tempted by her unwitting attraction.

She went to the foot of the bed and after touching the lid of her suitcase as though with affection, peered at the neatly trimmed lawns outside. A red admiral butterfly alighted on the windowsill. Eleanor nodded towards it, as if passing on some telepathic message, then shook her head knowingly. This particular messenger had appeared too quickly – it did not exist. There must be no communication with a mere mind fragment, she told herself.

"There is one success in being cured. But there is another

success in knowing you are cured, do you understand?"

She had understood, uplifted and refreshed, cleansed even, a whole person once more. Now her perceptions were correct. No longer did she need to build to see, or dissect to know. All just was, existing without internal aid. It was easy: the remaining vapour ghosts were disguised servants who simply needed to be told what they wanted to hear. She was Queen Eleanor of a lost domain in secret; and the darkness cloaked her child, wrapping her son Alastair in velvet protection, in preparation for reunion with him. If she tipped her head and listened intently, she heard insect preparers scuttling and tapping.

She awaited the arrival of her husband, eagerness tempered with patience – he had been due to arrive more than two hours ago.

William Stubb quickened his step with the gravel drive crackling beneath his boots. He waved away a bothersome fly skittering in front of him and looked up. The impressive sanatorium dominated ahead in the morning's pleasant sunshine. The building stood, resolutely solid, as if hewn from a single, huge mass of stone, as though concrete tentacles under it clutched the earth like tree roots would. Poplar and cypress grew to such heights that they peered over its roofs. Strange turrets and crooked chimneys broke the tile stretches there, with areas of brickwork beneath friable and decaying. Along the frontage stood tall fluted pillars and behind these were five doors, the largest one opening quickly. Four men, dressed in black, slid out. They moved carefully, each man bearing the corner of an oak coffin on his shoulder.

Wide steps curved up to the terrace; running the length of each side was a balustrade topping arabesque balusters. Conifers and exotic shrubs adorned each flank.

The pall-bearers came down the stone stairway with care, trying their best to avoid the sanatorium patients who were slumped on the bottom step. They manoeuvred their load towards a dark blue hearse sitting glumly to the side with its shafts attached to a snorting horse, the animal's bulky weight shifting on the gravel. The back of the hearse gaped open, ready to accept its mortal offering.

Though Stubb was a fair distance from the group, already he could read the words painted on the side of the vehicle, each letter larger than formality should allow: Nuckle's Funeral Parlour.

Some varieties of mind might have translated the morticians' activity as an omen, a message of portent even, but not William Stubb. His imagination had solidified years before and was incapable of buoyant meandering. Still he felt uneasy: he guessed that the very casket being loaded into the hearse was of his own making, maybe one of the last assemblages he had meticulously crafted. If he were to pull out the nails with pliers and lift the substantial lid – ignoring the rigid corpse within – tear the silk and padding around its sides, to leave the toffee-like bitumen to be scraped away, he might find his own monogram and a date carefully chiseled into the base of it.

How was he to explain to Eleanor that the mainstay of family life had begun to crumble shortly after her confinement? And now, upon her release, had finally disintegrated? His services were no longer required at Terps Joinery, Cabinetmakers to the Trade. All savings had gone. The house had been lost shortly after his redundancy, along with the major portion of his dignity.

An urgent voice snapped the quietness. 'Wait, wait, wait, wait, wait!' The white-haired Mr. Nuckle had trapped his fingers under the heavy coffin. 'Idiots – fools!' he cried out and then howled as he extricated the pulsing digits, tears forming behind his spectacles.

Stubb was nearing the commotion. 'Nuckle, want a hand?' he shouted over and gave a hollow laugh.

Mr. Nuckle strode around to the side of the carriage and gripped one of the brass lanterns mounted on its side.

'Do I know you? If not, you've no business with ours, so would advise you to walk away. Good day, sir.'

His fellow pall-bearers, nodding in agreement as though their heads were mounted on springs, muttered in stifled tones.

'You don't know me, but I know you,' said Stubb quietly.

A year before, Nuckle had found another supplier of caskets in the town of Smudge, forcing Stubb's village employer to sack many of his staff, William Stubb included.

'What did he say?' Mr. Nuckle asked one of his employees, who shrugged and was attentive to the casket in the back of the hearse. 'You said what?' he continued with a raised voice, massaging his bruised fingers. 'I recommend you keep opinions to yourself. We'll all be happy.'

The sturdy brown horse decided to shake its reins and the wooden wheels of the hearse creaked.

Stubb grimaced, and scratched one of his bushy sideburns. 'Go back to binding sheaves, you fraudster.'

Mr. Nuckle's white curls of hair wobbled as he shook his squarish head while holding an arm of his spectacles.

'What does he mean?' he said, his white eyebrows knitting.

His helpers pretended ignorance. Most of the villagers in Muchmarsh knew of the remarkable similarity of the funeral parlour owner with Mr. Badger, the farm hand, who worked for farmer Solomon.

Unsure as to the meaning of the insult, Mr. Nuckle bellowed back, 'I insist you go away or I shall be forced to … dump horse produce on your person, or some such.'

'Is that right?' Stubb replied, taking up an aggressive stance.

But then, slapping a palm through sultry air, he added, 'Forget it, I can't be bothered.'

As though by some divine link, with the switches of their brains tripping precisely at the same time, the two patients who lounged at the bottom of the worn steps began to rock from side to side with exaggerated movements. A third man, dressed in a white gown, ambling past aided by a nurse, shrugged off his helper. He proceeded to wave his spindly arms, counting beats with an invisible baton as if a conductor fronting an orchestra. He turned his attention to a hot air balloon floating above the virescent trees. The basket beneath the scarlet bulb held its traveller, seen as a spot of turquoise. With the gaping-mouthed patient diverted from his previous task of conducting an ensemble of two, the nurse took the opportunity to grasp his bony elbow. She led him away, the man's nose still aimed at the aerial globe.

Perhaps he had projected his entity, his affliction and personality to the passenger of that flying device and was, at that moment, peering down from amongst light cloud in a cyan sky to the grounds of the sanatorium. He would be seeing the noseless statues standing guard over the urns cupping their massed flowers, and the apple trees in blossom – white dots on the dominoes of grass; the artistic inmate – there to cure his obsession of carving statuettes from the chalk found in ditches – frantically scratching at the soil beside the west wall. The balloon passenger as patient would also be espying the hearse with its attendants, two figures sat nearby, with himself looking skyward. And another figure, marching briskly up to the crumbling stone steps before climbing the stairway that led to the sanatorium main entrance.

The ominous building swallowed Stubb, leaving those agitated convalescents and the gentlemen in black to swear and jostle.

After inquiring about his wife, Stubb was shown to a high-ceilinged corridor leading from the side of the grand hallway. Then to a room, plainly decorated except for a watercolour of Grinding Mills on one of its stippled walls. He sat on a plain chair with his gullet made of sand; he longed for a drink. A fresh and cold pint of Tanman's Quirly Ale would suffice...

He stood expectantly as a dull resonance reached his large ears. A figure, wearing a dressing gown and tapping an iron-tipped walking stick, shuffled past the doorway. The hobbling woman grinned foolishly to the wall coving above Stubb's head. 'Small town, nice place,' she bleated. Stubb ignored her, pursed his lips and sat again. If only the sanatorium staff would take him quickly to his wife, then he could leave this dismal abode with its strange echoes, and odours of urine and polish.

Stubb had much to tell Eleanor but when attempting to access the catalogue of the past year's events from his mind, he realized that much of what had happened had been swallowed, the memories somehow erased. All except one: he was prepared to admit that the house was no longer theirs, now belonging to strangers. That from today, Eleanor's new home would be his father's manor house in Muchmarsh. 'I'm going to find work again,' William Stubb needed to say. 'A fresh start for us as man and wife. Try for a family again.'

'Good morning,' said Eleanor, somewhat formally, as she stood by the framed watercolour, a white-coated doctor smiling behind her and a porter there also, holding her maroon suitcase. 'Have you brought Alastair with you; has he emerged from the darkness?'

Stubb gasped while the doctor looked surprised. All concerned believed Eleanor to be cured, finally released from her demons and delusions.

'Eleanor my love, you are free to go, today. We brought you

here to take away those wrong thoughts, remember? We've spoken about this: our son is buried in the family church crypt. It's a tragedy for us but we have no living child called Alastair.'

Eleanor forced an upturn to her appealing mouth and gently touched her brow.

'I know, I was only jesting,' she said.

CHAPTER 2

The Manor House

THEODORE STUBB DREW a final mouthful of smoke from his cigar and ground the remainder of it into an ashtray, his attention focused on a specimen in the ether bottle before him. He watched with fixed interest: the butterfly flickered and flashed in a dance of death, owning a grain of time before succumbing to the fumes. Clucking with delight, the collector picked up tweezers from amongst the paraphernalia of entomology scattered in a devious order on his workbench. He carefully extracted the insect from the bottle. Still the delicate thing waved its beautiful wings mimicking flight until a fine mounting pin, pushed through the creature's frail flesh, finally extinguished its last scrap of life. Who is to know whether or not that steel pin, thudding through its abdomen, produced a paroxysm of agony; a scream, instantaneous and fleeting, yet filled with so much terror as to raise the hairs on the back of one's neck? Theodore placed the impaled butterfly onto wet sand in the relaxing jar. His head bobbed in satisfaction. There, displayed on the bench in colourful extinction, was another new member to his extensive collection.

Not much sun intruded into the large and lofty attic of the manor house, though a block of light stood by the casement window at the far end, overlooking the garden. Theodore walked past the angled beams on a side of the attic to penetrate this brightness. He looked down through the window to the main lawn. Below, Brood the dour gardener was strolling across the turf from flowerbed to flowerbed, armed with a trowel and an insect spray. He was heading, past a distinctive statue, towards a lawnmower that stood by a gap in a flint stone wall. There may have been wrought iron gates there once; or a lichgate, now long gone, rotted to nothing.

The ancient wall divided the lawn from a small church hemmed with lopsided gravestones, those strangled by weeds. The Stubb family church, with a chapel and crypts within, had been abandoned many years before: the spire missing most of its terracotta tiles, stonework cracked and moss-covered, some of the arched windows boarded up, the oak door hanging open – held by a single iron hinge – graves untended. Eleanor appeared from the church entrance, carrying a hessian sack. Theodore set his attention, studying her form as intently as if she were one of his insects – his dark eyes made darker as his pupils dilated. The entomologist tore his sight away then, forcing his gaze to wander over the box hedges to the orchard and the vegetable allotments, then further still to the stiff stakes of a fence holding back the heath beyond. A spiky hedgerow striped it, where a cluster of beech trees stood as if a group of chatting people discussing the distant boulder-peaked hills wreathed in a morning mist.

The village of Muchmarsh snuggled in a valley. Orchards, fields, and tides of wheat lapped its perimeter. Untidy patches of forest and bush climbed the foothills around, an entourage hoping to reach the adjacent towns of Grinding or Smudge. Farmer Solomon's soil lay over to the left. On one of those fields beside a length of the disused canal, jump posts and marquees were being erected in preparation for the village's annual event. The early afternoon would see sorrel and skewbald mares, cattle and pet judging, races and shows, stalls and milling people, congregated there to celebrate Thimriddy Fair. Theodore cursed it as a waste of time and turned away from the attic window.

Presentation cases, as well as brass-handled drawer cabinets bought from a museum, stood in two regimental lines within the attic. They contained his private exhibition of thousands of insects, pinned and glued. Subtly tinted moths, arrays of butterfly varieties, armoured beetles the length of a finger to the size of small beads. Wasps, aphids, spiders and centipedes, flying creatures and crawling things all frozen in time – showing sapphire or mottled wings, mother-of-pearl shades, oranges, reds or yellows on their thoraxes and shells, speckled heads and iridescent eyes. Stored underneath the cases and on sturdy planks screwed onto the walls were flasks, bottles and flagons, filled with preserving fluids, animal specimens and other unknown organic forms floating within them. Theodore advanced along the sawdust-strewn aisle, touching the glass of the presentation cases. He liked to test with his finger for any dust on those protective panes.

Satisfied that all was as it should be, he returned to his oak bench. There he rubbed his palms together in readiness to prepare another insect despite his mind constantly preoccupied with thoughts concerning Eleanor. He must not allow his concentration to suffer by some unexplained obsession with his daughter-in-law, he considered. Even within his dreams he could never escape, her simple beauty magnified, her allure demanding. His lip twitched as it was prone to and upon touching his grey-flecked moustache, he reprimanded himself. It must be time to refuse the insects Eleanor brought him from out of the church; he must avoid her as much as possible, resist the temptation to spy on the bathroom from the door frame of the box room like some besotted schoolboy. The strong attraction to his son's wife must be halted somehow. Yet the more he dwelled on the problem, the more he lapsed into fictional romantic episodes. 'Get on with it,' he muttered irritably, then after raising the wick of a lamp, gently tipped a dead insect specimen onto blotting paper.

'Brood, have you another real spade? I seem to have misplaced the other one. My maid seems unavailable. I am also in need of more oil lamps. And do order extra boxes of candles from the candlemaker.'

After she spoke, Eleanor's pert chin rose by half an inch, and despite her face, overalls and overskirt smeared with grime and dust, she tipped her scarfed head to the side in an elegant fashion. She held a hessian sack and she placed it against the flint wall.

Brood was standing with his back to miniature rambling roses winding their thorny way over a potting shed. 'Don't know anything about your maids, miss,' the gardener replied, snuffling like a badger. 'Know for certain Mr. Theodore's maid won't be finding no spade or lamps neither. Why you're not stopped from spending allowances on so many candles, I don't have any clue. Boxes of 'em every week. No church needs that many, falling to bits or not.'

'You are, no doubt, playing games with me.' Eleanor held the knot of her scarf.

'I'll play any game you want.' Brood rubbed his stubbled cheek and with a tongue coated in spittle licking the sides of his coarse lips, his grip tightened on the handle of the trowel.

Eleanor quickly drew in breath, her mouth dropping open. 'How dare you be so … that's no way to talk with a queen; I must go now.'

Brood snorted. 'Wha'd you do in there every day? What's the point? Clearing some God house no one's bothered about. Last used by Mr. Theodore's grandfather and he won't be coming back in a hurry.' Eleanor was already walking over the bright lawn towards the back of the manor house. She must not explain to any smoke-spirited servant concerning her preparation for dear Alastair's return. 'Need help with your wash, you?' Brood called over.

Eleanor's steps had taken her to the carved base of the statue, a winged angelic messenger released from its block of white marble, standing with authority on the perimeter of the lawn and casting a sharp shadow. The renegade spirit which had been within Theodore's father had prompted Sir Bertrand Stubb to reposition the sculpted form – or rather have four workers move it inch by inch on metal rollers – from out of the church graveyard to where it now stood. Eleanor looked up to the androgynous, benign face of the angel, itself gazing at an orb ringed with laurel leaves in its ivory hands. And she whispered to it the promise to her son, 'For my dear Alastair, touching gentle flame to candle wicks, to light your way through the comforting shadows. You need not be afraid, I am waiting.' It could be harmful to talk more; only beetles and spiders, carefully swept from the crypt corridors, knew her secrets. Those others that had ceased to move – which had passed on the mission to their living brethren – could be preserved for ever in the manor house attic.

Eleanor gave a cursory glance to the back of the dark-bricked manor house, its many leaded windows decorated with carved granite, and unusual wooden relief panels lining the eaves. A slab of shadow cast from the house had fallen onto the blue slate tiles of the patio. Two ornate planters stood either side, containing a dazzle of flowered shrubs. And as she moved between them, into the shadow, over to a rose bush tethered to the trellis next to the kitchen back door, one of her phantoms walked out. To solidify the imagination, she need only name it. 'Florence; yes, Florence you are.'

'That's my name, madam.' The sketch of the maid became three-dimensional, even with a glint of the sun in her eyes as she left the shadowed area behind and moved onto the lawn. 'Can I help you?'

Of course you can, of course you must, was the thought snapping into Eleanor's mind. 'Run me a bath. I need to redecorate myself.'

Florence smoothed her white apron. 'Redecorate your ... I'm sorry madam but duties don't include running baths. I'll tidy your room if you want. Bring you a beverage; the cook's iced lemonade? Tea?'

'A lemonade. Then you must run the bath, not too hot, not too cool either. I will check, you know.' Eleanor began to remove her headscarf.

Florence sighed. 'I'll do it this once, then no more.'

'What is it with you strange servants and baths? Even my butler won't turn a couple of taps. Most discourteous and improper. I should report this to William.'

Florence ignored the idle threat, knowing it was Theodore's house and Pump the butler was employed by Theodore, not Eleanor's husband. 'As you wish, madam,' the maid replied. 'And as for Pump,' she continued, adding, 'Theodore's butler' with a firm voice, 'that's not his duty either. Anyway, he's afraid of water.'

'I've never heard of anything so ridiculous,' Eleanor replied. 'How does he wash? What's the matter with the little ghost?'

'A phobia, Dr. Snippet calls it. Had it ever since his father drowned. Water has to be in a shallow, coloured bowl, and he mustn't look. I really shouldn't have told you, madam. Me and my big mouth. I'm saying no more. I'll get your iced lemonade now.'

Eleanor lowered her voice. 'And if you find more clues to

Alastair's whereabouts, bring them to me, straight away.'

The maid, unable to stop a thought from being spoken, knowing of Eleanor's refusal to accept her loss, blurted, 'You hurt inside, don't you?' She inclined her bonneted head, her mind turning to her own estranged child, sadness sweeping through her like a cold wind.

'I don't know what you are talking about,' was Eleanor's abrupt answer.

Florence hurried away to avoid speaking further.

On impulse, Eleanor went over to the dried snail shells noticed the day before, hidden behind a row of plant troughs. Snail trails had made random patterns of silver swirls and zigzags on the patio slabs. Eleanor could see an important message, the dried slime glistening, appearing to be four traced letters of the alphabet. She spoke the word loudly with hope in her voice, confirmation in her heart: 'Soon.'

CHAPTER 3

The Pocket Watch

THEODORE LOOKED BRIEFLY to the mass of books lining a loft wall (jammed onto shelves made from rough and burled hunks of timber) and to the untidy piles of newspapers, sacking and specialist journals on the sawdusted floorboards. Half an hour had fled since he had looked through the gabled window – he decided to finish for today. The fact that it was time for Eleanor to enjoy her bath after poking around in the church ruin was neither here nor there, he insisted to himself. Upon leaving the insect-crammed space, he trod down the spiral staircase. On the walls of the descent hung more insects mounted in glass-fronted boxes, showing beetles, grizzled skippers and painted ladies, grasshoppers and wasps.

Pump the butler stood swaying gently with glazed eyes on the first floor landing, a foot idly shuffling back and forth over the burgundy carpet. The small man was dressed in a dusty black suit with a crooked starched shirt collar poking from it about his scrawny neck. He clasped a silver tray and upon that stood a cut glass decanter wrapped in a sheet of newspaper and a tumbler. Theodore groaned in annoyance. It was obvious that the fellow had spent his morning drinking again in the cellar. It had almost become accepted that the butler lived there amongst the cobwebbed wine collection, although on the strict provision that no bottles were touched.

'Your port, sir,' Pump announced in a slurred and quivering voice.

His master pushed him aside and retorted sourly that the fool should get about his business.

Theodore reached the top of the stairs, his lip twitching involuntarily. He paused to listen to the humming of a melody mingling with the sounds of splashing water, coming from the bathroom further along the wide corridor, and then afforded a smile to himself only. But catching sight of the butler staggering behind, whose thin top lip had also twitched as though in emulation, he growled and began the descent of the main staircase. The butler shadowed him like some faithful mongrel. The employee was oblivious to demands that he should go. Theodore drew a sharp breath for a final vocal attack whereupon the butler departed of his own accord, muttering and stopping to regain his balance by clutching the banister rail, all the while the hand gripping the silver tray bouncing as if it had a mind of its own. He reached ground level and disappeared down the cellar steps found via the panelled door under the stairs.

Theodore stood before the large carved stag beetle that acted as the wooden finial to the staircase newel post. It was a remarkably detailed piece of sculpture, created by his son William in a rare creative fugue while an apprentice at Terps Joinery. It was as if Theodore wished for some signal from it, an indication of his next course of action but with the tip of the left antler pointing towards the top of the stairs with the right tip opposing this, there was no decided choice presented. He tore his head away and walked past the grandfather clock and the drawing room doors, before turning into the reception room. There he gave a hasty glance to the mantelpiece clock before entering his study.

The study was a place of retreat – a book-insulated cocoon – to muse, or smoke and read. Two small circular windows high in one wall let in ungenerous light. A brass lamp lit by Florence an hour before stood on a mahogany side table; Theodore turned a milled wheel on it to make its flame higher. Then he took a briar from a rack hung above the bureau but promptly returned it to its notch: he rarely pipe smoked, and had changed his mind. And after taking hold of the creases of his flannel trousers, he sank into a leather armchair. Brass studs along its edge were cold on the backs of his legs.

The Theory and Practice of Medical Hypnosis lay on a side table. Although his sight had rested upon a brass container in the shape of a housefly beside the heavy volume, Theodore's vision clouded. Thoughts of Eleanor had unexpectedly taken hold again. Despite knowing that these particular ruminations bubbling to the surface of his consciousness – seemingly of their own accord – were irreverent and breezy, he encouraged their birth, making an effort to visualize them, to give them mental form. As from a seed bindweed germinates and grows, so his provocative thoughts over the last few months had been evolving into convoluted, shameful strands of lust.

Saliva thickened on his palate and his throat burned spontaneously with a flush. The reflections of a mature man should not develop into contemplations of adultery or sexual immoralities and yet incubated fancies, deep within, had grown to encompass such ideas. Was he not owed some recompense from his lodgers? Had he not fed and kept William and Eleanor for two months without mention of payment or consideration; given them pocket money and the run of the house? He believed that he was a fair man. Actions he wished to be fulfilled, he instructed himself, were legitimate and just. Eleanor would come round to welcoming his views, his advances, his gentle touch.

In the drawer of the side table was a mirror that Theodore used when trimming his moustache. He brought it out to inspect his reflection upon its uniform surface. There: he was still attractive, if not handsome; the impairment of a scar on his jaw, and a little overweight perhaps, but then Florence had never commented on these trivial matters – not that she would be aware enough to do so. The power of the mind, he thought, the power of the body…

The wings of the brass housefly were hinged. Inside lay a pocket watch covered with a silk handkerchief. The unusual object was his most prized possession; it was no less than an extension of himself, amplifying his powerful control and guidance of those weaker minds as he saw them, a potent reminder of his strength of mind and keen intelligence. If there was a choice required to be made between the pocket watch and his considerable collection of insects, the handmade marvel would be the one he would choose.

He opened the brass container and upon placing the handkerchief on his right knee, picked up the watch by its gold chain to inspect its front cover carefully, as if seeing the object for the first time. The intricate engraving on the cover was extraordinarily detailed, an apparent random and anonymous pattern containing swirls, leaf-shapes and meandering lines. But the closer it was held in front of the eyes, more details showed themselves within its minute chisellings and artistic scratches. Like ancient faces seen in rocks and tree trunks and leaf masses, so images came and went, forming and reforming, the longer it was gazed upon. Theodore held it a matter of inches from his brow, studying the masterpiece. And every time this happened, his mind would become faceted, with the incredible ability to think and analyse more than one subject at a time lit within his skull. Not only the concentrated analysis of the pocket watch cover, as well as a replay of past conversations with the beguiling Eleanor, but always the vivid memory of when he had purchased the watch twenty years before, in an antique shop in Grinding, all played in a different part of his grey matter. It was there in the cluttered shop, amongst the desirable items and pieces, he had been instructed by the fusty shop owner as to how he must inspect the skeleton watch face hidden beneath the fascinating cover. Had Theodore not prescribed to the procedure, he would have been refused the opportunity to buy the watch.

'Unfold the handkerchief and place it on your head; yes, as if you were protecting yourself from the sun. This must be done whilst you are comfortably seated, with no sharp objects about your person. Once you have had your fill of the exquisite engraving upon the watch flap, you must place a hand – like so – upon your forehead, ensuring the silk creates a lining between the skin of your skull and your palm – yes, this is necessary, believe me. Do you always wear your wig, may I ask?'

Theodore had been confused as to the sudden change in the man's instructions those twenty years ago. Then touching the judge's wig upon his own head, warming his ears, he had understood. With a desire to visit the shops in Grinding whilst taking a break from his dress rehearsal of Mrs. Walkbone and the Case of the Battered Punch Bowl at The Old Burly Theatre, he had forgotten to remove the formidable headpiece. At least he had remembered to wipe away the greasepaint. 'No,' had been Theodore's simple answer.

An unusual occurrence had distracted Theodore and the shop owner; they heard cheering and handclapping emanating from outside. They both looked through the shop window: a brass band had started its pompous tune, the members of it marching in consort down the middle of the gaslight-lined street. At their tail, a besuited gentleman had followed, a disdainful seriousness about him, necessary for his important task of waving a red flag in time with the music. Behind, with the occasional discordant tooted note from its horn, a metal construction similar to a carriage moved of its own accord, a man inside holding a circular object.

'What in the blazes name is that?' Theodore had said, consternation in his voice.

'That sir, is the newest invention being paraded. They call it a horseless carriage. No horses, yet it runs by horse power. Quite the conundrum.'

'Whatever next,' Theodore had replied. Returning his attention to the proprietor, he had asked if he would continue, whereupon the man did without hesitation.

'Prepare to be dazzled and amazed while you gaze upon the inner workings shown in this masterpiece; so much so that you will be mesmerized by the layers of exquisite clockwork and fine jewels set within.

Inevitably you will relax into this concentrated affair, whereupon your hand will begin to slip down, bringing the silk handkerchief with it, so that it may cover your sight, enough to sever the almost mystical attachment which you will have made. Five of your nicest silver coins please.'

Theodore's present moment returned, despite being enthralled still by the watch cover – the study and the books, the table beside, a feeling of the wing back chair about him. Today would not be the day for self-hypnotism. The watch as a scientific instrument needed to be utilized for a task far more important and useful, he rationalized. He quickly placed the almost paranormal timepiece into his waistcoat pocket, not bothering to button hole the chain.

He returned to the reception room and went to the door, opening it carefully as if it was a delicate thing, and stealthily moved his head into the lobby like some reticent animal, his dark eyes flicking. Satisfied that Pump was out of the way he crept out but froze as the noise of thumping wood kept tally with the beats of his heart. He remembered that he had instructed Brood to knock posts into the ground at the side of the manor house. The staccato ticking of the hallway grandfather clock seemed louder than usual as he listened for a time before walking stiffly to the stairs. He trod up the wooden steps of the creaking staircase as lightly as he was able.

The landing held the reverberant strains of Eleanor singing from the bathroom. As neat as a toothbrush Theodore's moustache was, and he stroked one side of it before going – without hesitation or indecision of any kind – to the bathroom door.

Pump wobbled into the hall from the cellar doorway with a grin and a pat on the bottom of the bottle he held. He slapped his numb feet onto the floor with a drunken discrimination. His game was to avoid the cracks between the striated marble tiles. Tiring of this, and without quite realizing where his own feet were taking him, he began to climb the hazy, undulating mountain of stairs in the invisible wake of his surly master.

CHAPTER 4
Ravishment

WILLIAM STUBB PULLED shut the door to The Bulldog Fish Tavern bar. After casting an eye across the village green, he began the walk home. The side of the public house with its mottled brickwork, and benches chained like dogs to its base, lived in Daisytrail Lane. As Stubb strode along the lane on his way back to the manor house, he looked up to the afternoon sky. It had collected a few infant clouds but still the day was warm. Cheering and whistling over the way – Stubb nodded as though to a companion – he felt in a fine enough mood; he would go to Thimriddy Fair.

He turned smartly on his heels and walked over the cobblestones that were beside the village green shops, and across the green, until he reached the alley. This would lead him to the field where the fruit and vegetables of the villagers, as well as the competition for the highest and most radiant sunflower, were under scrutiny from the judges.

⁂

Eleanor had stepped from the bath, streams of water running the length of her naked body, and had begun to dry herself with a towel, when a draught nipped her skin into pimples: the bathroom door was slowly opening.

Florence had begun wiping a duster over the furniture in the day-room when she paused; a shriek from some other dusty room had caught her attention but, upon continuing her work, she shook her head knowingly. Theodore might be calling her again.

She would often play his silly pastime – pretend to sleep before the swinging watch; overcome boredom at his mumblings and queer exhortations; prepare for the puzzling loss of time. Five minutes always becoming half an hour or more, and she would be left with indistinct memories of labyrinthine layers of embroidered metal. But all of it was worth the trouble for the sake of the money she would receive. Soon Florence would have enough saved for the deposit on a shop and could regain care of her miraculously-born daughter – whom others called illegitimate – who lived with her widowed aunt in Stillstone.

The wrangling in Florence's innocent mind as to how a young and virgin spinster such as herself could have conceived a child, was always ready to take over her thoughts after Theodore's music hall entertainment.

She decided it was not the master of the house calling though, or anyone else. More than once she had imagined voices in the manor house or heard her name spoken as if from afar by a gentle ghost.

Brood had finished twining wire around posts to form a fence when, upon rubbing his stiff back to a standing position, fancied he heard a shout. Scanning the first floor windows for a clue to its origin, he saw nothing out of the ordinary.

Thoughts concerning the utterance were dismissed immediately at the sight of the abundant growths of mottled ivy clinging to the red bricks of a side wall, even strangling a nest of chimney-pots huddled on the pantiles of the manor house. The ivy trails twirled and twisted, some of the leaves larger than a man's hand. It was time to cut the trailing tendrils back but he would wait until he was asked.

He retrieved a few garden tools and sauntered across the lawn to a corner of the garden, over to his shed almost hidden by enormous lilac bushes. To one side stood a roughly constructed rabbit hutch, the cook's white-haired pet inside, perfectly still except for its twitching pink-rimmed nose. Mrs. Wickling supplemented the gardener's food rations with sweets and cakes and, in return, Brood kept the straw clean and fed the animal with dandelion, mallow and clover.

As he neared the shed door his pace quickened for, like a wasp attracted to sugar water, he remembered he had saved the last food item Mrs. Wickling had given him as a treat. He was still pondering on whether to eat his iced cake or to leave the pleasure until the next day. Ducking his head to avoid hitting it on the lintel, he entered the wooden shed. He went straight over to the pastry, lying on a mucky shelf between a tin of cuttings compound and a small bag of fertilizer. Filaments of cirrus passed over the sun briefly, a chaffinch fluttered from the lilac bush and Brood, with his tongue to his lip, made his decision: snatching the cake from the shelf he put it to his nose to sniff its fragrance. Then each bite was taken with urgency, the cake soon devoured with a snuffling passion. He licked his grubby fingers and sucked the icing from the gaps in his teeth, staring without thought at the shed interior.

A wood burning stove sat to one side with a spade and a broom leaning against it. A small window was made smaller still by a calendar, four years old, curled and yellowing at the edges, covering half of it. Brood's bedding, which lined a quarter of the floor area, lay dishevelled and musty. An attempt at wallpapering the dingy wooden slats of the shed sides (with offcuts pilfered from the summerhouse) had failed shortly after the exercise; the majority of the paper had peeled away and lay in soggy piles around the perimeter.

The gardener was musing on the idea of brewing some tea, to be made on a small table scattered with sugar grains and tea leaves, when he sprang into life from his lethargy. In one swift movement he had taken hold of the spade, swung it as high as the shed ceiling would allow, and brought it down onto a rat, cleaning its whiskers by the stove. The floorboards shook and bottles rattled, and Brood condemned the existence of the creatures. He left the spade on the filthy floor. He would clean up the mess later.

❧

Evening was preparing to be staged. William Stubb arrived home with a vase and a tortoiseshell shoehorn held to his chest. In the hallway, he called out for his wife. There was no reply. He found the cook in the scullery, peeling potatoes by the iron sink. She passed a few friendly remarks before apologizing for her lateness. 'Got the vegetables from Tablet the grocer in Snoringham this time. The stagecoach needs a good talking to,' Mrs. Wickling said stiffly.

Ignoring the comment, Stubb said, 'Have you seen Eleanor?' The cook's only reply was a search for nude potatoes in the muddy water.

Stubb met the butler by the hallway mirror. Pump was sullen with his blob of a nose red; it burned from the day's drinking. He seemed unusually sober. 'If it wasn't trouble sir, I would like to have a word,' he said.

'Later, Pump. I want to find Mrs. Stubb.'

'It concerns your wife, sir,' the butler replied, and he looked furtively about him as if worried he was being overheard.

Neither of them spoke again until they were in the sitting room. The curtains were drawn for the afternoon sun had been hot. 'Well – I haven't got all week,' Stubb started.

Pump sat without permission but before Stubb could remark on it, the butler quietly spoke the words, 'For what I've got to say, sir, I think you'd better sit as well.'

The sitting room door opened with a rattle of the handle and Theodore bustled in. He nodded to his son but, upon seeing the butler who had jumped to his feet, exclaimed, 'What, you here? Get out.'

Stubb indicated with his hand for Pump to remain. 'I'm talking to him, father.'

'No,' bellowed Theodore, but continued in softer tones, 'I mean to say, Pump can gossip in his own silly time. I don't pay him to chat and sit in my chairs.' He glared at the servant who lowered his head.

Stubb tutted at the obstinacy of his father and asked him: 'Have you seen Eleanor?'

Staring malevolently at Pump, Theodore's florid complexion became redder still and with his mouth quivering, he swung around and hurriedly went out, the door closing behind him with a sound as though from a shotgun.

Stubb muttered, 'What's upset him this time?' and he continued with Pump, 'where is she; where's my wife?'

The butler pointed his florid nose to his creaking shoes. 'She's safe, sir; upstairs.'

Stubb became annoyed. 'Safe? What the hell is this all about?'

CHAPTER 5

Confrontation

TUBB NIPPED THE legs from a furred spider, one by one. With each fine, tiny limb flicked away, his clenched teeth tightened. The sounds of summer took second place to his senses; his whole being was focused on the task of destroying the arachnid between his fingers. He ground the remainder of the creature into the lawn with his heel and with the displacement of hatred finished, he fell back onto a white garden seat.

Nature slowly pulled the mist from his haunted eyes. The tang of newly-mown grass and the chatter of squabbling sparrows on the sundial temporarily soothed his ruptured emotions.

A bumblebee scored the air; Stubb stiffened his back. Childhood skipped from the lavender, hollered from the weathervane on the summerhouse: the pleasure he had received from killing the very things his father loved. Cabbage whites deprived of their powdery wings and the sound like crunching gravel when woodlice were crushed beneath a tablespoon. The spiteful wonder at earthworms, squirming and wriggling, attempting to untie the knots made in their slippery brown lengths.

It was a beautiful day with colours vibrant and rich. April showers had gone, leaving behind the deep hue of the sky to compete with its own reflection in the pond, where fantailed goldfish nuzzled in between the fronds of water grasses and bulrushes.

'*Tinn–saaal!*' – the call, then a yapping from the sunny heath way beyond.

Stubb sat with drooping eyelids, and palms pressed to his ears. He was unsure as to the course of action he should take. The situation seemed too complex to consider.

A decision: there was no alternative but for him and Eleanor to leave Muchmarsh, go anywhere to escape from Theodore. They could settle in Grinding, or even a town in another county. Surely the skills of carpentry were needed everywhere. It would not take long to awaken his hibernating talents. He was a perfectionist; he loved his craft, adoring every aspect of those coffins he made – the colour and grain of the timber, its tactile quality after being meticulously planed and prepared to a silk finish; the smell of the wood. His dovetails and joints had been beyond compare. Skills of other craftsmen would add more beauty to his works – the engraved filigree lettering on the nameplate, brass hinges set flush, ornate handles in the shapes of stags, galleons, or garlands. Often he had tended them up to the last moment, a coffin slid from under the beeswaxed cloth, leaving his revolving hand polishing no more than the air. Mr. Terps would have his caskets loaded without ceremony, stacked as high as the warped cartwheels would allow without buckling further, cover them with a chequered cloth, and transport them to Mr. Nuckle, or The Smudge Cremation Co-operative five miles north.

Stubb would sometimes mourn their departure and be gripped with resentment, complain bitterly about the insects, those creeping things, boring and chewing, spoiling his creations underground.

Through all of his reverie he had a nagging bundle of conjecture within. He was restless and a promise of a headache crossed his forehead. The sun was a hot compress on his scalp; he decided to go into the house but changed his mind as the portly man with a smirk smearing his face strolled across the lawn towards him. He willed the figure to return but his father advanced without pause.

Stubb shot from his chair with the intention of making a quick departure but Theodore, his voice flat in the heat, called over to him. 'Stay there, my boy, I'll have a chat.'

Contempt blemished each word Stubb spoke in return: 'I have nothing to say. Leave me alone.'

His father reached the wrought iron table and while mopping his temples with a striped handkerchief, sat on the chair that Stubb had vacated. 'Come now, William. Why don't you stop posing like a tailor's dummy and sit down,' he suggested. 'I'm sure we can come to terms with this little ... difference of opinion.'

Stubb ignored the advice and leant his weight on the table, gripping the edge of it. His lip trembled with his vehement reply. 'Difference of opinion?' he spluttered, 'You call abusing my wife a difference of opinion?'

Theodore motioned him to lower his voice and said, 'You have the matter confused and exaggerated. I have told you as best I can how this silly situation has arisen.'

'You've told me nothing.'

'My boy, I am afraid that young Eleanor has blown up this whole episode beyond belief; and as for Pump, why the little termite should stain my character with such incrimination I have no idea. Though we must remember, his faculties are shot; Eleanor's mental condition is still fragile. If your mother was still alive—' with this he clasped his hands as though in an act of devotion, '—she would rightly condemn you all for being distrustful and ungrateful. I have given you the freedom of the house, fed and cared for you; treated Eleanor as my own. And how am I repaid? False accusations, lies and smutty rumours.' He intimated a smile, and with deliberation extracted a cigar from the top pocket of his jacket and ran it between the tips of two fingers. Waiting for a reaction to his words he regarded his son from the corners of his eyes.

Stubb was staring hard at the ground. His father had, once again, destroyed the brittle structure of truth that had been constructed. Now all that remained was a mound of jagged possibilities, disjointed and uncomfortable, but then the words of the butler came to mind once more. He formed a sneer. 'You disgust me. If you weren't my father—'

Theodore snorted. 'You would kill me perhaps? Come now, boy, you're becoming quite melodramatic. Ah, Florence.'

The maid was tiptoeing across the lawn as though afraid she might damage the blades of grass. 'Your tea, sir,' she said politely, and placed a wooden tray in the middle of the table.

'Come closer, my dear – can't be afraid of uncle now, can we?' Theodore said, brushing his moustache with a finger. Stubb's head trembled. Everything seemed unwholesome today.

Florence stood next to Theodore. He rose and with clumsy fingers squeezing her hand, inclined his head to her bonnet and whispered. The maid gasped and from cheekbones to chin, she was suffused with pink. 'Off you go then,' Theodore called after her as she hurried away to the manor house. 'Don't forget now, will you?' Florence turned her face back to him with a look of confusion but gave no reply.

'Filthy swine,' said Stubb.

'You take life too seriously,' his father answered. He lit his cigar and paused to gaze at the coils of blueish smoke drifting lazily from its tip. 'William, my boy,' he said finally, 'love and life both take understanding. I have tried to make you realize this, but still you fail to grasp the concept. Do you see what I am trying to say? When your dear mother was alive...'

'I've had enough,' cried Stubb and he took a step away.

'Let me finish,' his father demanded. He stalled to draw on his unpleasantly large cigar.

How Stubb abhorred his father's monologues. His younger days were littered with such verbose renditions. He paced away from him across the sun-bathed lawn.

From the patio, he strode into the house via the French windows, through and out of the sitting room, into the lobby then on his way to the hall. A demanding pressure in his skull: he must search out the truth for once and for all.

CHAPTER 6

An Argument

STUBB LEAPT UP the stairs, taking them in twos.

'Eleanor!' he bellowed.

From the landing he stormed along the corridor, rattling past the bathroom and servants' rooms. Dusty and cobwebbed portraits hung on the walls in gilt frames. The pale, washed-out faces of his ancestors loomed large with animated eyes.

He flung open his bedroom door to find an empty bed. Back to the bathroom he went, and peered in. The smell of soap and condensation filtered into the corridor. He glared at the cool and white interior. Striding back across the landing he reached the spiral staircase and hurried to the top as fast as he was able, and stood before the heavy door of the attic. It was slightly ajar; he pushed it open.

A stale smell hung about, the same odour that had lingered for as long as he could remember. The same antique books lined the wall to the right, with the same dust of decades past; the same fireplace which had never tasted coal between the sloped rafters to the left side. The same clumpy workbench; the same rows of presentation cases and drawer chests running the length of the room, the only articles, in the dreary place, which received attention. The same insects, an abundance of entomological possibilities preserved, protected under glass; and Eleanor.

She was there at the casement window, her back to her husband, her palms flat on the windowpanes. By sliding one hand down, she let Stubb see a tiny scarlet balloon hanging in the sky; it would have him believe it still sailed its seas of air, tossed by an ocean of time and was visiting this present future from its passage over the sanatorium two months ago.

In the funereal silence of the attic, Eleanor could be heard to breathe deeply. Stubb's fraught emotions were caught unprepared: he felt compelled to run over and embrace her, sprinkle her graceful neck with kisses, stroke her hair. Snapshot memories moved dizzily before him – Eleanor laughing with happiness; picking an apple from a tree in Scripping's field; pretending to sleep, her simple beauty magnified.

Then Eleanor just a hollow effigy, standing in a foul-smelling room crammed with inanimate creatures which seemed to be waiting for a click of a finger, a signal for them to jump, slither and fly from their cases. The place was making Stubb uneasy. He was about to call his wife when, as if by intuition, she turned from the window to face him.

'What are you doing here?' she demanded indignantly.

'I might ask you the same question,' Stubb replied.

'Where did you get a key? This sty is always locked.' Eleanor threw him a haughty expression and flounced between the rows of cases. She brushed past him but he grabbed the top of her arm and pulled her back. 'I asked you where.' He set his mouth firmly and fixed her with a stare. A sparrow that had built its shabby nest in the rafters flew to a hole in the eaves.

'Let go!' Eleanor cried out, pretending pain. 'You may be a king but you're hurting me.'

Stubb removed neither his grip of her arm nor his gaze. 'Enough of your nonsense. Tell me.'

Eleanor threw back her untied hair and with her free hand brushed the remainder away from her forehead. 'You know there's a key outside the door. Besides, Theodore got me a spare one,' she admitted.

'You harpy,' shouted Stubb and he lightly slapped her face. Eleanor shrieked and clutched her cheek. 'That creep of a father defiles you, then gives you a key to see his damnation of an insect collection? You expect me to believe that?'

Eleanor had become limp in his grasp and she swayed, sobbing all the while. 'I'm telling the truth. It ... he told me he was trying to make amends; pleaded with me to forgive him. He was desperately sorry, thinking the bathroom empty; if only he could make it up to me, he said. He's promised to find Alastair.' Tears ran to her mouth, leaving glistening streaks.

Stubb tightened his hold on her slender arm. 'Make it up to you,' he chuckled sarcastically, 'we know what that means, don't we? You should know of a few more snippets of information I didn't tell you about, learnt during the enlightening conversation with the butler.' Eleanor's fraught crying was cut in mid-sob. 'For one, the household staff believe you are playing games with them, talking about a boy who doesn't exist; and are becoming weary of the way you order them about; and another thing, Pump has been keeping his ears and eyes open. You wouldn't give that drunken sod the credit, would you? He's seen my loving wife in my father's arms.'

'No, it's... he is...'

'He's seen my darling wife kissing my father and touching his fat, stinking body.' Stubb realized he was sweating. He wiped the trickles from under his chin.

'Never!' Eleanor yelled and she collapsed to her knees as though her bones had dissolved. 'It's lies, none of it true. He walked in on me, apologized, transformed into an insect, then the strange watch business; and then walked out again. That's all, that's all I remember. Yet you say Pump saw Theodore assault me. How would I not remember such a thing? This is all a really bad episode of the dream. Not like my good dream. This is a different, dreadful story.' She looked pleadingly up to her husband.

Stubb was in torment. He wanted to believe her; was it too late to patch the rents in the fabric of their marriage that was ripping apart? He tried to lift Eleanor but even her slim form seemed doubled in weight. 'Explain what happened,' he demanded then, his thoughts a blare of noise.

'I've told you. How many times do you want to hear?' Eleanor whimpered. She coughed and gulped, and paused to listen to the oppressive bulk of silence in the attic room. She heard Stubb's rasping breath, saw purple veins standing high on his forehead, gleaming with sweat.

'Yesterday, when you were drinking in The Bulldog Fish,' she began again, throwing an accusing glance before getting to her feet, 'I decided to bathe. I had finished, about to dress, when Theodore entered. He didn't knock. Look William, I keep on telling you all this.'

'Carry on.'

'He came in and apologized and said he had thought it empty. I said alright, but would he go. He didn't move. He stood there, you know, looking at me. I was holding the towel to cover myself, before you ask.' Eleanor swallowed involuntarily. 'Then he did a strange thing. He held out a pocket watch by its chain.' Eleanor stood as though transfixed, her eyes filling with more tears, the skin taut on the back of her pale hands held to her breast.

Stubb looked meek and suddenly weary. 'And then,' He said, with the words catching in his throat.

'For Godrey's sake, do you expect me to make up sordid detail? I can barely remember though I'm certain its thorax made a cracking noise...' Eleanor's voice trailed away.

'Pump was outside in the corridor. Florence was in the house.'

'Please, I don't know. I screamed when he first came into the bathroom, I'm certain.'

Realizing he still had a grip of his wife's chalk-white arm, Stubb released his hold. He wanted to cry out; Pump's account of the drama slithered into mind and began feeding upon his softened emotions, twisting them once more into the idea that Eleanor was deceiving him: she was the liar.

Some exterior force lifted his hand; it was as though he swam through the air, hover over to the other side of the attic, watch himself slapping her arm, again and again. 'Seducer; reptile!' he roared. Eleanor howled like a whipped animal; she wheeled around and out to the coiling stairs.

Stubb's chin fell to his chest. Wiping his running nose with his cuff, he also made his way to the landing. When in the corridor, he could hear Eleanor weeping incessantly from their bedroom. He stepped down to the hallway. He wanted The Bulldog Fish Tavern; he needed to get drunk.

CHAPTER 7

The Meeting

PONDEROUS WEEKS WITHIN bloated, routine months dragged wearily by. Each day held the common and conventional happenings of the village, save for the birth of Mrs. Codling's puppies; the feeble Thomas Cratch – sadly losing touch with mind and bodily functions – sent to Smudge Abode for the Elderly; the severe warning to Gerald Glister that should he be seen again anywhere in Muchmarsh wearing his flannelette pyjamas while walking his scruffy mongrel, he would be promptly arrested.

Although the village spent its life comfortably, tenseness and a sense of expectancy hung over the Stubb household like an invisible shroud. Eleanor would wander from room to room as though hopelessly lost in a maze, panic frozen to her face. Wherever possible she avoided Theodore, as did the butler. Florence was bewildered with the change in attitudes of the family; the gardener was unaware of any difference, although he was paid even less attention than the little he had become used to receiving.

The cook noticed: individual eating requirements were beginning to annoy her. 'They are all sulking like children,' Mrs. Wickling had said. 'More than likely it's over some trifling thing.'

Any of the spare bedrooms were too close to Theodore's or Eleanor's rooms and so Stubb's sleeping companions were trunks and suitcases in the box room. When the household slept, he would creep down in the night to eat like some foraging wild animal wary of sunlight. Having prescribed to the act of ignoring or evading his father and his wife, he found the process became routine. Even the aching within and hurt feelings from rejection (for Theodore and Eleanor were, in turn, ignoring him) had faded.

Half a year is a peculiar period, but only as much as time itself sometimes seems odd. Twenty-six weeks could spin past without much recognition of the fact; it could catch a person by surprise at the rapidity of their life. Or it could dribble away, every minute a snailing, painful existence with an acute awareness of each heartbeat, each tiniest event.

Summer had taken flight only too quickly – it had dragged away its canopy of verdure to leave the ochres, reds and golds of autumn. It was a particularly cold autumn that year and it, in turn, withered and died, leaving the corpse of winter across the land.

When Stubb met his wife in the sitting room by chance, he realized how much he had been missing her; it struck him how slowly the world had been revolving for one hundred and eighty two days. By knowing her daily routines, he had been able to avoid her for weeks at a time. Occasional meetings had been dissolved by a hurried acknowledgement with a restrained nod or a reticent verbal greeting. Situations requiring communication had been dealt with swiftly, resolved with the minimum of contact.

Eleanor had planned to go into Grinding, then decided to go later in the day; Stubb wanted to doze in a chair but had been restless.

His initial reaction upon entering the day room was to leave immediately after seeing Eleanor perched on the edge of the over-ripe settee, her hands cradling her knees. She wore a loose, flowing dress and had plaited her hair, the mahogany tail curling forward over one shoulder.

She looked up without surprise. An emulsion of a cloud, smearing the sun for most of the day, broke its surface briefly. An unusual brightness lit the room as though summer had returned; the crisp snow outside glittered.

Stubb sat and gripped the arm of the chair as if it were his jutting rock in the midst of a torrent. A handful of syllables had been exchanged between them over the months; this miserly situation lived on for a silent minute, each waiting for the other to speak. Eleanor fiddled nervously with silver bracelets about her wrist. Stubb sensed that something was amiss. 'I can't stay long,' he muttered.

Eleanor's cheeks became flushed; tutting then, she pulled the corners of her mouth up and said, 'Well, go. I'm sure I haven't been trying to see you for ten minutes in the last six months. What do I care?'

'I'm sorry,' was all William Stubb could say in return. He stood and moved to her side, and held her hands. His own were shaking.

Eleanor dabbed her misted eyes with a square of silk retrieved from her sleeve. 'I've missed you so. I've stayed awake some dream nights listening, you walking like a real lost soul. Do we have to carry on this way? I've been so lonely.'

'So have I,' admitted Stubb. It was then he wanted to smash the carapace he had made over his emotions; lay them bare, expose his true feelings that had been filed away, it seemed, an immeasurable age ago.

'William, I have something to tell you. It's desperately important for both of us. If you hate me after, still you must realize it was not my fault.' She began to sob quietly. 'Not my fault, you see.'

Stubb's eyebrows knitted in puzzlement. He spoke hurriedly, the tissue of his calmness tearing. 'Eleanor, I've had these months to think – I see that even after this nightmare, I still love you. I always have. Nothing can be worse than what we've been through already; so tell me.'

The grandfather clock in the hall did its best to cover the sounds of the weeping Eleanor but after its quota of four punctilious tones she still wept. 'I'm impregnated,' she whispered.

A misinterpretation, a joke, a mistake, anything but truth; Stubb paced back and forth in his new prison, trapped within her words, needing to hold back the walls from groaning closer. Eleanor ran to him and flung her arms about him. She was giddy with the same words as they jangled and rattled in her head, a devilish, echoing merry-go-round.

'Please love me,' she whimpered like a child. 'Our Alastair has returned.' Stubb pulled her arms away from him gently but firmly and went unsteadily to the door. 'Where are you going? Don't go; don't leave me. If it's not Alastair – if it's a rogue insect, coiling inside, using suckers and feelers, I'll kill it, William, I'll kill it!'

She reached out for him imploringly but froze when he snapped, 'Don't touch me.'

Stubb dragged her last words with him as he trod up to the box room. A manic babble swamped his mind, and above it all, the shrill voice of Eleanor, the same phrase repeated over and over, 'I'll kill it, I'll kill it, I'll kill it—'

CHAPTER 8

Decision

I'LL KILL HIM, Stubb thought. An obvious solution; and after his father's death was achieved, all problems would evaporate soon after, he was certain. He was surprised the idea hadn't struck him sooner.

His usual afternoon nap had been interrupted by this inspiration and had brought him to wakefulness with a jolt.

He rubbed his sticky eyes and although they were open wide, he stared blindly upwards as he lay on the mattress. He must try to think logically, unemotionally. If he were to entertain the concept of murder then he must decide on how the deed was to be accomplished. It would have to be a guaranteed method that was both easily executed and foolproof. Nobody should get even a hint of a scent.

A certain death would be to somehow fill Theodore's lungs with a noxious gas – rip the oxygen from him and be done with it. Slitting his throat would be a more practical way but certainly a messy business and it would leave too many palpable clues to be found. An arranged accident could be the answer: pushing him through a window, or an unfortunate slip of a handsaw. At that moment, Stubb realized in an instant that thoughts of murder had not been fully absorbed, either consciously or seriously, and the potential of it stung him. Kill his father? How could he ever consider such a savage act? He plumped his pillow, sat up, and after rubbing the top of his balding head as if to impede similar thoughts, leant over to a small cupboard that stood on the floorboards beside him. Yet after pouring ale from a terracotta bottle retrieved from it, the ratchet of his mind clicked on...

The murder would bring his wife and himself closer, as they used to be, he was sure. But what if they were simply to leave, get away from everyone? This ageing possibility was quickly dismissed. They had no resources to start afresh; they would have nowhere else to live. Stubb wanted a house – the house in which he sat; and after all, the property would become his once Theodore was dead. 'His death,' Stubb mouthed and the suggestions of murder came to mind again: slitting his throat; gassing him; throwing him out of the window – he knew they all sounded ridiculous.

His relationship with Eleanor still hung on by threads. Some drastic action needed to be instigated, and as soon as possible, to save their marriage from plummeting to its destruction. But was there no alternative to patricide?

The embryo who would become Alastair, curled in Eleanor's womb, appealed to the depths of his being, pleaded with his instincts, justifying its existence. No matter which man was the sire, it wanted to leave its watery dungeon, feel its heart beating in the outside world.

Whether or not Stubb was the father, the fact remained that Theodore had abused his wife; and the knowledge of that sickened him. If Stubb was honest with himself, he knew his own disturbed mind needed purging, Eleanor had to be avenged, and told the answer to their problems – his father must die.

His wife was not due back into the house until early evening. Stubb had no alternative but to wait.

He was fretful and restless: he got up and, to pass some of the time, opened one of the chests stored in the box room to inspect its contents. As he pulled up the lid, an odour of mothballs and dampness rose from the clothes and objects stored inside. Sequined pantaloons, a toreador's jerkin and white pigskin gloves; a waist sash, burgundy capes and a judge's wig; a revolving cartridge pistol in its brown leather holster; a stringless violin accompanied by a block of resin; a papier mâché mask and other strange theatrical creations. After inspecting some of the items more closely, he tired of the diversion and so closed the lid of the chest and lay on the mattress again.

Stubb had been sleeping lightly. He awoke with a start to find the afternoon sun had slunk below the horizon, leaving the full disc of a moon glowing with a bright light. It had begun to snow again. He fumbled for a match to light a candle then from its glow, reached for his bedside clock. It was seven-thirty.

He pulled on some clothes then walked the corridor to the main stairs, all the while suspiciously eyeing closed doors and unlighted corners. He would not want to meet Theodore. It was going to be uncomfortable enough speaking to Eleanor again. To the six months of his solitary existence, he had added still another two weeks of hurtful glances and refusals to discuss matters concerning the child. Though to achieve this, he had resumed a cryptozoic existence, sleeping during daylight hours, and pacing the house or roaming the quiet and dark lanes of the village during the night.

He had grown to enjoy the darkness. The humming wind and the empty streets and lanes, the countryside asleep under its blankets of moonlit snow, and the whooping owl or barking dog were all parts of the whole: the beauty of the night. Clumping upon snow-compacted cobblestones or trudging over snowdrifts, he had the opportunity to think on his circumstances, and there in those cold and vacant places he realized, even after all that had passed, to be without his wife would be empty and meaningless.

As was her habit on Thursday evenings, Eleanor sat at the kitchen table to read the latest edition of The Grinding & Smudge Recorder.

'Hallo,' said Stubb softly as he entered.

For a moment, he thought there would be no reply, until she looked up from her newspaper, and said, 'You are William.'

Stubb inspected the gentle structure of her face both with affection and concern. 'How have you been?' She shrugged. 'I wish we could be friends,' he said.

An unexpected yearning washed over him and as though Eleanor had read his thoughts, she rose from her wooden chair by the plate cupboard and rack of saucepans, and went to him. Stubb put his arms about her waist and they kissed. Her lips tasted of rosehip tea. For him, the kiss was an unusual sensation, having been deprived of this simple pleasure for so long.

'What can be done?' asked Eleanor plaintively. She parted from him. 'Do you want me to get rid of—?' Her sorrowful eyes dropped to the mound she carried.

They sat, facing each other across the pine table.

Eleanor's taut features softened and she gently smiled so as to break the beginning of a flow of tears.

'I want to keep him, insect legs or proper legs,' she said quietly.

'I want us to have the child too,' Stubb replied, 'but on one condition.'

Eleanor gave a short laugh as the elation of the moment overtook. 'Anything to keep my baby. We have wanted Alastair back for so long, and he could be like a human being again. I'm going to Martha May's Wool Shop tomorrow and start knitting right away. Not long now, two months more. Tell me the condition, William, it can't be much.' Her delighted face had cracked the mask of grief she had been wearing for so long. 'Can it?' she said, her voice tinted with laughter.

Stubb's eyelids fluttered involuntarily. He fiddled with a cup handle. 'The condition is you agree we get rid of my father.'

'What do you mean?'

'I mean that we kill him.'

She let out a shriek and turned away as though afraid to look at her husband. A pause before she said, 'You can't mean it. Stoop that low to murder? Never!' She thumped the table with the outstretched palm of a hand.

Stubb examined her expression, gaining distinct evidence that she feigned shock. Still he continued, 'The only way out. Think, this will become our house, with our servants, and we'll regain the complete happiness we deserve.'

Silence while Eleanor's disposition seemed to reflect some inner conflict.

Scratching sounds from over by one of the snow-rimmed panes of the kitchen window; Stubb ignored them.

Finally, Eleanor spoke again. 'Yes, you're right. Together, as it used to be. You and I, with our lost Alastair, now found. Agreed.' She nodded sagely and her alluring eyes were alight as she gazed about the kitchen as if she already owned it. 'How do you propose to destroy him?'

'Poison,' said Stubb, the method dropping into mind from nowhere.

'Will it be painful?' Eleanor said, as if enquiring the price of a shop item.

'Not much,' he lied. 'A quick and peaceful death, I reckon.'

'I hope not. I hope he suffers; hope he screams in agony. The pain should be too much for him to bear. I hate him, the cockroach!'

Stubb was taken aback by her vehemence. 'Is there something else?' he mumbled, his tongue suddenly losing the ability to make words properly. 'More you've not told me?'

Another vague sound from the direction of the window.

Without effort, another hidden fragment of Eleanor's memory illuminated. 'Dreadfully sorry, quite forgot to tell you about his stinking breath and what he whispered before he swung the watch.' She sniffed. 'Alright, there is one thing more. It came back to me recently. He…'

The back door rattled and swung open, singing on its hinges, Brood stepping into the kitchen from the cold garden.

'What the hell are you doing here?' roared Stubb.

'The master lets me come for my nightcap,' Brood said. 'A bit earlier than usual, you.'

'Never mind your impudence. Have you been listening to our conversation? If so, there's going to be trouble, do you hear? Now go back to your poky shed.'

Brood snorted. 'The master lets me…'

Stubb was glaring at the gardener. 'Get out.'

'The master…'

'You obstinate oaf. Well, if you aren't going, we will. Come along, Eleanor.'

She carefully replaced the few strands of hair which had strayed onto her cheek while staring hard over to her husband – an attempt to transmit some silent message.

'No, William, my gardener and I are fine.'

Stubb growled but knew not to press the matter; he realized her intentions. He and Brood disliked each other. For him to find out how much the gardener had overheard would be a fruitless task. Stubb hurriedly left the kitchen without speaking further, turning only to give Brood a look of disgust.

The gardener remained standing by the open doorway smacking his gloved hands together – cold air invading the kitchen – looking to Eleanor without expression. Still it was snowing; spots of white were melting from his dark overcoat, dripping to the tiled floor, joined by more droplets falling from the brim of his battered black hat.

'Close the door, for goodness sake. The talking wind is quite bitter tonight,' said Eleanor abruptly, tugging at her shawl.

Brood did as he was asked and after, stepped back onto the same spot he had previously occupied. 'Evening, Miss,' he said. It seemed an inappropriate time to greet her and, for that reason, Eleanor pretended not to have heard by intently examining her newspaper. 'Evening, Miss,' Brood repeated.

Eleanor looked up to glare at him, wondering if this servant was stupid. She gave a clipped reply then began preparing to ask him how much he had overheard.

Brood brushed away a trickle of water that ran down one of the creases in his cheek. A polluted puddle had formed around his leather boots. 'Not a nice night, Miss. Cold. I hate the cold, can't stand it, see. A cold, cold night. All the washing stiff in the morning.' He grinned, exposing his crooked and yellowing teeth. Leaden eyes, normally dull and devoid of gaiety, glistened while a streak of watery fluid leaked from his nose. His sight dropped to the curve of Eleanor's bloated womb, his blistered lips curling oddly. She caught the leer and pulled the chair she sat upon further under the table to hide herself. 'Looking tired, Miss,' he said and taking a glove off, lethargically scratched the warts that grew in profusion on the back of his hand. He sneered. 'Winter, takes it out of us; can't get warm, see. Worrying, getting cold in your bed, you.'

Why couldn't this abominable man go? She had to ask the question first though, but before she could speak, Brood persisted. 'If you ever need extra warming—' Eleanor's mouth dropped open in surprise. The impudence! 'You can always—' don't say anything, it would only promote an argument, 'get

48

more blankets from Florence. I'll drop her a word, Miss.'

Eleanor shrieked the gardener's name in frustration at listening to his continual insinuations. 'I am trying to read this thing – this newspaper. Stop your talking, I would be most grateful.' She heaved a sigh, her heart thumping heavily.

'Reading, yes, I can see that, Miss.' He wiped a drop of water, fallen from his hat, from the tip of his nose. Another droplet followed and he ignored it. 'Seen the master lately?'

'What do you mean by that?'

'Nothing, only,' he sucked air between his teeth, 'I want a few words with Mr. Theodore, that's all.'

She was beginning to think that he had heard all of the conversation with her husband. 'Get your tea or whatever and be quick about it,' she demanded. She closed her tired eyes and felt herself sway. Her heart now seemed to have left her chest and taken residence in her throat. 'Do that; now.'

'Alright, Miss.'

'I am Queen – Mrs. Stubb, do you hear me?' Her eyelids sprang open, eyes stabbing at the gardener. There was no visible effect.

Brood went to the kettle and clutching it in his large hand, proceeded to fill it from the hand pump which stood in a corner, in preference to the taps over the sink, those installed with the new plumbing system a few years before.

Eleanor was in the grip of panic. Concentration had started to waiver. The beginning of dreaminess, as though the whole of the kitchen – with its stove, pantry and copper skillets – was becoming insubstantial, as if one could pass a hand through it all as if a phantom projection. Only Brood seemed to hold his solidity; a finished, moving, dark sculpture within the sketch about him. She closed her eyes once more to dismiss these unsettling visual fallacies.

Quickly, Brood stepped over from her right to immediately behind. She twitched in surprise as his body weight, on his hands pushing down, weighed on the back of her chair, tipping it slightly. Her every muscle had become tensed while she attempted to see him without turning her head.

The gardener spoke softly and slowly with a syrupy whine. 'Now if you're unhappy – and I'm not saying you are, Miss – but let's say you was and help was required, don't be afraid to ask.' He licked the saliva that was about to dribble down his chin back into his unsightly mouth.

'What are you trying to say?'

'Any unhappiness, and you needed some help, you can rely on me. Always willing...' he infuriated Eleanor with his long pauses, 'to give you... you know, assistance.'

Glancing at dirty marks on the stone floor left by his boots, she said, 'So you can help, can you?' The remark had meant to sound casual but had become thin and whiney. Her face was chalk-white; dizziness overtaking. The kitchen had become superficial.

Brood went to the stove and placed the kettle on the hob and then turned to Eleanor, his grating voice forming an invisible band of metal across her forehead the more he spoke.

He said, 'Must do something about those rats. Shed's infested with the blighters. Saw another one last night, biggest I've ever seen, almost as big as a cat; and it had bloodshot eyes, and long fur, and teeth you could saw wood with. Having a nibble at my biscuits. Soon put a stop to that. Crept up behind it, and wham!' Eleanor jumped to her feet and spun around to face him. 'I belted it with a spade. Squashed flat, it was, innards all over the floor.' He spoke then in hushed tones as though passing on confidential information.

Eleanor inclined her head and leant forward so that every

syllable he spoke would be heard. Brood's tongue clicked before he added, 'Of course, did that to all of 'em, there'd be a right mess. Blood and gore everywhere. Think of the smell in my shed. Has to be a better way.' He spoke his next sentence clearly, enunciating each word with rare precision. 'What's needed – for the problem – is – rat poison. Outside my shed.'

Eleanor swallowed nervously. 'Goodnight, Brood.' She walked wearily to the kitchen door leading to the lobby, clutching her swollen belly as if it might drop.

'Nightie night, Miss,' Brood answered with a grin.

Eleanor met the maid in the hallway. 'Real Florence, have you seen my husband?'

'Are you alright, Mrs. Stubb? You don't look very well.'

'I'm fine. Where is he?'

'He did say he was going to The Bulldog Fish, madam.'

After thanking the maid, with her whole body weighed with tiredness and her mind disoriented, Eleanor trudged up the stairs. She needed her bed early that cold evening.

CHAPTER 9

Rat Poison

THE FOLLOWING CHILL morning, Eleanor had returned from the village shops in a content mood. She opened the gate at the side of the snow-spattered manor house.

Remembering her conversation with Brood the evening before, she hurried over the whiteness of the garden away from the house. After glancing up at the graceful marble statue holding a small pillow of snow, she found her way to the gardener's shed, snow-laden branches of the lilac bushes trying their best to disguise it.

Despite the cool sun being swaddled with gunmetal grey clouds, a tin can beside the battered door of the shed glinted in the bleached air. It stood on sheets of newspaper. Although a snowfall had ceased only twenty minutes before, both can and paper were dry. A symbol printed on the tin can's label, seen as an acorn perched upon crossed swords, was suddenly translated into its actual image of a skull and crossbones. Eleanor pulled her scarf tighter about her neck and marched briskly away and back over to the manor house that stood starkly against the plain sky.

She stamped her booted feet onto a metal grating in front of the kitchen door. When inside, warmth in the kitchen ate the chilliness from about her. The smell of roasting meat: she was keen to peek inside the oven but decided she must change into dry clothes first; snow had found its way into her overboots and thick coat. She went to the scullery and deposited those articles into a cupboard before going up to her bedroom.

Stubb was asleep in their four-poster bed, an extra woollen blanket covering him. She smiled. It was nice to have him back with her. One by one the loose ends of her marriage were being untangled and made fast. And soon Alastair would be cradled in her arms. Eleanor was convinced of her future loving delight, no matter how many legs the child possessed. Not long for everything to be as it used to be.

She crept about the room so as not to awaken her husband but as she passed the side of the bed an arm shot out and gripped her wrist. 'I thought you were asleep,' Eleanor said and she gave a coquettish laugh.

'Lightly dozing really; trying to keep warm,' Stubb answered. There was a moment of quietness until he continued, 'It's good to see you content again. You're looking lovely, even if you have forgotten to take your scarf off.' Eleanor looked coy but then grinned while untying the headscarf knot from under her chin. A sudden movement from within her womb but she ignored it.

'Been visiting Mrs. Crowpack?'

'Not today – I felt like a walk; such a fresh, alive morning.'

Stubb nodded but then his brow creased. 'I felt guilty leaving you with Brood last night; did you find out if he overheard?'

'Yes, all of it, I'm certain. Or at least, enough to suggest we use rat poison. That servant man gives me the shivers.'

'But of course. Why not? I've read about that sort of thing. By administering doses over a period of weeks into food, small enough not to spoil the flavour, the victim gradually deteriorates day by day. Later on, he might catch on to what's happening, by which time he's too ill and weak to do anything. The person simply fades away.' Stubb's eyes glazed over as he pondered.

'Yes, fading; I knew your father hasn't been real, all along. You don't mind our gardener knowing?'

'Why should I? When we've got the house, I'll sell all of Theodore's junk from the attic and then Brood can live there instead of that stinking shed; perhaps more wages. He's no fool, Eleanor. He knows the advantages; he'll keep his mouth shut.'

They both fell silent. The clock beside the bed ticked its monotone, marking the seconds until Stubb enquired casually, 'What were you about to tell me yesterday before we were interrupted?'

His wife's face became a shade darker. 'Don't know. Couldn't have been important.'

'Come now, I need to know what else my father spoke about that's such a great secret.'

Eleanor sat on the edge of the bed. 'Alright, I will say,' she began. 'It is such a great secret. I'm sure you didn't want to know how much your phantom of a father hates you. Before the insect beast hypnotized me – so you say happened – he gave me a proposition. He asked if I would marry him.'

Stubb laughed and wrinkled the top of his stumpy nose. 'Is that all? Should have guessed the old man is losing his marbles. How can he marry you when we are married?'

Her words were clipped. 'That's the whole point. He wants to marry me after your death. He wants to kill you, William. It's almost funny if it wasn't so tragic; both of you want to kill each other.'

Stubb gritted his teeth. His father's death would be painful, he would make sure of that. 'Brood keeps rat poison in his shed. On a shelf somewhere at the back.'

Under normal circumstances, I'm guessing,' she answered.

'What do you mean?'

'He's has been leaving the tin outside, and not hidden either.'

'I see,' Stubb said, 'so I suggest we take it,' then adding quietly, 'before anyone else does.'

CHAPTER 10

The Notes

THE NEXT DAY was even chillier than the day before. Icicles had formed along the eaves of the manor house and under its window ledges. Eleanor had returned from visiting the rickety Mrs. Crowpack. It was against Dr. Snippet's instructions to go outdoors but as well as Mrs. Crowpack looking forward to the visits, the old lady had been feeling unwell. Eleanor now saw herself as a practical and down-to-earth queen, who cared for the solid, elderly ones; who had learnt to run her own baths, one who even shopped for groceries.

Upon approaching the gardener's shed, she grasped her coat as her heart seemed to miss a beat: there was no tin can to be seen. Nothing by the shed door except for three piles of newspapers, each pile tied with rough string.

She padded across the snow towards them, heaved the papers away, and gasped with relief when she saw the silvery container that had been hiding behind the piles as though for warmth. A scrap of folded paper was held to the lid by an elastic band. Her breath quickened and condensed the more into a fine mist. She was locked in a moment of indecision. Then, glancing about her and seeing the white garden containing no other living thing, she bent and snatched the tin from the ground. The metal was cold, even through her woollen gloves. She pulled the folded paper from the lid and pushed it into her pocket, and bundled the tin into her bag before hurrying into the house.

'Afternoon Mrs. Stubb. It's properly chilled. You look frozen,' said the cook gaily.

'Good afternoon, Mrs. Wickling. Yes, it is cold in this world.'

'Luncheon won't be long. I've made your favourite sweet.'

'Summer jelly?'

'No, jam roll with cream,' the cook replied with a bemused tone.

Eleanor put her shopping bag on the chair in front of her and pulled the fingers of her gloves to take them off. The cook steered her generous bulk around the kitchen table and tottered up to the bag. 'I'm sure you remembered my liver salts,' she said as she began to extract articles from the bag, placing them on the table.

'If you don't mind,' shouted Eleanor and upon grabbing a jar of face cream preparation from the cook's hand she threw it back into the bag. She winced when the glass jar hit the tin can and gave a dull chink. For her, the noise seemed to echo about the kitchen and scream 'Poison!'

The cook's mouth drooped like a child that had been reprimanded. 'Well, really.' Mrs. Wickling trotted over to the stove whereupon she began to vigorously stir a concoction that had been bubbling and spitting there.

Eleanor snatched up her shopping bag and left the kitchen quickly, walking past the scullery to the day room.

The day room was one of those places that most of the household passed through but did not use: Eleanor had taken to keeping some indoor plants on the windowsill and her few books on the dresser. Florence would come in to dust and polish but even then only once in a while. Eleanor would use the room to sit and commune with her unborn Alastair or to read or wile away the hours, knitting and planning her child's future.

She was about to walk through to the lobby when, upon

giving the room a cursory glance, she decided to unload the items of her bag and hide the tin of poison. She sat on the chair that stood by the window. The chair had been the first item her husband had made during his apprenticeship with Grandfellows Carpentry Trade, even before the days of Terps Joinery. Although it was a lovely article, its creator could not say why one leg was a fraction shorter than the other three. A wedge of wood had been placed under the shorter leg, as a temporary measure, to stop the chair from rocking. But like many other tasks, Stubb had never found time to rectify the fault.

The chair rocked slightly as Eleanor placed her weight onto the seat. She leant over and peered at the shorter leg. There was no wedge – in place of it was a wad of white paper. She was intrigued and so retrieved it. Turning it over in her hand she decided to replace it, thinking that Florence had lost the wood and the paper was her substitute, when she spotted the wedge lying on the carpet further under the chair. She remembered then the folded paper that had been attached to the tin by an elastic band and she took it from her pocket. The chair was pulled over to a marquetry-lined mahogany table. There she straightened her back when she realized that once more she had been slouching, a pose she was prone to take with the additional weight carried. The little being inside her gave a hefty kick and she gave an exclamation of surprise.

The papers were opened out flat onto the table and she saw that they had similar writing upon them although both were quite illegible. It looked as though the scrawl was the result of someone in a hurry or of poor penmanship, or indeed both. It did not help that the ink had got wet and was smeared in places.

She took one of the pieces to the window where it could be deciphered more readily. Gradually she could understand a few of the words though not enough to make any sense of the whole.

She was not going to be beaten by this intriguing problem. She went to an oak bureau and took out a pencil and a sheet of crisp paper and, seating herself once more at the table, began to translate the scribble into intelligible words. The cryptanalysis threatened to take her the rest of the afternoon but she was determined to understand the characters.

As the sense began to emerge she shook with an impassioned anger. Eleanor screwed both pieces of paper into a hard ball and stuffed them into her shopping bag. She left the day room behind her, puffing in an intense irritation. She would prepare herself before dinner.

CHAPTER 11

Arsenic

FROM DR. SNIPPET'S examinations and with a speck of sixth sense, he had surmised that the birth of the child would be slightly premature and that the happy event would take place in no more than six weeks ahead. The doctor insisted that Eleanor spent more time resting. On no account was she to attempt anything strenuous, including any work in the abandoned church, although she insisted all had been completed there.

She sat up in her bed while Dr. Snippet bumbled from his black bag to the bedside cabinet and back again. A constant mumbling emitted from him. He idly scratched his balding scalp and then, as though he had only noticed her for the first time, looked up in surprise. His features warmed into a smile. 'Ah, Mrs. Eleanor,' he said cheerfully. Large spectacles were pushed further up his angular nose. Placing a finger upright as though testing for the strength of the wind, he added, 'and how are we feeling today?' He did not hear her reply for she spoke softly. She did not feel very well. 'Excellent, good,' he muttered.

He sniffed and seemed satisfied with himself for finding the item that had been apparently hiding in his doctor's bag. A stethoscope was extracted and held between two fingers and at arm's length as though it could whip up and give him a nasty bite. 'Now Mrs. Eleanor, I wish to examine you if I may.' He gave a lopsided grin.

William Stubb entered the bedroom. The doctor was ignored as Stubb walked quickly up to the bedside.

'Eleanor, I must speak with you,' he whispered urgently.

'Dr. Snippet,' she mouthed without sound, flicking her fingers towards the muttering gentleman, who was now stalking about the room inspecting this and that like a curious child. A patterned vase was balanced precariously on the palm of his hand and he peered at it over the top of his spectacles.

He was oblivious to the presence watching him until Stubb spoke: 'Doctor, if you would not mind, I wish to have a word with my wife.' The man addressed smiled benignly and placing the free hand behind his back, remained where he was. 'Alone,' added Stubb, precisely.

'Ah,' Dr. Snippet exclaimed as if he had thought of the answer to a particularly intriguing puzzle and then with a nod, walked out into the corridor.

'How are you feeling?'

She smiled. 'As well as can be expected, I suppose. Alastair keeps giving me twinges.'

Stubb was patient. 'Eleanor, we don't even know if it's a boy.'

'But I know. It is my baby Alastair come back. Even the doctor tells me so. By the way, did you know that your insect father is paying Dr. Snippet?'

'I did. It's the least he can do. Did you get it?'

'Yes.'

'Good. Where is it?'

'Standing by the shed.'

'What do you mean?'

'I mean it is standing by the shed. I got it but then I put it back.'

'Why? Have you changed your mind?'

Eleanor stared hard at him. 'No, but one thing is certain.

We're not going to use that poison from our gardener. We'll have to buy a tin, or make some.'

'But whatever for? What's happened?'

Eleanor looked serious with her fine brow creasing. She sat up in the bed and without twisting her body, put her hand behind her, placing it under the pillow. She withdrew two balls of paper and put them onto the counterpane and replacing her hand, extracted a third note.

'What are these?'

'Why don't you unfold one and read.'

Their eyes met and Stubb bent to pick up one of the collection. He pulled it out flat, ironing out the creases with the palm of his hand. He placed it closer to his face and began to read Eleanor's translation under the scribbled words. His features changed gradually from amusement to a look of disgust. Stubb looked up. 'Why haven't you shown these to me before now?'

'Because I was going to ignore them until I found the third one in my coat pocket this morning. Besides, I didn't want to upset my king unnecessarily.'

Stubb resumed reading. 'The dirty swine,' he said. He clenched his hand into a fist; and the paper was crumpled to a ball again. 'So that's how Brood wants repayment for his favour. I should have guessed. A question remains though: if the so-called favour is not repaid, will he say anything to Theodore?' He shrugged his shoulders and answered himself: 'It's a possibility but even if Theodore did know, he wouldn't know how. We will have to think about that later. The immediate problem is, what to use now.'

'Why not buy it from the chemist?'

'The one along the Grinding Road? He knows the family too well and it might cause suspicion. He also knows Brood is the only one to buy the stuff.'

'You could go into Grinding town tomorrow. If it was bought at one of the large stores then nobody would ask questions.'

'True. I think that could be the answer.'

The doctor returned uninvited. Sticking his head around the door, still the smile engraved upon his pasty face, he said, 'Good afternoon, may I examine you, Mrs. Eleanor?' as though he had at that moment arrived at the house.

Stubb threw an impatient glance at him and answered for his wife. 'If you want,' he snapped.

'Thank you, thank you,' replied the doctor and he entered. 'And how are you feeling today?' Eleanor tutted at his forgetfulness. He examined her swollen belly with his fingers. Whispering and muttering still, he returned to his bag. He began to take out green bottles of pills, tweezers and tins and glass tubes and strange metal instruments. He had lost something in the depths of the bag once more. He placed the extracted articles in a neat line on the ottoman standing at the foot of the bed.

Stubb rubbed his jaw thoughtfully. Perhaps he would not have to go into Grinding after all. Eleanor gave him a sidelong glance. 'You have many things there, doctor,' said Stubb amiably. 'You must be very clever to know what does what.'

Dr. Snippet grinned. 'All has to be learnt, Mr. Stubb. Now I remember my university days in Pellingshaw Mews—'

'Yes, I'm sure you do, but for instance what is this strange substance?' Stubb picked up a glass bottle from the ottoman.

'That is known as a purgative compound. Administering doses of up to…'

'I see. Most interesting. And what about that one?'

The doctor chuckled. 'The little tin? I keep my blackboard chalk in there.'

'This one?'

'A urine sample.'

'Oh. And this? It looks a strange liquid.' Stubb picked up a thin glass vial.

'That, Mr. Stubb, is an arsenical solution. A very useful substance. Patients with asthmatic conditions find it most beneficial.'

Stubb licked his lips. 'Is it strong or a weak concentration?' He bit his lip. He thought that he had said too much even to the absent-minded man but Dr. Snippet merely raised his generous eyebrows.

'It should really be back in my laboratory. It is concentrated. For that, one must be careful; there is enough there to fell ten men. It is quite amazing how much I can fit into my bag.'

The leather bag in question received an affectionate pat and then the doctor, tiring of the conversation, returned to his search for the particular tablets prescribed to Eleanor. 'Here we are,' he exclaimed triumphantly and clutching a bottle in one hand proceeded to replace the articles from the ottoman with the other hand.

Stubb could not wrench his sight from the vial of arsenic. 'Dr. Snippet,' he stated quickly. The doctor looked up. 'I noticed your interest in that antique vase over there.' He pointed to it and placing the palm of his hand on the doctor's back, guided him firmly away, towards the object sitting in a wall recess. 'This,' Stubb explained with false pride, 'is a very old vase.' What else was he to say about the monstrosity? 'I'm sure you will agree that it's a very fine specimen, probably one of a pair. They were given to my great grandfather's wife as a wedding present—' and thus he continued, enthralling his learned listener with its varied and colourful history. He heard Eleanor ruffle the bedsheets.

After his monologue, and ascertaining that the doctor did not have the cash on him to pay for the article, Stubb immediately changed the subject. 'Well doctor, I presume that the tablets you hold in your hand are for my wife.'

'How right you are. Indeed, yes.' The doctor trotted over to the bedside and murmured instructions to Eleanor and giving her a tap on the head and collecting up the last of his medicines and instruments, he bade farewell and departed.

'Did you get it?' Stubb asked his wife excitedly.

She smiled proudly and withdrew the corked glass tube from behind her pillow. Stubb took it and held it up to the light.

'When is the deed to be done?' Eleanor melodramatically questioned. To have been told that she had been defiled, ravished without permission, let alone without consciousness, had polluted her mind more than she would ever care to admit or know.

'In a month's time,' said Stubb slowly, still inspecting the liquid. 'Theodore has planned a party in the new year. I have something to say to him.'

'Are you mad? It will turn into a fight. My king in battle with an insect, I'm sure of it.'

'I am going to express my most humble apologies for the dreadful misunderstanding that has been made. I will say that you have, after all this time, confessed the truth. I'll beg him to forgive me and when that's done, I shall ask that we are guests at his party.'

'You won't convince him. He – it – will never believe you, William.'

Stubb sat on the edge of the bed, gently resting Eleanor's head on his chest, and he stroked her hair.

'There is nothing to worry about. He will believe me. I'll twist him around my little finger, you'll see. It's going to turn out just the way we want.'

CHAPTER 12

The Party

THE AIR FELT heavy; dark clouds blanketed the sky and covered the full moon. It was a stormy night and a sudden change of temperature had softened the ice and melted the snow into a slush. The heavens rumbled ominously. There was no wind: the trees stood pensively as Muchmarsh slept under the hood of darkness, though a mewling baby broke the quietness from its cot in a cottage and farmer Solomon awoke with a coughing fit. A rag-tailed fox, stalking the empty lane, blinked up to the farmhouse; the sky rumbled again.

The splattered marble fireplace in the drawing room, with its aging and bequeathed plushness, was full with burning logs that popped and crackled and threw their cherry redness about the place from behind the fireguard. It was pleasantly warm. A hearty guffaw from the drawing room was dampened as the first thunderclap bellowed its arrival; a mighty vociferation that sent cats scurrying behind dustbins and other animals deeper into the earth to their lairs and burrows.

'—and then I said to him, in no uncertain terms, if you don't get your backside out of that door, I'll take it out for you.' A round of laughter filled the room. 'And I haven't seen the ridiculous fellow since,' chuckled Theodore and he looked smug as there were more happy smiles. Then a pause was created by all: taking a sip of brandy or a swallow of fortified wine, or warming their toes by the fire, suddenly finding the chandelier of immense interest or perhaps a sudden lapse into thought to mull over the progression of the evening. But as quickly as they had fallen into silence, conversation sprang into life again and a mumble of voices from the party guests grew to a babble.

'Not quite like that,' Mr. Parsley was saying, 'but more like this.' He put two fingers to his head and waggled them. 'It was a queer thing to watch, I can tell you, and then this other fellow dressed in purple appeared and came up behind him with a sprig of holly and – what was it now? Ah yes, a knife and fork and some rope and he says, "a sprout of holly to beat him, a knife and fork to eat him. Tie you up with string till you appear next spring." Most peculiar it was. They call it the Oak Leaf Day Ceremony.'

'It sounds right strange, I agree. But where does the oak leaf come into it?' enquired Mr. Taper.

'I wish you could tell me. I asked this oldish chap and he says the custom has been going on every year for as long as he can remember, and his father before him. He reckons it's pagan.'

'Does he now,' Mr. Taper replied, eyebrows bouncing. 'That's like this chap I used to work with—'

A thin lady with a long nose pushed her way between Mr. Parsley and Mr. Taper. 'Work you say?' she exclaimed. 'I used to be the manageress of the big firm in Grinding. I was very important. I held a lot of responsibility. And I would still be there if it wasn't for my elbows. Dr. Snippet tells me I have particularly fine elbows though somewhat sensitive. I am sure they all missed me when I had to leave there; the big firm in Grinding, I mean. Still, life is cruel.' Elsie Snicker lifted a finger and coughed delicately.

Mr. Parsley slipped away. 'What firm was this?' asked Mr. Taper.

'I said, didn't I? The big firm. The big firm in Grinding.' Her possibly refined elbows were flaunted with an untranslatable gesture.

'Oh, the big firm,' Mr. Taper echoed. 'You mean the textile firm. A huge place. My brother's friend's mother-in-law used to work there. Perhaps you knew her.' He took a sip of wine and brushed back his sculpted black hair – clumped with a homemade hair cream – behind his sagging ears.

'The textile firm? I would not work there. Only the lower classes work there.' She gave a cough again and upon seeing that Mr. Brittle had stepped over and stood beside her she frowned and walked away, as though on stilts, with a sour look upon her.

'What has she been telling you?' said Mr. Brittle with a knowing grin. 'That she used to be a trapeze artist in the circus? Or the one about her rich uncle who's about to pop off and leave her a fortune?'

Mr. Taper winked at Mrs. Musty the vicar's wife and she waved in reply from across the room. 'She was a manageress of the big firm in Grinding,' he answered.

'Oh, that is a new one,' replied Mr. Brittle.

All conversations were curtailed then as Theodore's bellowing voice filled the room.

'Ladies and gentlemen – that's it, settle down. I am most pleased that you could all come here, collected tonight; a post-seasonal treat as it were. It's also a type of celebration for I am pleased to be on happier terms with the son – of my dearly departed – and daughter-in-law. We did have what you might call a misunderstanding,' his eyes twinkled wickedly as he fingered an arm lining of his tweed jacket, 'and I don't mind telling you it had got quite out of hand. Still, that is all in the past. Here's to you,' he announced to William and Eleanor, and he raised his glass in a gesture of a toast. 'The two finest people you could ever wish to meet.'

He hiccoughed and tossed the remainder of the liquid from his glass down his throat; and after, wiped his wettened moustache. The majority of those congregated followed suit while others sipped coyly or did not drink at all but nodded affectionately towards the couple.

'Hear, hear,' someone shouted.

Stubb forced a smile and showed it to the gathering. He was standing beside the seated Eleanor who tried the expression but could not sustain the mask. Her countenance showed confused hatred as she blinked at her father-in-law.

'I say, Theodore, what's this all about? It is all very well toasting these two fine people but what is this misunderstanding of which you spoke?' said the very tall Mr. String, the barrister's clerk. He realized his protruding top teeth were showing too much and he covered them with his upper lip.

'You mean to tell me, Archie, that you haven't heard about it?' Theodore answered in consternation, as though he thought it common knowledge.

Stubb was jolted from his sleepiness. 'The old fool is drunk,' he whispered to Eleanor.

'Yes, do tell us,' chimed in Mrs. Musty. She liked to hear of anything with the vaguest hint of scandal.

'There is nothing much to say,' Theodore said. Stubb gave a sigh of relief. 'But if you really want to hear.'

'The idiot never gives up,' whispered Stubb. 'Look here, father,' he said aloud. 'I don't think they want to know.'

'But they do, my boy. Did you not hear them ask?'

Someone in the room tittered. Stubb stood erect and faced Theodore as though ready to pull a gun from a holster on his hip. There was silence but for the crackling logs in the grate and the grumbling sky outside.

Then Theodore submitted suddenly with a devilish grin upon his face. 'I'll tell you what, William. If I might – shall we say – give the wrong interpretation to the interesting story then you tell it.'

Before Stubb could reply, inebriated hecklers encouraged him with flippant remarks. 'Yes, tell it, Stubbo.'

'Come on Will.'

'Let's hear it,' added Mr. Parsley before placing a piece of cheap cheese on his tongue.

As though to hinder any words that might stray from his mouth, Stubb tightly pressed his lips together. He felt his face glow. His father was becoming an embarrassment and Stubb's distress was exacerbated by the expectant faces of the guests looking upon the proceedings as a party piece.

Theodore's wicked mood prompted him to speak again. 'Alright William. I'll make you. I will make you tell it.' There were gasps and surprised glances within the assembly. The suggestion was insufferable and Stubb's mouth unlocked.

'What in hell's name do you mean by that?' Would Theodore actually use physical violence in front of the guests?

'I mean I will hypnotize you.' That's all, thought Stubb then, his ridiculous game of swinging the watch. Although his father's prized possession might have been instrumental in the ravishment of his wife, he still believed that – providing it was used on someone who was not unwell or with a strong mind – no harm or real change would come of it. 'I will put you under my control,' Theodore continued, 'so you would have no alternative but to tell the whole, sorry story. I could even make you run up and down the stairs without your shirt, shouting "I'm a mongoose".'

The majority of guests burst into hearty laughter.

'Well really,' remarked Elsie Snicker.

Mr. Taper passed a comment to Mr. Brittle that it was turning out to be a very entertaining party indeed. It was then that Theodore decided he had teased his son enough.

'Alright old boy. The story can keep for another time.'

Several people who had held their breaths breathed again and the vicar's wife wrinkled her nose in disappointment.

'Anyone for more?' Theodore wiggled his glass between two fingers.

Conversation was reborn and it buzzed about the room as everyone exchanged remarks and mingled or followed Theodore to replenish their glasses.

A laughing Mr. String bounded up to him. 'Oh, do let me have a go,' he said with glee.

'Have a go of what, my hat?' answered Theodore. Mr. Brittle chuckled.

'No, this hypnosis lark. You can have a go on me if you like.'

After consideration, Theodore concluded that to "have a go" on Mr. String would prove a fruitless exercise. As well as being enthusiastic, one's subject needed to be malleable, a particular type for post-hypnotic suggestion to have effect, and he felt that the lanky man before him would not be suitable. 'Afraid not, String. Now, who wanted sherry?'

'What about me then?' suggested Mr. Taper. Any answer that might have been was lost as Mr. Brittle shouted, 'Elsie, she would be good.' The lady in question snorted and made the point that refined ladies did not indulge in party games.

'None of you, forget it,' Theodore said loudly but then he saw a man who seemed to be curling in on himself in a darkened corner of the room where light from one of the gas lamps did not reach. Mr. Badger, the farm hand, had not moved or spoken for most of the evening; and his host had quite forgotten he was there. Mr. Badger seemed transfixed by a framed painting of a hunting scene: an olive and tree-lined landscape, a stylized rampant horse with others rearing or heads turned to their mounts – red-jacketed noblemen, with cream jodhpurs and pitch black boots, blowing horns or pointing to their quarry, the fox skulking low and terrified as it made for cover.

'Mr. Nuckle,' Theodore called over, 'would you come here?'

'That would be Mr. Badger,' the brilliant Mr. Peake remarked.

Although Badger had been intent upon viewing the work of art, so far the proceedings had not missed him. Realizing the intention and not wishing to participate, he turned in his seat as though preparing to make a dash to the door. White curls of hair wobbled as he shook his head and he whispered in reply, 'No thank you,' and he removed his spectacles as if by not seeing his audience as clearly, they would not see him so well either. But before he could distract attention away from himself, his arm was taken and he was led unwillingly to the group who were planning the pastime.

A plain wooden chair had been procured and it stood at one side of the room. Some guests lost interest or, not realizing what was happening, were busy chatting, forming an aural backdrop for the events to follow.

'Sit down,' Theodore snapped harshly to the timid man.

'No, I...' He was pushed onto the chair by eager spectators.

'This really isn't going to hurt you.' Theodore placed a hand into his waistcoat pocket and extracted the pocket watch. Unattaching it from the buttonhole he held it by the long chain and showed it with an outstretched arm to those assembled. Most took a step forward, the engraved pattern upon the hinged lid attracting them. 'No nearer,' Theodore ordered.

All seemed startled at his strength of voice, and the intrigued guests complied, looking sheepish, nonetheless awaiting the unknown spectacle with anticipation.

CHAPTER 13

Hypnosis

'L ET US BEGIN,' Theodore murmured to the quivering Mr. Badger whose wide, almost tearful, eyes watched every move.

He spoke to the assembly again. 'At no time should your sight stray from Badger or Nuckle, whoever we have here,' he commanded. 'Looking at the watch will only, let us say, spoil the experience.' Now holding the chain by two fingers, he carefully opened the cover, making certain that no one, other than the farm hand, would see the magnificent interior of the watch. Theodore was preparing the words of his particular oration, an impressive mixture of circus patter and pseudo-science.

It was totally unnecessary, as he knew. The skeleton watch with its fine movement, to be seen performing as if in a type of fascinating and compelling dream, more than enough to lull any mind into a warm state of satisfied numbness, preparing it for an easy acceptance of any suggestion given.

He swung the watch before the man's face but he would not look at it.

'Come on, play the game,' someone shouted.

Without a conscious decision, Badger's attention fell upon the swinging timepiece and a comforting, low monotone of a voice settled into his ears: 'You have had a long tiring day, Badger,' left, right, left, right, 'stacking hay, through the day, stacking hay, through the day,' left, right...

A voice from the gaggle of guests: 'I see, like counting sheep.'

'Shut up now – so weary, extremely tired,' left, right, left, 'you feel relaxed, your muscles are gently settling into a luscious pasture, one after the other. The lids of your eyes are weighed down with gunshot,' right, left, right, 'so heavy, you want to sleep – to rest your eyelids,' left, right, 'you want so much to close your heavy eyelids...' left, right, left, right, 'you hear my voice, only my voice of authority and understanding, only my voice...' left, right, left, right, left, right, left.

The watch as a pendulum swinging, the murmuring stream of words soothing and running over Mr. Badger, oozing over the man's consciousness turning to treacle. Already swamped by the tiniest of cogs moving in regular and fascinating ordered patterns, and jewels of the highest distinction, seeming to pulse with a lustred glow. And even as Badger's eyes left the swinging pocket watch, cogs still remained, as if his brain might be composed of clockwork and he had authority over his sight to look inward upon it. One by one the guests had ceased to talk until the only sound was Theodore's soft, ponderous words recited to the man who sat with a straight back, hands on knees, his mouth gaping open, and his eyelids finally shut.

'There,' voiced Theodore. Someone began to clap but a 'ssshh' curtailed that.

'I am not sure this is right, you know,' Reverend Musty commented but his usual stentorian pulpit tones had inexplicably left him and his voice had trailed off into silence. A log spat in the grate. There was a chink of glass and a stifled cough.

'You are in the deepest of sublime trances, Badger, and you hear only my voice. My important voice which has become your voice, your beloved grandfather of the voice, whom you trust implicitly and rely upon. Do you understand?'

A slow, breathy reply issued from between the subject's lips. 'Yes, of course I understand.'

'Good. Now, what should we do?'

'Make him dance; a sort of happy, funny dance?'

'Let him climb onto the roof and roar like a lion.'

'Quiet everybody. Badger, when I snap my fingers, your eyes will open and you will be a parrot. It will be as if you have always been a parrot, a large, red plumed parrot in a jungle of wild and damp growth, and you will be calling a lost mate. Your partner has been missing for many a year; you must attract her, with your colourful feathers.' Theodore paused and then clicked his fingers. Instantly Badger's eyelids sprung open, bright eyes wide and staring, his white curly-haired head twitching comically from side to side. He clambered onto the chair and sat on his haunches, preening the feathers which only he could see, producing an extraordinary noise from the pit of his chest; a squawking, howling row that covered the laughter of the delighted guests. But then over the cacophony Theodore's voice bellowed, 'when I snap my fingers again Badger, you will be as you were.'

With the click, the farm hand had retaken his seat in the proper manner and closed his eyes once more.

'Let us have something a little less noisy,' Mr. Brittle suggested.

'Quite right,' agreed Theodore. 'I will implant another thought into his half-pint mind and awaken him then. Badger, can you hear my voice, which is your grandfather's voice?' With an affirmative answer, Theodore pronounced, 'I am going to awaken you shortly. When I click my fingers once, you will not remember anything of what has happened.' Theodore had plans for embarrassing Mr. Nuckle in the future, use him for his own amusement when he felt the want, and so he added: 'But if I click my fingers twice, you will become … a talking bird, the parrot who knows much language.' The unimaginative Theodore was running out of ideas. 'You will have an irresistible urge to... to... play out your innermost desires with no conscience.'

'What does that mean?' someone queried.

'Obscene urges?' somebody else asked.

'Haha, who will know? Now I really can't think of anything else at the moment. Perhaps he will dash to the nearest jungle and begin a life of novel freedom of speech to convince some lost birdy mate. Who knows? An element of surprise. Besides, I'm getting bored with this and quite thirsty,' and with that said, without thinking of the consequences, Theodore clicked his fingers twice.

Badger's eyes opened wider than ever and they were instantly attentive. To the immense disappointment of those gathered he flicked and twitched his head nervously about him, thanked Theodore for not hypnotizing him after all – albeit in a peculiar high and strangled type of voice – and then resumed his position in the corner of the room.

CHAPTER 14

The Perpetration

THE FOCAL POINT of the evening bowed his bubbles of hair and fixed his attention upon a pastel whorl on the carpet, gentle clucking sounds emitting from him until those about lost interest and dispersed to islands of chatting guests. Theodore, still unable to find his butler, was once more pouring drinks from a bottle taken from a large oak cabinet.

You haven't done it yet,' Eleanor whispered urgently. 'What are you waiting for, my king? You have had all afternoon.'

Stubb put his arm around her shoulder and crouched to speak into her ear. 'I've told you not to worry. I haven't had the opportunity today, Pump was floating about. The one time I want him in the cellar and he doesn't stay there. Don't worry, there's plenty of time. Theodore gives guests the cheap stuff. He wouldn't waste his decent port and whisky on this crowd. He'll have his favourite drink when they've all gone.'

'Now,' demanded Eleanor. 'Now is the time. See for yourself, the cockroach is too busy chatting to impress the vapours, and moving his segments. He won't worry about you.'

Stubb studied Theodore who was engaged upon pulling the brown belt of his trousers tighter about his large belly while talking to Elsie Snicker.

He stood. About to make his way to the study, he was abruptly stopped by a peculiar occurrence.

The chair, which had been placed for the entertainment fifteen minutes before, had been put back into the centre of the

76

room and Badger, his face lit with a strange light, stood upon its seat. Wildly gesticulating, his arms flailing about him, he began to sing in a cracked voice: 'When I was a birdy sailor, A sailor I would be, sailing across the heaving oceans, sailing across the warmest seas, Until one day I found my true love, *bererrrk...*'

'Hooray!' they shouted. 'Bravo!' Theodore's back was patted and he was congratulated on the accomplishment. A desire to entertain and express his parroty love in song was being fulfilled for the meek Mr. Badger.

Stubb felt a nudge to his arm. With a quick nod to his wife he strolled across the drawing room, passing behind his father, and throwing light remarks to groups of guests who stood holding their drinks and encouraging the exuberant farm hand.

'William, my dear boy,' said Reverend Musty.

'Good evening to you, vicar. Sorry I can't stop. I have an errand to run.'

'I believe that you have yet to meet my niece, Isabel. Isabel, this is Mr. Stubb.' He raised his voice against the clamorous chanting and laughing behind him. 'Say hello to Mr. Stubb.' The plait-haired girl remained silent.

'It's very nice to meet you, Isabel, now I really must—'

'Pleased to meet you, Mr. Stubb,' Isabel began quietly and she curtseyed. 'It's my birthday tomorrow; I'll be seventeen.'

'Oh, really. How nice for you.'

Stubb watched nervously his father's steps. Theodore had turned and was walking past though his attention and mirth was directed towards Mr. Badger. This man had quietened, though was enthralling his audience with a stream of peculiar and rude anecdotes, with much gaiety and enthusiasm in his newly-acquired high voice, interrupted with bird calls of shuddering intensity, much to the delight of his audience.

'Tell me, what does it feel like to be a successful woodcarver?'

Isabel enquired softly with obvious admiration. She fluttered her eyelashes through her plaits and scratched her pug nose, and Reverend Musty looked on proudly.

Stubb replied crisply: 'Miss Isabel, let me make it quite clear that I am no longer a woodcarver, nor can it be said that I am in the least successful. Now if you will excuse me, I have an urgent errand to attend to,' and he turned and walked away.

'Well, really,' said the Reverend.

Standing in the lobby, a coolness immediately dismissed the warmer layer that Stubb had acquired in the drawing room. He heard the muted conversation of the guests, the guffaws of his father and the voice of Badger floating high above all others.

He listened for any sound of the butler or maid: all was clear. Another clap of thunder boomed outside. There was a pattering of rain on the porch and sounds of the gusting wind gaining in strength.

Passing quickly through the reception room he came to the door of the study. He grunted after trying the handle. The door was locked. He swore under his breath, cursing his forgetfulness.

Then he remembered there was a spare key under the clock on the mantelpiece. As he approached the clock, the door he had previously come through from the hallway, opened quickly. Stubb turned at the noise of the hinges singing. He felt his face redden.

'Hallo old chap. Looking for the maid, you know. Theodore sent me on the assignment.' Mr. String grinned and winked. His voice lowered. 'To be truthful old bean, I volunteered for the task myself. She's a bit of a cracker, your maid, what?' His protruding teeth stuck out almost horizontally as he shoved his head forward, his eyebrows twitching.

'I'll be bound,' laughed Stubb, playing the ridiculous game. His collar felt sticky and his face still burned from his blush.

'She's not here though,' he remarked hurriedly. 'Perhaps in the kitchen or one of the back rooms.'

'I say, the back room,' said Mr. String with glee and he winked again. He left the door ajar behind him, calling as he went, 'Tally ho!'

Stubb sighed and wiped his damp brow. He closed the door to the hall and then, collecting the key from under the clock, walked over to the study door, unlocked it and entered.

Stale tobacco and an odd perfume came from the books and the few animals heads on the walls. Time was not to be wasted. He went straight to the drinks cabinet, opened it, and drew out a decanter of tawny port. He placed it on the table and fumbled in his pocket. His heart gave a jolt when he could not find the vial of arsenic but a thorough search revealed that it had been hiding in the jacket lining. He retrieved it and held the glass tube up to the light. The contents looked no more than water. He removed the cork stopper and without hesitation, poured the liquid into the decanter.

He put his nose to the decanter lip. There had been no visible reaction. He had expected it to bubble or change colour. However, he considered that it did smell differently and so he left the cut glass stopper off the decanter for as long as he dared, in the hope that the new odour would disperse. Finally replacing the stopper, he swilled the mixture around. Perhaps Theodore would be too drunk to notice.

He chewed on his lip. It was done now, he could not go back. Or could he? He considered the idea of tipping the concoction down the drain and be done with the whole affair. But no, he said to himself. He had come this far. He would see it through to the end.

He replaced the decanter into the drinks cabinet and gave the room a final inspection. Satisfied that everything was in its place, the light in the gas lamp was extinguished and the study locked.

The noise of the gathering in the drawing room seemed louder than ever though evidently Badger had ceased his farcical cabaret. Florence came into the hallway from the kitchen, giggling and flushed. The laughing Mr. String was following her. Upon seeing Stubb, the maid brushed over her apron with an edge of a palm. She tipped her head respectfully. Without thought, Stubb demanded, 'Florence, I would take that silly grin off your face and take in my father's special reserve port.'

She curtseyed and turning her head to giggle at Mr. String again, entered the drawing room.

'What a cracker,' said Mr. String and he followed her in.

Florence collected a few empty glasses as she approached Theodore. She waited for an opportunity to speak.

'I suppose I am. There can't be many people who can boast of having a collection of over forty thousand insects,' Theodore was saying. 'Though curse the Brindling Entomological Society for not recognizing me. I'll show them.'

'Why don't they recognize you?' said Mr. Brittle.

'Never mind why,' Theodore snapped. He inhaled from his cigar.

'Excuse me, sir, but if you are ready for your special port,' said Florence. Mr. Brittle's eyes lit up.

Theodore snorted. 'Who told you that?'

'Sir, Mr. Stubb asked me to—'

'Well, he should know better. You are a maid, do you hear? I will have the port later and the butler will bring it. Now go and tell him as much.'

Florence, looking decidedly upset, curtseyed and went.

'My, you are jolly good with your staff, may I say,' said Isabel.

'Don't I know it,' Theodore said to everyone but the girl.

Mrs. Musty was seated in a large armchair in one side of the room.

Theodore left a group of guests and made his way over to the vicar's wife. 'How are you, my dear lady,' he enquired very loudly, bending down and pushing his face close to hers.

'Quite well, I might say, Mr. Stubb.' She smiled sweetly.

'What else might you say then.' Theodore snuffled with amusement and breathed alcoholic fumes into Mrs. Musty's face. She attempted to maintain her smile but failed and held her nose. Theodore lowered his voice to a more personal level. 'I wonder if I might ask you something, my dear Mrs. Musty?'

'Of course you may, my dear Mr. Stubb.'

Theodore grinned. 'Do you mind if I sit where you're sitting? That's my favourite chair, you know.' He belched so loudly that it seemed to have the strength to cause him to sway backwards.

Mrs. Musty stood hurriedly to her feet. 'Don't you think you've had quite enough to drink?' she stated and walked quickly away to find her husband.

Theodore fell into the vacated armchair and let his eyelids close for a couple of minutes, opening them in time to see the butler stagger into the drawing room, his nose seeming to glow with a light of its own. Before he could reach his master, Reverend Musty and his wife stood rigidly before Theodore.

'Thank you for a pleasant evening but I feel we must take our leave,' stated the reverend and he gave a creaking bow. The rain doubled in strength outside.

'So soon?' Theodore spluttered and he wiped his mouth with the back of one of his hairy hands. He snatched up a bell which stood on a table beside him, ringing it with a type of annoyed enthusiasm.

'You rang sir,' Pump said quietly.

Theodore's eyes focused onto the butler. 'I most certainly did. The reverend and his wife,' and he indicated with his hand, 'are leaving. Show them to the door will you,' then he added as an afterthought, 'and anyone else who's going. And when they've gone bring me my most excellent port.'

'Goodnight to you, sir,' said the vicar formally, fingering his collar. 'Come, Matilda,' he pronounced to his wife. 'Come along, Isabel.'

Despite his sciatica, Badger had been bending over, ostrich-like, in an attempt to peer at the back of Elsie Snicker's shoes in search of feathers though the young woman, quite unaware of the farm hand's strange behaviour, had stepped back and accidentally kicked him in the head. Badger stood and somewhat dazed, retired to his corner, wondering whether he had consumed too much sherry, though still clucking all the same.

The party was ailing. Conversations were still-born and patience grew to infancy only. Finally the celebratory atmosphere was killed: a drunken Theodore floundered to his feet, and swinging an arm about him, said loudly, 'I wonder when this damnable crowd are leaving.' There were gasps and embarrassed coughs and upon asking the maid to fetch their coats, the majority of those assembled prepared themselves to depart.

Mr. and Mrs. Parsley felt that it was time to go as they had a long day ahead of them tomorrow. Mr. Taper the cobbler expressed great apologies for not being able to stay longer and Elsie Snicker and Mr. Brittle passed by Theodore without bidding farewell, following the remainder of the guests out of the room.

The maid served the guests their coats from the doorway of the dining room whilst the butler stood as a swaying coat-hanger with six or more items clutched unceremoniously in his hands and a steeple of hats balanced upon his head.

The reverend and his wife stood on the porch steps with a hope that the rain would lessen. They began to twitter together of the rudeness they had been subjected to, competing in sound with the hissing downpour.

Isabel, who had been inspecting the images of ants in the stained glass about the imposing front door, looked bewilderingly to Badger for he was slowly raising and lowering his arms.

'Uncle,' she finally said in a dreamy voice, 'Mr. Badger looks like he's trying to fly.'

With a hint of impatience, Reverend Musty replied from the open doorway, 'Pardon, Isabel? What do you mean? Now I think we really must go. We're going to get soaked but that's the way it is. Say goodnight to Mr. Badger.' With that said he stepped back into the hallway, took hold of Isabel's hand and pulled her into the night rain.

Though the fire had maintained a comfortable heat, it seemed colder without the room's former occupants. Stubb returned from his bedroom to find that all of the guests had gone save Mr. String, who was involved in chasing a foreign speck in his drink with his finger.

Eleanor was gazing into the fireplace, perhaps too afraid to look at Theodore for he was pouring himself a glass of port. Stubb was transfixed; he could not drag his sight from the glass. Theodore held the concoction up to the light of one of the gas lamps and Stubb held his breath; then Mr. String walked out of the room, thinking of higher pleasures, followed by the intoxicated butler.

'An exquisite drink. A toast to both of you,' Theodore said loudly. He sent the glass at arm's length in a semicircle about him and brought it to his lips and Stubb heard a clink as it touched his teeth. Theodore paused. Stubb was on the verge of crying out. His father lowered the glass and rang the bell twice. The butler appeared again, surprisingly quickly. 'Pump, get my best cigars, and both of you – you're not drinking. Where are your glasses?'

The butler left yet again to leave Theodore smirking at his son and daughter-in-law.

'Yes, let's get a drink,' said Stubb to his wife, his voice shaking uncontrollably.

'That would be nice,' Eleanor answered in a surprisingly calm manner.

When they had finished pouring drinks from a bottle of red wine, Pump returned, clutching a pine box. He lifted the lid and offered the selection of cigars to Theodore who carefully selected one after much consideration as though choosing a particular chocolate. The butler bowed, leaving the room in an ungainly fashion, and headed for the cellar.

Theodore bit the end from the plump cigar and spat it into an ashtray beside him. 'Must keep the place tidy,' he chuckled. He lit the cigar with a taper, the flame taken from one of the candles in a candelabra on a side table, and after pumping volumes of smoke, raised the glass to his lips once more. 'Here's to an excellent party,' he declared and he consumed all the liquid in the glass in one swift movement. Stubb and Eleanor were as sculptures, motionless and staring. Theodore smacked his lips and looked inquisitively to his son. 'What in diamond's name has got into you?'

'Nothing, I mean, what do you mean?'

'You're not drinking, boy.'

Stubb took a sip quickly and with a shaking hand he dropped the glass and it smashed onto the carpet, leaving a pool of blood red wine by his feet; and then his father stood upright.

CHAPTER 15
A Death

'IAM AFRAID I don't feel very well,' Theodore muttered and he touched his mouth gently and coughed as though clearing his throat. But then, wheezing and gasping for breath, he fell onto his knees. He swallowed constantly and gulped in air to his heaving chest. 'I can't breathe,' he croaked, clutching and clawing at his throat. His eyeballs rolled upwards, leaving the bloodshot whites of his eyes twitching. His tongue hung from his mouth like an obscene red slash. He gurgled and tried to push fingers into his throat while the other hand still grasped at his stout neck. He fell clumsily, face-down, onto the carpet as his rasping breath became shortened and laboured. He stretched out his arms; with a fearful cry of agony his whole bulk overturned ponderously like some great ship sinking beneath the sea and – limbs pulled as far away from his body as was possible – the arms and legs flayed about like a beetle on its back. Then, with his inflamed eyes staring and his mouth gaping open and dribbling, his tongue lolling and his belly heaving, he emitted a shrill shriek. So sharp and sudden was the shriek that it turned Stubb's limbs to water; so acute and abrupt that it seemed to take on solid form and hang in the room like a serrated rag, then to vanish as quickly as it had appeared. His back arched so that only his head and heels of his brown shoes touched the floor until his weight dropped and he became limp.

Theodore lay on the carpet, motionless.

Eleanor peeked through her fingers that were plastered

across her wide eyes. 'Is he?' was all she whispered.

Stubb could not answer. What had he done? Watching his father's death throes, he had seen it as an unreal dream but as he stared hard at the body of Theodore on the drawing room carpet, the reality exposed itself in a vicious instant. He, too, fell to his knees like his father before him and wept bitterly, his eyes stinging.

Eleanor held his quivering head to her side while stroking one of his impressive sideburns and said, 'There, there, William, all over. The old slimy cockroach is dead. He wasn't real anyway. It's all ours now. It was always ours, wasn't it? Our palace stolen from us. We have everything again. I have my Alastair. We're going to be so happy.' She grinned when an idea came to her. 'We'll sell the rotten insect collection in the loft. Dead creatures can't help. I'm sure it's worth a bit.'

Stubb stood and drained the liquid from Eleanor's glass and he wiped his face with the back of his hand. 'What do we do now?' he whined, clutching his sideburns.

'Get rid of this damned insect, that's what,' Eleanor hissed and she bent down to Theodore's pocket watch which dangled onto the floor, unbuttoned the chain and placed the watch into her cardigan pocket.

The door swung open and Stubb gasped. Eleanor blinked at Mr. String who was chuckling as though he had heard a rude joke. 'My dear William and Mrs. Stubb,' he said, 'I cannot express how much I have enjoyed myself but all good things must come to an end. I'll be taking my leave over yonder hills. Where is Theodore? I must thank him also.' He glanced down and his sight fixed onto the prostrate body on the floor behind Stubb and Eleanor.

'Oh,' he said simply. Stubb shouted gibberish and Eleanor put a hand to her mouth; Mr. String began to laugh. 'I knew the old boy had a bit too much, even for him. Told him to watch it,' he said.

Eleanor was quick to take the opportunity of the moment. 'You wouldn't help us to get the poorly insect up to a spare room, would you, Archie?' She pouted her lips and fluttered her eyelashes then pointed to her large mound.

'Why, of course,' Mr. String replied. He gave a short bow and with a dry chuckle he skipped over to the body of Theodore. He was joined by Stubb who was shaking gently.

'I say, are you alright? You look a bit green around the gills.' Stubb nodded. 'Let me see now,' said Mr. String, 'I'll take his head and you can take the legs,' and before Stubb could argue the barrister's clerk was heaving Theodore from the floor with his hands under the man's armpits. Stubb gripped his father's ankles and with a loud, 'Heave ho!' from Mr. String, they lifted Theodore, and both grimacing with the effort, carried him out into the hall, leaving Eleanor in the drawing room.

'By Jove, he's a dead weight,' Mr. String remarked. Stubb grinned weakly.

Taking the proceedings at a slow pace, they carried the body to half way up the staircase whereupon they propped Theodore on one of the steps. They rested. Stubb suggested that they should change ends and thus done they carried on. It was when Stubb's shaking arm muscles gave way and Theodore's head was dropped with a dry thud on the edge of the banister that Mr. String said, 'Careful, old boy. A bit of life left in the old man yet.' They both wiped their brows and continued their task. Upon reaching the landing it was agreed that after carrying fifteen stones of weight between them up a flight of stairs they deserved another rest. Theodore's eyes were open though the pupils had given way to white; he gazed sightlessly to the spiral staircase that led to the attic. Dribbles of saliva were drying on his chin. Stubb groaned when he thought he saw his father's chest rise and fall but he knew it was a trick of the dusky shadows. Ignoring the remark from Mr. String of 'He's gone a most peculiar colour, don't you think?' Stubb watched closely, and sure enough Theodore's chest was still.

'We'll put him on a spare bed,' Stubb decided and felt he needed to add, 'he can sleep it off there.'

Eleanor retrieved the cigar from the carpet and disposed of it. She picked up the silver tray and placing upon it the decanter and glass from which Theodore had drunk, took them to the kitchen and washed them out thoroughly. She felt happier than she had been for a long time. She knew all along that Theodore had been a renegade insect. The massive walking cockroach had ceased to be, perhaps now ready to join the attic collection.

On the way to the study, she began to hum Badger's odd tune and she gazed about her as she went, as if in awe of her surroundings. When in the study, she replaced the decanter into the cocktail cabinet.

She looked down to her mound and as though her clothing and flesh were made of glass she saw her baby, curled contentedly in her womb, cocooned and waving six legs. Then, distinctly and precisely, she believed that the being spoke to her. 'Mummy,' she heard as a soft whisper. She felt lightheaded and dreamy until a knife-edged pain seared through her abdomen and she nearly dropped the tray: labour pains, so soon despite Dr. Snippet telling them the birth would be at least another few weeks ahead.

Eleanor made her way to the hall – hunched over and with teeth clamped – but could go no further. She pushed a potted plant out of the way and lay the tray onto the hall stand to grasp her swollen belly. A burning and ripping within her womb spread to the tops of her thighs and to her chest. She stood panting for a while, riding the pain, then began to walk laboriously up the stairs, moaning softly, 'Fire, fire.'

The strength to call out had gone. Her legs were as heavy as if weighed down with lead and yet her head seemed weightless and detached from her body. She even gave a chuckle when the idea of giving birth to her insect child on the staircase struck her as amusing but the blazing stabs returned, and winded her.

She reached the landing and was met by her husband and Mr. String. 'My, they're dropping like flies,' laughed the barrister's clerk.

'So soon?' Stubb cried out. Eleanor was overcome with the throbbing, shooting pain and she could not answer. 'Don't stand there like a bag of sawdust, go and fetch the doctor. Quick!' yelled Stubb as all Mr. String could do was stare from one face to the other. Then his skinny legs flinched into motion and he bounded down the stairs at an admirable speed and ran across the hallway. He wrenched open the front door and ran out.

'Come then, my love. Slowly does it,' Stubb murmured, placing his arm around her shoulders and guiding her up the stairs.

Mr. String was back in the hall, calling. 'I say, William old boy, doctor who?'

'Dr. Snippet, you rotten bean pole. Now go.'

'But I don't know where he lives.'

Stubb growled. 'Monstrous fool,' he shouted. 'Bacon Cottage, Pindle Lane. It's only around the corner, over the other side of the green. Go.'

And Mr. String was gone.

CHAPTER 16
The Deal

'I THINK, MR. STUBB, there is nothing more we can do,' Dr. Snippet said, almost sadly.

'But the labour pains.'

'There is no more to worry about, I assure you. They will not start again until quite a few more hours. Then you will both have a gurgling child before you can say Jack Hodgson. About seven o'clock tomorrow morning, I would estimate. I had a feeling that the child would be early.'

'When can I see her?'

'I have given Mrs. Eleanor a mild herbal medication to make her relaxed. She needs rest. Now I must be going, though I will be at this address if you need me.' He handed Stubb a rectangular card. 'But I am sure there will be no need for that. Even so, the number of the telephone is there.'

'A telephone machine? We don't have such a thing.'

'Not a worry; I would advise you, Mr. Stubb, to catch fifty winks and I will be back in four and a half hours' time.' He patted him on the back and departed.

Stubb felt exhausted but he knew that worse was to come. He went to the kitchen to make a cup of tea.

While sitting at the kitchen table and sipping the beverage slowly, he began to think. His immediate problem was the disposal of the body. He could hardly bury it in the garden. Could it be burned? He rejected the idea as he had no means to implement that.

As he thought, his mind ran into absurdities of which he could not rid himself, as one is prone to do with the onset of tiredness and when emotions have been agitated. He shuddered as a new voice promoted the theme that the disposal of Theodore would be easier if he was cut into small pieces. Stubb imagined throwing them, as though bits of bread, to the ducks on Laughing Pond, then pictured slices of flesh and whole limbs hanging in a butcher's shop; a leg here, a lump there, with the severed head sitting on a marble slab, sightless and drained of blood. He groaned and rubbed his tired eyes to rid himself of the gruesome images.

Something had to be done quickly: if the body was kept for a week it would surely begin to decompose; for a month, to smell. It seemed a peculiar situation: there on the first floor (he looked to the ceiling as though he could see through it) lay a woman due to give birth and a dead man.

How would he explain a missing person to the authorities? No letters, notes, explanations, no spoken intentions of departure, no body, no funeral.

Funeral: the word unlocked a door within him and an image appeared of Mr. Nuckle, outside the sanatorium eight months before, loading a casket into the back of a hearse. The undertaker was well acquainted with the gardener, that much Stubb knew, and he surmised that any friend of Brood's would not possess a total honesty. Besides, while working for Terps Joinery, he had heard rumours of Nuckle's business procedures which implied a tarnished character. Could he be persuaded, with selected words and the right amount of promised money, to take the body without questions asked? There was a good chance. It was maybe his only chance.

He drank the remains of his tea and managed a wry smile.

He would pay Mr. Nuckle well for disposing of his father. He would visit him tomorrow.

The silence of the kitchen was becoming more oppressive by the second. He stood and paced the stone floor, then made another tea. It remained in the cup with the milk forming a white skin on its surface. Still his mind would not rest. It was becoming as though his weary senses could hear cells within Theodore's body emitting a sigh, one by one, as they gave up their life. See fluids draining down under the insistent force of gravity; smell the organic structures decomposing with the inevitable entropy – to wait until the next day was proving to be impossible. It would have to be that night.

He left the kitchen and got his thick overcoat for, though the rain had stopped, the sound of the wind wailing told him it was bitterly cold. He found Florence and informed her that he had to go out on urgent business. She was to listen for any sound from Eleanor. If there was any trouble she must fetch the doctor. He gave her the address. She was told not to disturb Theodore under any circumstances. 'Why would I do that at this late hour, sir?' she said.

Stubb walked across the short gravel drive to the already opened black iron gates, the hinges of both rusted solid long ago. The dark clouds which had marred the night sky had passed over and had been replaced by feathery formations. They would have more snow the next day. The slush on the pathways was beginning to freeze.

Brushing down his hair that was blown in all directions by the wind, he walked briskly past the snow-covered tree branches along Daisytrail Lane, on his way to Stutter Lane, with a feeling of joy in his heart. He had forgotten his trembling shock at the sight of his dead father and he thought only of the future. It would be good to be content again.

A row of modest houses slept along Grinding Road. Stubb checked the undertaker's address in his notebook then studied each house in turn. The dwelling with the correct number stood with a bay window and purple door, and snow-laden bushes in the garden. Shrugging his shoulders and pulling the belt of his overcoat tighter about him he swung open the gate and marched along the path to the door. A sign was on the ground partly obscured by milk bottles. He read the sign and muttered the words: 'Chapel of Rest, Paradise Cottage, Grinding Road, Muchmarsh.'

He pulled the bell knob and a tinkling sound came from inside the house. He rubbed his hands briskly together to bring some heat back to them then snuffled impatiently. After counting ten taps of his big toe on the inside of his boot, he pulled the bell knob for a second time. There were shuffling noises from the interior. The door creaked open a fraction and a pair of bespectacled eyes peered cautiously from the gap.

'What is it this time of night? Don't you possess a watch? If you do possess one I strongly recommend that you look at it and when you realize it is later than you imagined, you will go away. Now, goodnight to you,' said an irritated voice.

Stubb was embarrassed for he had had no thought for the time and he said, 'I am sorry to disturb you at this late hour but I have urgent business. I'm sure you remember me.'

Mr. Nuckle opened the door wider and said, 'What of it? What if I know or don't know you? Coming here to my house, a total stranger at twelve o'clock at night. I've got a busy day tomorrow, I will have you know. A lot of arrangements to sort and I need my sleep like any hard working man and you stand on my doorstep talking and keep me up. Anyway, who are you?'

'Mr. William Stubb, a previous employee of Terps. I was

reminded of you by Brood,' and he felt it best to add, 'a fine fellow if I might say.'

Nuckle's hand relaxed visibly at the gardener's name; the joints of his fingers that curled around the door had been almost as white as his curly hair. He sighed a long, relieved sigh as though ridding himself of some mental burden. 'Be quick about it,' he snapped, with a hint of suspicion still. He opened the door wider and Stubb saw the small man possessing large, sorrowful eyes which were obscured for a moment when his spectacles reflected the moon. The similarity to Badger was remarkable; they must surely be twin brothers and yet he knew there was no family connection. Stubb almost expected Mr. Nuckle to begin singing or squawking, as Mr. Badger had done two hours before.

A dog barked in the distance at the silent alleys and lanes.

'It concerns my father. It was a dreadful business but the honourable gentleman passed away quite suddenly two days ago – or was it yesterday? You see how grief has confused me so.'

'Can't you see?' spluttered Nuckle angrily. He jabbed a finger at the sign by the milk bottles.

'See what? I see your sign.'

'Of course you do. It's the sign I took down three days ago from the rest chapel. I've forgotten to take it in, that's all.' The time had come for him to do just that and he bent to retrieve it; and clutching the article in one hand, began to push the door closed.

'Wait,' Stubb said quickly, stopping the door with his foot. 'Are you saying that you're no longer an undertaker?'

Nuckle shook his head. 'I have had my fill of that lark. Sold the plot, sold the stock, sold the horse and the cart. Sold the lot. So I'm getting out before it's too late.' Stubb decided not to remark although his mind bounced through possibilities of the man's meaning. Maybe he had been correct in his estimation of his character. 'I am going into the catering business,' Nuckle announced proudly. 'I have bought a place overlooking the green. Now, goodnight.'

'But my father, he needs burial.'

'Well, you'll have to find someone else then, won't you? Goodnight to you, Mr. Pub.'

Stubb ignored the mistake and stood his ground. 'Look here, Mr. Nuckle. I will pay you double your normal charge. Triple even. Please, one more transaction before you give up your fine profession.'

Nuckle looked pensive but then rubbing his unshaven, bristly chin, a tentative interest lit in his eyes. He finally opened the plain door to his terraced house. A musty but aromatic scent clung to Stubb's nostrils. There, on the unvarnished floorboards of the small hallway, were sprays of dried carnations and sheaves of lilies, green wreaths with dessicated roses and pansies about them, bouquets, posies and baskets, flower cushions and pillows, heart-shaped floral arrangements and pots and glass vases filled with cream and white petaled dehydrated flowers, orange, purple and red. All of a sumptuous garden's bounty seemed to be there, along with larger presentations that Stubb could see through a gap in the doorway leading to the front room. And even while he stood outside, the powerful odour of the blooms, all in different states of decay, some already dried and fallen to pieces of potpourrie, made him feel unusually light-headed. A pile of sympathy cards, almost as tall as the funeral parlour director, stood in one corner, the striated paper column made up of deckle-edged and black sided card.

Come in quick; quickly come in,' Mr. Nuckle said, his voice hushed and urgent. 'But only if the price is right,' he added.

CHAPTER 17

Spectre

ELEANOR FELT AS light as a gas. The herbal infusion that Dr. Snippet had prescribed was making her weary and with feelings of intoxication yet sleep eluded her. She had become hot and restless and confused. She weakly thumped her pillow into shape and sat herself up with the certainty that Alastair would be released from her soon, along with the small fire in her womb becoming extinguished.

***

Brood curled his lip in contempt. He remained motionless with fingers splayed and arms outstretched as though imitating a tree. His breathing was slow. He stared without expression at the rat which twitched its whiskers and seemingly glanced innocently up to him whereupon the animal resumed eating the cake which had been left on the shed floor as bait.

It was another cold night and the gardener had found that he had been unable to sleep. He hated cold more than anything; he resented coldness even more than William Stubb and the rats. After finding more sacking to cover himself he had slept fitfully but only to have been awakened by scratching and scurrying vermin, so keen were his ears to the night sounds.

The gardener moved a fraction of an inch at a time until his hand rested on the end of the spade, leaning in the corner of his shed. He held his breath and waited with patience for the moment when he would squash the life out of the furriness which dared to sit on his floor and eat his cake.

He raised the spade, level with his head, in preparation to strike. But before he moved further, the rat emitted a squeak, its skinny body shaking violently, its red pinpoint eyes flaring until it fell onto its side. It opened its mouth to show rows of fine, pointed teeth until they were covered by blood that sprang from inside the starched body. It had happened in a moment.

Brood stared, baffled and annoyed. Baffled because he could not remember lacing the food – indeed, why he would have spoilt one of his much-loved cakes with poison – and annoyed because he had been deprived of the pleasure of destroying another of the loathsome creatures which inhabited his territory. He cursed and flushed, and kicked a workbench when he was reminded that Eleanor – or whoever else had taken it – had returned the rat poison. Then on the impulse of the moment, he pulled on a shirt and overalls and put on his boots and gloves as well as two coats and went out into the night. Another rat appeared from behind the mechanical lawnmower.

❦

When the sun sleeps and it has taken with it the colours of day, it makes way for darkness to creep over the landscape, painting the legacy of the sun in sombre, darker colours – smoke-black, umber and ebony. Evils, real and imagined, thrive. It is the time when children are pushed shaking and crying from their nightmares into the worse nightmare of the darkness where the fear of the unknown is born. Fear lives in the cobwebs, steely grey, and in shadows that hang like waiting bats in holes and corners and caves.

The drapes had not been drawn and the moon shone an eerie

glow into Eleanor's charcoal-shadowed room. It painted objects with a silver tinge enabling them to be picked out in detail while others were smothered in blackness.

Eleanor felt lonely. She was about to call her husband but changed her mind when she felt it to be childish. Her loneliness had become companion to nervousness then, for her familiar companion, darkness, was playing tricks on her. Was that a balloon of light, a globe of brightness which contracted and expanded and was floating to the ceiling? The more she strained her head forward to pierce the night in the room, the more the hazy shape lost definition. She felt tearful and suspiciously kept her fatigued eyes to it. It was then she realised it was nothing more than a lampshade stored on top of the wardrobe. She could even see some pattern upon it.

Her eyelids became weighty; a lethargy swamped her and she had no choice but to close her eyelids. Wriggling further under the covers, she tried to find sleep.

A noise then, she was convinced. With an effort, she scanned the dark bedroom for its source. She whimpered. Upon hearing her own voice she felt foolish. It was the worst thing she could do, she told herself, to let panic take hold on the important occasion of a queen giving birth to her child. A high royal privilege, to have been chosen as a channel for the reincarnation of her darling Alastair. Her work of lighting the way in the church had not been in vain.

The dark shapes still floated and swam, swirling and congealing, dissolving into granular and fluid whorls. She was well acquainted with interiors as black ink, night during a day, sacred dust and insect envoys busy with their assignment, the frozen tombs and crypt corridors hidden from the sun. Despite this, Eleanor still let out a short cry; it seemed evident that a human form was there, standing in the corner of the room beside the door. Perhaps one of the stone figures forever asleep on one of the crypt caskets in the church had become alive, animated and in a visiting mood. She could make out a fraction of a shoulder though the rest was lost to the heavy blanket of the night.

In a weak and tremulous voice she cried out, 'Sir Bertrand? William?' The figure seemed to sway. 'Who's there? Who is it? I command you tell Queen Eleanor.' Her voice sounded listless. There was no answer except for the ticking from the clockwork beside the bed. This is becoming ridiculous, she thought to herself. Perhaps it was knowing that her father-in-law – the massive cockroach with hidden antennae, mandibles and cold, compound eyes – lay dead only a few rooms away that was stimulating her imagination to frightening images.

Obscure meanderings filled her mind. The form etched faintly into the purple-black appeared to shift, to change position as though transferring the weight of a body from one foot to the other. Eleanor's breath quickened and though her fright was growing into a tight thorny ball within, she was finding it increasingly difficult to keep her eyes from closing again as the herbal concoction that the doctor had prescribed took a firmer grip over her consciousness.

The doorbell rang. Pump slept in an alcoholic haze in the cellar. He stirred at the noise but, failing an attempt to raise himself to a sitting position, fell onto his back and tittered before plunging into a bottomless sleep.

Florence – still awake after clearing and cleaning the aftermath of the party – ran to the front door. The clanging bell was insistent and it had been obvious to her that the butler was not going to answer. Upon opening the door a fraction the identity of the person that merged with the night was unknown but when the visitor stepped forward from the darkness of the porch and said, 'Miss Florence?' she opened the door wide.

'What are you doing here at this time of night?' she whispered, trying to sound annoyed but failing, with a grin on her pert face.

'I have returned on my snow-white charger from over gale-lashed mountains, storm-rent forests and torrents to steal more of your exquisite kisses and to take my fill of your passionate embraces, my lady,' gushed Mr. String and he gave a theatrical bow.

He stepped into the hall without invitation and puckered his lips the best that he was able over his prominent teeth, advancing upon Florence with stick arms outstretched and his sparkling eyes tightly shut.

'If you don't mind,' she said, curtailing his amorous ways with her hand, 'Mr. William Stubb will be back soon. Leave be.' She spoke seriously but spoilt the effect by giggling. 'You are a one, Beany,' she added.

'Come now my princess, my pearl, my beauty. We will go straight away to my glittering palace in the sky. Besides which I want to show you my bric-a-brac.' His eyebrows twitched in unison and he laughed heartily. He pulled Florence gently to the door.

'No, wait. How long will we be? Mr. William has had to go out on urgent business so I have to look after Mrs. Stubb, you know.'

'Ah, that is so. I do hear that her offspring is due to arrive into this mad turmoil of life's rich tapestry in three weeks' time.'

'No, this morning. It's early.'

'Oh – I see.' Mr. String appeared disappointed.

'In about four hours, I believe.'

'So there it is.' His long face brightened. 'Time is ours for the asking. You, my dearest, will be back in the twinkling of an eye. Come, I have my magical carriage awaiting us outside.'

Florence was convinced. 'You've borrowed the new-fangled machine again from Barrister Leggit?' she said excitedly. 'Alright Beany but wait a moment.'

She fetched her coat from the cloakroom and ran back into the hallway to Mr. String who was tapping an arm and staring at the ornately coved ceiling. He bowed again to an invisible audience and with a jolly, 'Farewell, mortals,' to his own reflection in the wall mirror, shut the front door behind them. They skipped down the snow-mottled gravel drive to the open gates like children playing truant.

Eleanor was trying to catch her breath that had become sharp and shallow. Pains that felt as though they were ripping her flesh rent through her body yet she remembered enough to know that the final contractions of labour were still to come. Through watering eyes she saw the shadow figure move to the end of the four poster bed, by the ottoman. Still she could not recognize the identity of the shape cut from the fabric of the night.

She was petrified with fear. 'Who is it? What do you want?' she wailed. There was a guttural chuckle, a disembodied voice as an answer. Eleanor howled and covered her sight. 'Please leave me be, whoever you are. Go away, get out of my chamber,' she whined in between gasps, as the pains spreading their tendrils through her loins became even more insistent. When the shadow swung from one side of the room to the other, she flinched and began to gabble a prayer of appeasement to the horrid moving shadow; but rather than dissolve the shape into nothingness it stimulated more laughter. Eleanor's face creased in horror and her head, with hair loose and tangled, bobbed from one side to the other in an attempt to identify the unknown spectre that had felt it right to visit her. Was this some sort of punishment from a phantom guardian of the crypts?

An urgent, whispered voice, insistent and an opiate to her already drugged and ill brain; it was difficult to make out any of the words as dark and frightening as bats but the more she listened, the more those syllables became pleasant sounds, as beautiful as butterflies.

She began to doze as they floated and flitted and stroked her jagged fear. She was succumbing. 'No,' she cried weakly. She was not going to be fooled into sleep by an evil demon. If the creature wanted her soul, her tangled thoughts told herself, it would have to work harder than that.

It was then that the throbbing in her womb ceased temporarily and she found herself more awake than she had felt that evening. The deep velvet voice stopped as well, as if the cessation of pain was a signal; and Eleanor moaned in relief.

It began again straightway: the whisper rising to a mutter seeming harsher, more insistent. As she felt pains returning in waves, blood pounding her temples and sleep pulling her from awareness, Eleanor realized she could understand what was being said.

'Why did you kill Theodore?' the ethereal voice demanded. She stiffened her whole body so much that she pulled the muscles in the calves of her legs, already sore from bed cramps, and in the back of her neck. She sobbed fitfully. What retribution was to befall her? Her throat was sealed and she swallowed spasmodically as the voice demanded again, 'Why did you kill Theodore?'

Her emotions were in turmoil and with her bewilderment they swung from one extreme to the other like the pendulum of a clock: at the one moment fright gripping her while weeping and wailing from her pains, then in the next instant laughing, wide-eyed and bewildered. She heard an utterance, a querulous whine but realized that it was she who had spoken. She continued, 'I'm sorry. Queen Eleanor didn't mean to kill him. It was all a dreadful mistake. Cockroaches aren't meant to die. We wanted to frighten him, that was all.'

'But he did die. You killed him, you and your husband.'

'Yes we did. No we didn't. I don't know, at least, I didn't – it was William. It was his idea. Yes, he did it, he murdered Theodore.'

'How did he kill Theodore?' the disembodied voice asked as the speaker covered himself totally within the folds of the night.

'Yes, that's right. William killed him.' Eleanor felt dopey and listless. Was this some dreadful nightmare? She was sure she was feverish. To prove the point she felt her brow. 'He murdered Theodore,' she said in a singsong voice. She saw a child on a swing. The child wore a pony tail tied with a ribbon and was swinging from the bow of a beech tree and she sang to the bluest of skies. Eleanor asked of the image of her past self, 'How did you kill Theodore?' As the memory faded she explained, 'Eleanor killed Theodore. Brood gave her some rat poison but she didn't use that. Oh, no. She poisoned him with arsenic because she hated him, every part of his filthy shell. She wanted him to die in agony because ... because he stole Alastair, gave wrong commands to the spiders; she was glad when he did go. Then Alastair returned, here within me, safe and warm and protected.' She smiled into the darkness: she cried bitterly then did both at the same time. She tried to pick up the shattered pieces of her senses and put them together but was dazed and muddled.

'Eleanor, you owe Theodore everything. What did you use? Tell me again.'

Eleanor moaned and gasped, 'Arsenic. It was a painful death, wasn't it. Wasn't it?' She listened for a reply. The wind breathed through the trees, their bare branches groping to the heavens in the hope of catching the bright stars. She listened intently and gasped as contractions were becoming prominent with positive pulses, stronger by the moment.

The demon had departed and returned to his lair in the depths of a red hell. She had beaten him. Her soul was safe; Alastair was safe.

'Your baby,' rumbled the voice. Eleanor twitched and screamed and began to pant rhythmically. Her baby; the demon must not have her baby. Don't let the monster know it is winning. Laugh in its bloated, devilish face. Laugh...

Eleanor laughed in a way she had never laughed before. She threw back her head and with her mouth open wide emitted a piercing gale of derision, tears flowing down her cheeks, along the creases that her face made as pain came and went and came, then she cried out, 'Leave my baby, leave my baby, leave baby!' and she cackled almost insanely.

❦

The doctor stood on the doorstep of the moon-lit manor house. He looked nervously at his watch. He had wanted to be back earlier but to administer words of comfort to a woman who had been made a widow within the hour could not have been rushed. He rang the bell. Florence appeared beside him and gave a furtive wave to Mr. String in his borrowed motor car, passing the gates on his way along the dark lane. 'Good evening Dr. Snippet; or I should say good morning,' she said cheerfully.

'Ah, my dear, hello. I have come to deliver a child. It is Mrs. Eleanor, you know.'

'I've this minute thought I would tell you to come.' Her lie passed without comment or suspicion. 'I think it won't be long now.' She produced a key and opened the door.

Once in the hallway, they stood facing each other to glean an explanation as to the screams interspersed with a croaky laughter that came echoing from upstairs.

'My goodness gracious, she's started,' the doctor said and he moved quickly up the stairs, clutching his brown calf hide bag. He made his way to Eleanor's bedroom and was followed shortly by Florence who held a trimmed lamp. The radiance chased the dirty shadows away and as they fled they took with them the ghosts of the night. The doctor gasped in surprise and the maid muffled a cry by smothering her mouth with a hand.

Eleanor had bandaged herself with the bed covers; they had become bound tightly about her. Though screaming in agony, still she laughed, her previously clear complexion a blotched and wrinkled face of a clown. Beads of blood sat along scratches in her cheeks that had been made with her own fingernails. Her hair was a dishevelled mess.

'Clean linen, hot water. Plenty of it and hurry,' Dr. Snippet demanded.

CHAPTER 18
The Missing Body

STUBB WAS PLEASED. It had been a successful transaction with Mr. Nuckle. It was arranged that the body of Theodore was to be collected the following night. He walked briskly along the dark Stutter Lane past shuttered windows and snowy lawns, on his way to Daisytrail Lane via the village green.

Upon entering the manor house he found it in silence. One of the drawing room doors was ajar. Florence and the doctor were seated by the fire, a fresh log of ash burning within it, and they spoke in conspiring tones. They did not hear Stubb enter, so engrossed were they in their conversation. A creeping feeling that something was amiss: 'Doctor, my wife,' Stubb blurted out.

Florence stood hurriedly and looked embarrassed. Stubb ignored her and the doctor rose from his armchair.

'Where have you been?' he demanded, his usual mild manner replaced with annoyance.

Stubb clicked his tongue. 'I … I had urgent business to attend to,' he said.

'Urgent enough to leave your wife as she gave birth to your son?'

Stubb looked bemused for a moment and then he smiled and it widened the more. 'A son, you say – wonderful, wonderful, that is wonderful!' He gave a shout of glee and could not help but chuckle whereupon, seeing Florence's surprise, he contained himself and said to her, 'I think you had better go. You should be in your room at this time anyway.'

Stubb sat opposite the doctor in his father's favourite wingback armchair after dragging it nearer the fire guard. He spoke in a confidential way. 'Dr. Snippet, I trust my wife is safe and well.'

'As well as can be expected,' came the quick reply. The doctor looked grim. 'I have placed her under light sedation. She has been through much more than any other young woman in her position. Time heals, they say. Let us hope that is so.'

'What are you saying? What do you mean?'

'I mean, Mr. Stubb, that something or someone has frightened Mrs. Eleanor out of her wits, to such a degree that the birth of the child was brought on even more prematurely by her acute fright. When I arrived here, the woman was half out of her mind. You know yourself that your wife has had a record of mentality upsets and on that score she is very delicate.'

'What can be done?'

Dr. Snippet gave a drawn-out sigh and looked to the coloured tufts of carpet as he spoke. 'With the terrible scare that she has undoubtedly encountered, coupled with the fact that it was a difficult birth, I can only suggest that you pray.' He looked up from the floor to fix his attention onto William Stubb. 'And you had urgent business to attend to,' he said with an unusual bitterness.

Stubb could not hide his guilt. He knew that he should have waited until the next day to see Nuckle but to live in a house that contained a dead and murdered body had been unthinkable. 'How was I to know she was going to give birth while I was away?' he muttered feebly. 'What could have frightened her?'

'I have no idea. Your maid tells me she heard nothing out of the ordinary and that your wife was sleeping soundly until the final labour pains came. I arrived then.'

'She is going to be alright isn't she; she's going to be well...'

'As I have said, Mr. Stubb, I cannot say. All we can do is wait and see the outcome. She has suffered a condition that we call eclampsia. Violent convulsions and so forth. Being of a nervous and, may I say, unstable type of person to begin with, her physical and mental state is somewhat worrying.' Stubb lowered his head and covered his brow with his hands. The doctor continued, 'Now if you will excuse me, I must go. I have other calls to make tonight but I will return in the morning's light to check her progress.' He stood. 'She will not awaken until then and I would not disturb her,' and he added firmly, 'I insist upon that. Goodnight to you.'

'Goodnight,' murmured Stubb, deep in thought.

Once Dr. Snippet had departed, Stubb poured himself a drink and sat back in the armchair with a mournful expression haunting his features. He slowly sipped from a glass of whisky. A terrible fright, the doctor had said. But what could have frightened her? Or whom? As he stared at the flames of the fire, he cursed himself for not being with her. Then impulsively he stood up and placed the unfinished alcohol upon the side table. He must visit Eleanor despite the doctor's advice. He was also keen to see his newborn son; to see them for a few moments surely could do no harm.

He tiptoed up the stairs, trying to calm his excited breathing at the prospect of seeing his child. He paced along the paneled corridor, past a stunted suit of armour and the morbid portraits, and stood outside their bedroom door. The baby inside would be a strange being; a small and fragile thing, almost as a doll, he knew. A paternal desire took hold but then, with his neck muscles stiffening, the dark thought that there was no hope of the child being his came to mind; he decided that to see another's offspring from his wife would be too painful an experience. He would heed the words of Dr. Snippet and leave Eleanor and the child to sleep.

A hasty decision came to mind: he would take a look at the body of Theodore. Why, he could not say, for the idea repulsed him yet some inner pressure urged him on. He went to the spare bedroom where he and Mr. String had laid the dead man. Lighting the oil lamp that stood by the door, he entered. The bright flame licked the walls and ceiling clean of the dark and spread an orange light over the bed.

Stubb gaped. He put his head to one side and laughed although he did not know why. This nervous reaction was broken by a shriek and he nearly dropped the lamp. In a blind panic he ran out of the room and tripped over a chair that stood in the corridor. The lamp spluttered and he righted it, leaving it on the carpet. He stood up, panting hoarsely, his throat drying.

Brood had returned to his ramshackle shed some time before, breathless after walking in the night chill and wind. He was becoming worried. Determined to sleep, he lay on his bedding but still his mind refused to relinquish its consciousness. He walked four paces the length of the shed before his vision fell upon the stiff body that lay on sacking. As though willing it to move, Brood held his gaze to it for a full minute.

He reached for his spade. He would bury the body that night. Sleep would not be accessible until then.

Stubb was frantic with worry. Surely it was not possible to lose a body? He began to search each room, pulling open wardrobe doors and even cupboards, the ottomans and large oak boxes. He stood in the box room after exhaustive investigations, and after a fruitless search in the chest with the theatrical costumes within, he was unsure as to where to look next.

An idea came to him. He walked hurriedly along to the main

bathroom but the place was empty, a dripping tap there marking the seconds. Cursing and moaning, he ran down to the hallway to continue his search. Once he had made his way through the lobby and into the kitchen, he found the maid.

Florence was content with the progression of her romance and a contented happiness kept sleep from her. She hummed a jaunty tune while waiting for the kettle to boil on the range. She looked up without expression as Stubb bustled in. 'Is there anything the matter, sir?' she enquired.

'Nothing,' Stubb snapped but then, making a sudden and hasty decision, exclaimed loudly, 'Yes, a problem. I want you to take the baby to Dr. Snippet's house. Wrap it up well or whatever you have to do. Give it a sweet pacifier.'

'Surely not now, sir? And the child is too young for a pacifier.'

'Now, yes; ask the doctor to contact his nurse to look after it until tomorrow.' Florence looked confused and stood staring at Stubb until he shouted, 'Well, go on then, do as I say!' Florence shrugged her shoulders before running to fetch her coat.

Stubb looked with bewilderment about the kitchen then marched back to the lobby and into the hallway. The grandfather clock struck one; Florence had forgotten to unscrew the striker hammer. He watched the maid as she trod lightly up the dark oak stairs to collect the infant.

'Stupid of me,' he muttered and he hit his forehead with the palm of his hand. In his blind panic one of the more obvious places had been overlooked. He ran to the cellar door that stood under the staircase and pulled it open. The descent on the basic wooden steps was taken with care for they were steep. He told himself to calm down, to pull himself together and try to think logically.

There was a glow, dull but definite, coming from below him. Stubb heard the shuffling of feet; he ducked to avoid hitting his head on the underside of the staircase and, upon reaching the bottom of the rough steps, he discovered the identity of the dusty cellar's inhabitant.

'What do you think you're doing this time of night, Pump? For God's sake man, do you never stop? It's gone one in the morning.'

The butler turned at this outburst and as he did so took a stout brown bottle from one of the racks which lined the cold stone walls. I'm getting drink, sir,' he replied and grinned foolishly.

'Getting drink? Getting drunk more like. I think you've had quite enough. Now leave this cellar right now and get to your bed. I'm quite aware that my father used to sleep – sleeps until well into the afternoon after his social evenings, and all of you take advantage of it, staying up to gracious knows what time in the morning. But it's got to stop, do you hear?' Pump nodded. 'Put that bottle back into the rack.'

'Yessir,' the butler answered humbly, 'but this bottle isn't for me.' He was finding it difficult to speak clearly or focus his attention.

'Don't give me that, you impudent little man. You are nothing but a drunkard and why you have not been told to pack your bags years ago I've no idea. Put it back this instant and get to your proper bed.'

Pump replaced the bottle. As he began to mount the steps, Stubb, curious to know what the butler was wining on, had taken the returned bottle from the wine rack.

'Wait a minute. This is my father's special reserve port.'

'That is correct, sir,' Pump replied. 'I told you that it was not for me.'

'Then who is it for?'

'Why sir, you know yourself that nobody else drinks the

special port.' He swayed and steadied himself on the side of the damp cellar wall. 'Your father told me to get a fresh one for him.'

Stubb did not seem to understand. He asked the butler to repeat himself then queried, 'how long ago was this?'

'A few minutes ago, sir.'

Anger swarmed through him. 'You drunken imbecile; you moron! Are you mad? Go, get out of my sight before I...' but Pump had scuttled away and clumped up the wooden steps.

Stubb slumped onto a barrel and buried his head in his hands. What was happening? Then his mind, a stagnant black pool, became disturbed as if by a drop of fresh and clear water: someone was trying to break him. It all added up: frightening Eleanor; taking his father's body; bribing the butler. There was only one person other than his wife and himself who had known of the planned murder. The picture was becoming clearer. It was obvious: Brood was going to blackmail him. Did he really think that he could do that to William Stubb?

He stood and felt a surge of triumph and he climbed the steps up to the hall, smiling artfully. A stop would soon be put to the gardener's game. He had no doubt in his mind that the next day would reveal all. He expected a note under the bedroom door. He snickered. If the gardener believed he could blackmail him then the man was yet more stupid that Stubb believed.

When he was in the hall, Florence called out to him from the open main entrance, the child hidden in blankets in her arms. 'Are you sure, sir?' she said.

'Of course I'm sure,' he replied in the most kindly voice he could muster.

'Where is Miss Eleanor?'

Stubb looked to her questioning face then to the precious bundle held to her chest. This charade is an easy one to play, he considered, and said, 'You know where she is, don't you? You have seen her when you fetched the baby,' then shouted with annoyance, 'who is paying you to play this game? Tell me now!'

Florence was hurt by his words. 'I don't know what you mean, sir; Miss Eleanor's not in her room and the baby was in one of the spare rooms.'

'Go, will you?' Stubb demanded. After the maid was on the gravel path, he closed the door.

He had an idea: he went to the day room to check for any notes; but there were none.

His mind would be less fuddled tomorrow. He remembered the scotch which he had left unfinished in the drawing room and decided to drink it before retiring. Then he would sleep in the box room so as not to disturb Eleanor.

CHAPTER 19

The Astonishment

ROOD SWORE TO himself that he would somehow get even with Theodore for harming him. Had he not feared for losing his job he knew he would have retaliated and inflicted a serious violence upon his employer. He rubbed his aching and sore arm.

He felt his eyelids grow weighty with the moonlight glowing into the shed creating a pressing mass upon them. He dreamily wondered at the shouts of pain and laughter he had heard coming from the manor house while taking a night stroll in the late evening and he felt saddened when he had come across the stiff body of Snitch, white with ice. He had become fond of Snitch, although he would never have admitted to it. Mrs. Wickling's rabbit – allowed by Theodore to be caged in the grounds of the manor house – had been a good animal. How it had escaped from the straw and newspaper-stuffed hutch beside the shed was a mystery. As Brood finally secured unconsciousness, he felt satisfied that the day he was leaving behind did not have many loose ends. He had cleared his shed guttering of snow, killed and disposed of two rats and pruned a hawthorn bush near the summerhouse. Only the stiff body of Snitch – laying on sacking at the end of the shed interior – needed to be buried under a pear tree near the statue on the lawn, when light found the morning.

Stubb stood in the drawing room. The fire had burned down considerably and the logs lay broken and disintegrating in glowing embers. His eye was caught then by a cord of smoke that rose and curled in the air. It came from one of the wingback armchairs by the fireplace but with its large back facing Stubb and thus obscuring its occupant.

'Who is there?' Stubb demanded. 'If that's you, Pump, you will be deeply sorry.' There was no answer and Stubb advanced further into the room. He was puzzled: he sniffed and smelled smoke from Theodore's best cigars. He strode impatiently up to the chair.

The occupant turned his head and smiled. 'Good morning,' he said.

'My God,' shouted Stubb aghast, and his scream was like a woman's shrill voice. 'No, it can't be, you're dead. I killed you!' His eyelids stretched wide as he stared in terror. He fell backwards and staggered to keep himself on his feet. He shielded his eyes with his arm as though afraid to look. Theodore had nestled his large bulk into the armchair, thoughtfully puffing on his cigar. 'Dead,' whispered Stubb. Was it some grand delusion created in his own head? He moaned in disbelief and he looked his father over as if expecting him to vanish as a mirage.

Theodore remained and he seemed amused. 'What on earth are you talking about, my dear boy? Dead? As you can see I am as alive as you are. Kill me, you say? No, my son, you haven't killed me. Here, touch. Flesh and blood and as solid as you standing there gaping like a bulldog fish. Sit down.'

Stubb sat on the chair opposite Theodore, with his wide eyes still haunted and frightened. Holding his head and pulling at his sideburns, he groaned. Was this some gruesome dream?

'Do tell me what this is all about,' Theodore said with mock concern but then he chuckled and stroked his moustache.

Stubb was confused. His head was reeling. He rubbed his smarting eyes and said, 'You haven't seen Eleanor, I hope?'

Theodore did not seem to hear his question. 'Your remark

interests me. Do I owe you an explanation as to why I'm seated in front of you? I think not, nevertheless I will endeavour to explain. You see, William, I am dead after all.'

Stubb stiffened. 'What are you talking about?' He met his father's unblinking gaze.

'I mean, I'm deceased. I no longer exist in corporeal form on this earth. You've been reading too many ghost stories; should I be some wavering phantom walking through walls? What do you think?'

'I...' Stubb began. Could it be true? He had seen his father die before him. 'I'm sorry I killed you,' he muttered without thinking on what he was saying.

Theodore's stony face broke, emitting a loud guffaw. Stubb realized in an instant that he had been made a fool of. 'You—' He jumped to his feet, threatening two fists.

His father's derision vanished as quickly as it had appeared. 'Sit,' he ordered. Stubb did that, grimacing and muttering under his breath. 'Alright, I will tell you the truth, though why you should know, I'm not sure. You deserve nothing from me.' Stubb did not comment. 'Let us begin at the beginning. If you were to cast your mind back to younger days when your dear mother was alive and if you were to sift through that cupboard you call your mind, you will find a compact box of irrelevances which you have no doubt stored away. And upon sorting it you would come across a piece of information that I used to be a reasonably successful actor. I made a living. Did you not use to enquire of your mother as to my whereabouts when I was touring with my company? Still, that is beside the point, you were no more than four then. The point I am trying to make is that as you have seen, time has not dampened my acting skills.' He paused and coughed. 'Mind, if it wasn't for Brood, I wouldn't have been acting.'

'So it was the gardener who let on?'

'After some persuasion from myself. His arm should still be hurting from when I, unfortunately, nearly twisted it out of its socket. He was going to blackmail me. As for Mrs. Wickling hiding the rat poison for you...'

'She did no such thing.'

Theodore paused. 'Ah, I'm not totally perfect all of the time, you see. Shame about her rabbit then. What is certain is Brood telling me he knew of someone who was going to kill me and that if I didn't pay up some stupid amount, he would not disclose information. Have you heard of anything so ridiculous? As if I didn't know that you would try. Yesterday night at the party, I told Pump to get fresh port, with the laced drink still sitting in my study, because I reasoned that you would poison my favourite tipple. So obvious. I have since discovered that you used nothing less than arsenic. What a waste of good port. And there you have it, my boy, I am as dead as you are. My educated guess is that you have paid a wasted visit to a certain Mr. Nuckle.' He puffed on his cigar and added, 'This business of dying as it were, certainly opened my eyes to a few things. For instance – Eleanor.'

Stubb's heart pounded heavily and his whole body seemed to flinch with the dull, thumping beat. 'Careful what you say. Have you seen her? Is that why she was in such a state?'

'I paid her a visit and, yes, she was in such a state – of joy. You see, she loves me as much as I love her. She has covered it well.'

Stubb, with a look of disgust upon him, replied, 'You Medusa. I don't believe anything you say; you are a liar, a scoundrel and a twister of words. I love Eleanor and she loves me; never you. Do you honestly think that you are capable of loving? You are nothing but a filthy, vile old man.' His voice had risen to a shout as his hands gripped tightly onto the sides of the armchair.

Theodore licked the butt of his cigar and smelled the smoke that rose from its crimson end. 'Dearest Eleanor. She was rather concerned and I must tell you, in all confidence, something which might upset you. She wants to leave. She asks, nay, pleads, that I should marry her so that we can get away from this pimple on the map and start a new life together. She, myself – and our child. Now at Dr. Snippet's; am I right? I know I'm right, Florence told me. So, so, so, my dear, dear boy, Eleanor doesn't want you.'

Stubb was on his feet, his body shaking with rage. 'I can see why I tried to murder you,' he yelled and he threw a punch at Theodore's face and ran out of the room and up the stairs. He had to see Eleanor. As a red welt began to glow on Theodore's cheek, he dabbed it with a handkerchief and smiled knowingly.

Stubb lit a lamp. The eyes of his ancestors flickered into life from its light, the paintings of those long dead seeming more than paint on canvas. He pushed the bedroom door open and entered.

CHAPTER 20

Fire

A FTER RUBBING HIS stubby fingers in front of the decaying fire, (the fireplace flanked by porcelain tiles showing ladybirds on twined stems,) Theodore strolled to the hallway. He chuckled when he heard a shout from the top of the house and the thumping of heavy feet.

Stubb was sobbing, panting and shouting, after discovering that Eleanor was not in their bedroom. 'Where is she? What have you done with her? Eleanor, Eleanor!'

He ran from room to room, shrieking her name. A pale moon dodged behind a cloud and a stray dog scurried across one of farmer Solomon's fields. The wind was beating with a muffled hand against the window panes.

'You blaggard!' Stubb screamed to Theodore. He dithered for a moment, unsure of where to look but then, flinging himself from the landing and nearly losing his balance, he clattered back down the stairs, retaining balance at the bottom by clinging to the stag beetle finial. 'Father, where are you?' He ran into the dining room but found it unoccupied, and then back into the hallway, in time to see the maid opening the front door after returning from Dr. Snippet.

Upon catching sight of Stubb she was taken aback. His hair was tousled and his eyes seemed buried deep within his drawn face that was grimy and tear stained. He ran to her and gripped her by the shoulders. 'Where is she?' he shouted.

'You're hurting me,' Florence whined. Stubb shook her.

'Where is who, sir? Miss Eleanor? I don't know. Please...' She grasped his hands to stop him shaking her the more but then Stubb released his hold and bounded upstairs. Florence became tearful and decided that enough was enough. Buttoning her coat again and replacing her hat, she departed, taking satisfaction in slamming the front door closed. She was sure that Archie String would let her sleep in his guest room until morning.

Stubb grabbed the lamp which he had left in the first floor corridor and went up the spiral staircase which led to the attic room. On the small landing at the zenith he tried the door and found it would not move. Infuriated at such a detail, he kicked it and unlocked it – for the key was in the lock – and after a swift twist of the handle, pushed the door open.

The musty and dry dust smell that had always lingered seemed overpowering. Moonlight was reflected in the panes of glass which protected the insects. Taking a step into the room, Stubb held the lamp up high and saw that the place seemed empty save for the books in their bookcases and the two rows of presentation cases.

'Eleanor,' he called out. There was a scratching noise from somewhere in the shadowed interior. He took a pace forward, looking cautiously about him and swung the lamp from left to right. His shadow behind, huge and grotesque, mimicked this and bobbed from one side to the other. There was the sound again from over his left shoulder so he turned quickly on his heels though still not fast enough; as he did so, someone brushed past and the black door was shut. Hearing the grating of the key turning in the lock he ran to the sealed entrance and pulled on the handle. The door was firmly locked.

'Father. Theodore, is that you there?' he shouted. He shivered for already the chill in the attic was making its way through his jacket and beige shirt. He placed his ear to the door and heard a muttering from the outside. 'Theodore, listen to me. I've found Eleanor,' he lied. 'She is safe. This sort of thing will solve nothing. Let's talk the situation over sensibly. Only, let me out.' The wind of the night was the only answer. Upon listening again he heard a muffled scraping noise as though fingernails were scratching wood. 'This whole ridiculous business has gone too far,' he shouted with annoyance. 'Theodore? Can you hear me?' He sighed with his vexation and pounded on the door with his fists, the sound multiplying about the attic room and then silence. 'I will get you for this,' he threatened.

He turned away to stare at the shadowy walls. He quickly decided that, with no means of escape, he would have to find the warmest place to sleep for now he expected to be there for the rest of the night. There was a suitable spot not far from where he stood, the corner to the left of the door by one wall of books, well away from the draughty window. He found pieces of sacking and wound them about his chest and legs and lay on the sawdusted floor – piles of newspapers and journals and sawdust about him – put out the lamp and curled into a ball. He sneezed and shut his eyes.

Sleep eluded him. His mind would not rest; questions irritated and ran circles in his head. Where was Eleanor? What had gone wrong with the plan? Why didn't he deal with Brood to ensure he wouldn't have opened his mouth? Why hadn't he realized his father was feigning death when he had carried him upstairs? Why couldn't he have seen Nuckle the next day and so been with Eleanor? Where was Eleanor? And still his mind bounced to consciousness and to the eternal questions then back again into disturbed sleep.

Brood cursed; he found himself awake. Keenly aware of the sounds of the night, he had been aroused from sleep by distant thumping noises and shouts within the moaning wind. He pulled on overalls and boots and a grimy duffel coat – tightening a belt around it – and opened the door of his shed, then looked across the dark garden to the manor house. The statue on the lawn appeared ghostly and glowing. The gardener scratched the warts on the back of his hand. Only a bat swooped over the snowed roof tiles on its way to the abandoned church, and the sound of a night creature whooping from the heath during a lull of the whistling air.

Now that he was awake, he decided that he should not waste the opportunity to bury the rabbit. It didn't seem too cold, despite the white layer of snow covering all, glowing in the moonlight. He went back into the shed and fetched the dead animal, and hung the slim form from his belt. With spade in hand, he trudged across the snow, heading for the pear tree.

Stubb awoke with a start and sat up, brushing aside the sacking. A noise: the key slowly revolving in the lock. He stood and placed himself at the side of the door with his back and arms flat against the rough plastered wall.

It was then that he decided to light the lamp and position it on the other side of the entrance so that he would see the enemy clearly, with himself hidden in shadow. He fumbled in a pocket and brought out a box of matches. And at the same time as the thick timbered door clicked open, he struck a match. There was a low, sugary voice, calling softly. 'Eleanor my beauty, it is I, Theodore. I have come back for you as I promised. I know you are calmer now amongst our friends. We'll find our little baby together.'

Stubb was surprised at his father's words and had not realized that the lit match had slipped from his fingers onto the dry sacking. It caught light and burnt a hole quickly, a bright circle of flame. The door opened wider and from a strand of moonlight that came through the window at the end of the attic, Stubb could see his father made silver with a leering smile upon his lips and his arms waving and outstretched. 'My darling Eleanor, here amongst our family. Not kept for long, were you?'

Stubb pounced and grabbed Theodore by the wrists and with all of his strength pulled him into the attic. As Theodore tottered over the floorboards and fell heavily against a presentation case, Stubb ran out onto the landing and then, pulling the door shut behind him, turned the key. His father had given a yelp of surprise and a groan when he had hit the boards. He picked himself up, touching his nose and chin gently, stepping over to the door. 'Eleanor, stop playing games,' he said loudly. 'Be a good girl and let me out.' He did not wait for an answer for long tongues of flame appeared suddenly as they consumed the sacking and ate the dark shadows in the corner of the room. He shouted but Stubb did not want to hear for he was already in the first floor corridor looking for his wife.

'Fire, fire! Let me out!' pleaded Theodore, a panic engrained within his being. He began to stamp on the sacking but already the flame had lit a pile of old papers and was singeing the sawdust and running quickly along the ancient dry wood of the bookcase on the back wall. As he wafted some of the newspapers in an attempt to extinguish them, the fire was taking a firmer hold of the books at a surprising rate, aided by a small fireball made as the sacking and newspapers and heap of dirtied sawdust that had not been cleared away, burst into golden light. Now burning on one side of the bookcase, the summit was almost reached and the top rows of antique leather volumes began to burn, along with the rest there, producing a peculiar odour, making the bookcase crack and creak. Theodore ran to the case and clawed at the books, trying to pat out the blaze with the palms of his hands but even as he did so, the fire was spreading the more. And throwing the smouldering volumes to the floor only made matters worse as the parched layer of sawdust caught alight, sending fingers of flame in all directions over the floorboards, the smaller particles of sawdust popping and sparking like fireworks. Theodore ran to the casement window at the other end of the attic in a frantic attempt to find some implement to beat out the fire, but there was nothing. The flaming tongues had taken a firm hold of the bookcase and it burned with a steady light. It was becoming hotter from the timber and paper and wood chips being eaten by the fire. Theodore pulled off his jacket and tie and undid the top buttons of his shirt. He whimpered and stood dazed, wasting valuable time, hypnotized by the dancing and flickering swords of light.

Prompted into action again he ran back to the bookcase and pulled out more of the burning volumes and threw them to the floor. The fire coursed across the floorboards and had reached the other bookcases and the scattered piles of journals and documents. Flames were gaining strength in one half of the attic and he cried out. The blaze flexed its orange muscles in reply and licked greedily with its many spikes of yellows and reds as the fiery form became stronger still. Bottles of ether, formaldehyde and isopropyl alcohol fell from their burning shelves, some rolling away, others shattering upon impact with the floor, their preserved contents of slugs, frogs and other small animals scattered, the great puddles of flammable liquid immediately igniting before they could seep into the wood and gaps of the floor.

Theodore ran to the entrance again and hammered with his fists upon the door and threw horrified glances behind. With a mighty whooshing the bookcase at the back there burst into a solid wall of flame. The fire which had crawled across the floor began to lick at the legs of some of his presentation cases containing their dessicated contents. He ran over to the new fiery offspring, shielding himself from the hot wall of light and he stamped upon burning floorboards. He was forced to step back as more of the legs of the cases soaked in flammable liquid caught alight, the flames spreading quickly over them. There was a loud report as one of the panes that covered his collection cracked with the heat.

Flickering spikes danced and jeered before him and at one point in the room had gained such a hold as to brush the rafters of the roof. Cobwebs there shrivelled in the heat and dry twigs of one of the old nests caught alight.

The bookcase burned avidly now and sent out showers of sparks that danced and twirled in the hot air like fireflies. A reeking stench and billows of thick smoke was the prelude to total conflagration. Theodore rattled the door handle and bellowed at the top of his voice until he was exhausted. Resigned to death by cremation, he slumped onto the floorboards like a crumpled doll, his fingers raw and bleeding and his eyes staring and bloodshot. The side of his face and his hands were badly burnt. Jumping shadows mocked the flames by casting their spider legs over the walls and rafters, following the waving and twirling movements of the fire.

Theodore cowered under his workbench and sucked on a stinging hand and in perfect unison a bead of sweat and a tear fell to the floor.

Bright light glowed from the attic window and smoke swelled out in cumulations before vanishing into the night. Brood threw the spade down to the bare earth he had uncovered and hurriedly grabbed a bucket which stood on the snow-smothered patio before loping across and over to the kitchen door. He could see the gas lamp in the kitchen was lit. He beat urgently upon the door pane and blew into his hands and stamped his feet. The temperature was becoming too cold again for his liking. 'Come on, come on,' he muttered. He crouched and peered into the kitchen through a slit that the window blind did not cover. He could see the edge of the stove and the row of pans but, by pressing his nose harder onto the cold frosted glass and twisting his head, he saw Stubb slumped across the pine table. Brood beat upon the door again and rattled the handle.

Stubb's eyes sprang open. He cursed bitterly for allowing sleep to lure him away from his search for Eleanor. He looked at his watch. Five minutes had been lost. 'Alright, I'm coming,' he said irritably. Then he brightened suddenly. Had Theodore locked Eleanor out of the house; was she trying to get back in? When he had unlocked and opened the door, the gardener pushed past him and went straight to the hand pump. He furiously worked the handle while scowling at Stubb. The water gurgled and Brood, placing the bucket under the now spurting spout, demanded, 'Don't stand there, you. More buckets, anything. Fire in the attic.'

Stubb stared for a second but then was motivated into action, and scuttled across the kitchen into the utility room in search of more receptacles. He found two more buckets there which he left for Brood to fill, insisting the new sink taps were used instead of the hand pump in the kitchen. But already the gardener was moving fast and was standing by the carving of the stag beetle in the hallway. He ripped the rabbit carcass hanging from under his belt and flung in into the corner by the hallway mirror. On he went up the stairs with the two filled buckets and, at the same moment, Stubb wrenched open the door to the cellar: more buckets and helpers were needed.

Pump was asleep in his domain, curled under a moth-holed

blanket. Stubb shook him violently and kicked his feet. The butler grunted and yawned and upon opening his eyes and seeing Stubb standing over him, fought his way from the blanket and staggered to his feet. 'Sir,' he said wearily, 'I haven't been drinking, honest.'

'Never mind that now, man, there's a fire in the attic.' Pump looked blank-faced. Once Stubb had taken an iron bucket from a corner of the cellar and pushed it into the butler's hands, he began to run back up the steps.

Pump remained where he was standing. 'What's this for?' he questioned, holding the article away from him as though frightened of it.

'For water, you idiot. Now come on, hurry.'

The bucket fell to the rough stone floor with a clatter and Pump's body shook. He crammed his fingers in his mouth and whined, 'Water? No, I won't come. I can't help you, sir. Can't stand the stuff.' Frozen with fear, he held tightly onto one of the wine racks as though expecting Stubb to drag him away.

Stubb could not waste any more time. He sneered and shouted, 'You snivelling baby. You haven't heard the last of this.'

Returning to the kitchen he found that Brood had still not returned and so quickly filled two buckets with water.

It was then that he heard loud footsteps clattering down the stairs, barking and grunting and squealing as if made by animals, then a pause, followed by the front door singing on its hinges before the sudden slamming noise as it was shut in haste...

Stubb took the two filled buckets to follow in the gardener's footsteps, water slopping onto the marble tiles of the hallway as he went. The front door seemed to beckon. 'Eleanor,' he cried out for he guessed that from wherever she had been hiding in the house, she had now run out in terror.

The attic room blazed with light. The rafters smouldered and the bookcase and books were ablaze and the insect cases crackled furiously. The floorboards burned and there was choking smoke. It was very hot. The gardener had flung his buckets of water onto one of the bookcases and although the fire had ceased in a section it had spluttered angrily then burst into flame again. Stubb threw his water load over the floor. A stinking fog of blackness was produced and it grew to fill the room.

'Brood, more water,' he shouted above the roaring of the fire. Both left the attic, coughing and with their eyes streaming.

It became such that whilst one was fetching filled buckets the other fought the flames and thus a crude rota system was formed. The stair carpet was drenched where, in their hurry, water had been slopped down its length. Brood suggested that the water would be more easily obtained from the bathroom. Stubb agreed and wondered why he had not thought of that before.

Stubb felt that they were fighting a losing battle for, upon throwing their bucket load onto the fire, it would die but then spring up again in another part of the attic. Both laboured boldly, soot and dirt smearing their faces, their arms and legs aching and their bodies heavy with exhaustion. When the blaze seemed firmly under their control, they allowed themselves to rest for a few minutes only.

It was after half an hour that the fire was finally vanquished though even then it hung onto life by a thread. As Brood and Stubb stood gazing forlornly at the wreckage, a spark would wink weakly and then flare into life but only to be drenched by water from a filled bucket at hand. Wreaths of gauzy smoke drifted, the rest having made its way through the opened window and burned holes in the roof. Some of the roof tiles lay about them amongst the debris. The gardener rubbed his smarting eyes.

The books lay half eaten by fire or scorched on the sooty floor and on the blackened remains of the bookcases. The room held an acrid stench. Scraps of paper that had been shrivelled to a wafer thin ash would float and drop to the ground and disintegrate. A large gaping hole had been made in the charred floorboards and much of the floor was unsafe to walk upon. The insect collection was destroyed, if not by the fire then by the two who had fought valiantly to save the attic and thus the whole house from burning to the ground.

To curtail the progression of the flames, cases had been hacked from the floor with an axe and flung into corners of the room which had been untouched by the blaze. Shrivelled paper, charcoal and exotic butterflies, caterpillars and beetles – insects of all shapes and sizes – lay scattered throughout the room, burned, charred, squashed or black with soot.

Stubb wiped his brow with a dirty hand, smearing more soot onto his grimy face. He glanced at Brood who had acquired a similar disguise.

'Theodore,' said Stubb as he gazed mournfully at the mess. Where could he have gone? How had he escaped? If he had been consumed by the fire there would surely have been some remains.

'Where is the master, you?' asked Brood suspiciously. He remembered the noises that he heard coming from the attic.

Stubb thought quickly. 'He was called away tonight on urgent matters. God knows what he's going to say about his insects. They were his life's work.' The gardener nodded slowly. Then Stubb said, 'Brood, was the attic door locked when you first came up here?'

The gardener appeared confused by the question but finally answered, 'When I got here, the door was wide open.' He turned and said, apparently to the charred rafters, black and stark above him, 'I think it's wise we all get some rest, you.'

Stubb nodded in agreement, too tired even to answer. They filed out of the fire-swept attic. Stubb was the last to leave and he looked at the destruction for a few seconds but hid it by slamming the charred door shut. How did Theodore escape? he wondered again. Where was Eleanor?

CHAPTER 21

Aftermath

WINTER PREPARED TO leave the village to aggravate
warmer parts of the country; although it left an
acquaintance of rain to ensure that Muchmarsh did not
give welcome to the next season yet awhile. A dull day was
marked by starlings studding the bare trees on the village green,
the silhouettes of the birds on those branches looking like black
pods of seaweed.

Stubb sat on a settee in the front room of Mr Nuckle's
terraced house. 'There was nothing else I could have done,' he
said and shrugged.

Mr. Nuckle screwed up his nose and scratched his ear. 'To
be honest with you, Mr. Stubb, I hadn't wanted to do the job
anyway, seeing as I am going into the catering trade.' He rubbed
his hands together as if in excitement at the prospect. Both men
sat in silence until Nuckle said, 'And you say that arrangements
for your father's body are no longer needed because there is no
body?'

'Yes, I told you, the police have no qualms about the matter.
As far as they are concerned everything is cleared up. The letter
that Theodore left behind before he emigrated explained all.'
It had taken him many hours to forge the writing though he
had been pleased with the fictional story which read as fact; a
persuasive result. 'So no dead body.'

That's most strange after your insistence of a corpse, but if
you are happy.' Stubb grimaced while Mr. Nuckle continued,

'And now that you're leaving, what's to happen to the servants? If you don't mind me saying, all the years they've been there; just asking, just wondering.'

'When they heard I'm selling the manor house – to Dr. Snippet – a few threatened me. Would you believe it? They spun the old story, you know – they had been there for years, dedicating their lives to the Stubb household; they deserved more than that; they had nowhere else to work. But with money considerations offered and with persuasion most of them went without trouble.'

'Most of them?'

'Look, can we move this column thing out of the way, I'm getting a stiff neck with peering around it.'

'If we must,' Nuckle replied and he moved the large sprays of blooms in their vase from the top of the wooden plinth, placing that on the floor next to others, and moved the plinth to the side.

Stubb sneezed while watching the fine pollen and fragments of dried leaves floating in shafts of light that came through the front sash window into the room seemingly dedicated to horticulture. They moved as bright spots within the sun's ray like stray molecules, or tiny organisms swimming under a microscope.

'Thanks. Now where were we? Oh, yes: most of them. Your friend Brood was particularly difficult.' Stubb pointed with the cigarette to his puffed and blackened eye. 'Well anyway,' he said. 'Thanks for the coffee. It's a very nice beverage; much different from tea, isn't it? I must be away soon. I'm to view a certain property again this morning.'

'Where are you going to live now, Mr. Stubb? I mean to say, what with your recuperating wife and a baby to support you'll be after a fair-sized place, I expect.'

Stubb stared dreamily to the scattered petals strewn over the floor. 'Just me and the child, with the help of a registered nurse,' he answered. 'The sudden disappearance of my father has, I am afraid to say, had an adverse effect upon my wife's health. She has always been very sensitive. She is getting better, at her Uncle Thomas's in Smudge.' Stubb blinked rapidly and uncontrollably while speaking the lie.

'I see. Let us hope she recovers soon,' replied Mr. Nuckle. 'By the by, what are you both to call the little one?'

Stubb's mouth distorted into an unknown expression. He had thought long about the name and was certain that Eleanor, wherever she might be, would be more than happy with his final decision.

Stubb was about to answer when his good hand dropped to his side. Then feeling a newspaper in the settee on which he sat, he casually withdrew it, hoping to use the article as an excuse to ignore any more questions.

To his surprise he found that he had withdrawn a magazine from its hiding place, the cover of which featured a cleverly detailed print of a half-naked woman, her lower half covered with billowing cloth, standing in a ballet position. The image appeared vaguely absurd. There was a look of wide-eyed excitement upon the model's face. The banner at the top read "Natural Lady Luck". Stubb, holding a curiosity, was about to flick through the pages but was rudely interrupted as the magazine was snatched from him by a red-faced Mr. Nuckle.

'I see you have found my study book,' he muttered hurriedly. 'I am of an artistic mind – in my spare time, you see,' he explained. 'So full of life, not an ounce of rigor mortis to be seen. Supple joints, flesh alive, wonderful spirit activating the sculptured bodies to dancing forms; you understand, I know. But if you don't, there's no matter.'

Taking the confiscated item to a corner of the room, he moved away vases of bright but drying flowers so he could pull a cupboard door open. But as he did so, he was detained in depositing the magazine within its interior by a pile of similar magazines plopping to the floorboards from the top shelf.

Understanding Nuckle's embarrassment, Stubb said, 'Now I really must be going. Goodbye, Mr. Nuckle,' and with a wave of a hand he quickly wove his way between the clusters of drying flowers and walked into the hallway of the small house. Before opening the front door to depart, he turned back to say, 'In answer to your last question: the child is called Alastair.'

Thirteen Years Later

CHAPTER 22

Thimriddy Fair

ALASTAIR ENJOYED EATING a plum. It had been worth saving the payments from Mrs. Battlespoke for cleaning out her chicken coops, regritting and restrawing them. A month of coins had been enough to buy his treat of delightful plums, sold as a side product by the toffee apple man from his three-wheeled bicycle basket.

Walking at a brisk pace, Alastair was soon across the village green; then through and out of the alley that was between the ironmonger's and the wheelwright. Mrs. Frill hung out from one of the windows on the other side, striking a dust-filled mat with a beater.

Alastair trod along the track running between the banks of bushes. He found a stout stick with which to hack aside any obstacle in his path. He came across a horse chestnut tree and he tried to knock conkers, wrapped in their spiky sheaths, from its branches.

Without success, he strode on, tentacles of a wild rose bush from the undergrowth seemingly attempting to trip him. He gave them a hefty whack and, while humming random notes of a ballad he had heard on his father's wireless set, turned sharply to his right through a gap in an overgrown hedge and entered one of farmer Solomon's sheep fields.

The day promised to be filled with interest for it was the morning of Thimriddy Fair. The tea marquee and the large open tents had already been erected, areas decided upon and roped off for the different events. The brightly coloured flags hung motionlessly: there was no breeze and the sun was beginning to feel warm. Sammy Solomon was hauling jump poles for the gymkhana and he whistled tunelessly while his brother was happier to chat to Cynthia Musty, the vicar's daughter. Other children with smudged faces gambolled to and fro, frolicking and chasing each other with their laughter floating high above the murmur of activity and the occasional shout and the dry clunk of wood against wood.

A sparrow swooped down in a wide arc to collect the crumbs that had fallen from the blackcurrant pie which the rotund Mr. Spittle was eating with much enthusiasm. Currant seeds spotted his face, juice smeared his lips and puffed cheeks, the remainder of the pie crammed into his toothy orifice. The day that he learnt not to eat his own produce would be a day indeed. He casually wiped his mouth with the back of his hand and yelled, 'Get a move on there lad, we haven't got all day,' to his assistant who was carrying more pie-loaded trays into the tent. The baker took another of his baked marvels.

Mrs. Goodwithin gave a shrill shriek of pain and the birds pecking the grass flew up with a flurry of flapping wings. Everyone preparing the field looked away from their allocated tasks and several people ran over to where she lay. She had tripped over a guy rope and had twisted her ankle.

Alastair stood and watched the sudden emptiness in the middle of the field and it was to him as though time had ceased to flow. Those standing in the tents had taken the opportunity to rest awhile and they remained motionless. A group of people stood in tableau around the prostrate figure of Mrs. Goodwithin. No bird flew in the sky and as the sun dipped behind the slip of a cloud and the vivid green of the mown grass became a shade darker, a sense of expectancy descended upon him. The few seconds in which all of this occurred seemed to stretch to an age and yet, at the same moment, it was no time at all. Amid the absence of life – this apparent ceasing of time – Alastair's lip twitched involuntarily for, like the cloud that had passed across the warming sun, a greyness spread over his thoughts. He viewed the scene as if through the wrong end of a telescope and heard his laboured breathing and his heart beating close and interrupted by a quick, saw-edge sound – like a sharp drone of a wasp – that prickled his hearing.

Then, as if by some divine cue, the elastic space of time retracted to its proper length. The group who had stood immobile around Mrs. Goodwithin moved into life and helped the stricken lady to her feet. The world breathed again. As Alastair shook his head and frowned at his sudden experience, Colonel Midwitty began thumping the uprooted stake back into the ground with a mallet. The guy rope was tightened and Mrs. Goodwithin, hobbling and tearful, was helped to the refreshment tent.

Alastair took another plum from the paper bag and bit into it. His eyes focused onto the hill in the distance, shrouded in a light morning mist, where the Reverend Musty's church stood. He looked away and shuddered, though he did not know why.

Upon the punctual arrival of twelve o'clock the organizers and helpers had put the finishing touches to the tents and stalls, the tea urn had arrived at last, the sun shone especially for the occasion and Reverend Musty – now a serious and worried man – had unenthusiastically declared the fair officially open.

Alastair mingled with the crowds who whistled and jostled and jangled their money, between stalls and small tents.

'Hoopla, hoopla,' a cheery gentleman sang. His cheeks burned red and he grinned at Alastair. 'Hoopla, sonny?' he asked of him. Alastair shied away and continued his intrepid journey through the forest of people. Upon reaching a particularly thick knot of spectators he stood on tiptoe and craned his neck in an attempt to see over their shoulders. They were gathered around the main arena and from the exclamations and shouts of encouragement it was evident that the tug of war had begun. Alastair could hear dry soil pawed by heavy boots, and grunts of exertion.

'Come on, George, you lazy soul!'

'Pull, pull, pull.'

'Muchmarsh, Muchmarsh, ra, ra, ra—'

'Excuse me sir, but may I squeeze in there?' Alastair said. The man to whom he had addressed this question looked down over his nose and moved slightly to the left but, with a quick shuffle, resumed his original place.

'Move yourself, Stillstone.'

Alastair wove his way through the villagers and visitors from the towns to a refreshment tent.

Surprisingly there was no queue, no doubt many people's attention drawn by the tug of war and the steam engine which was chugging into the field from Marshmallow Lane. He marched up to the trestle tables and glanced at the plates of cakes and sandwiches and biscuits laid out on embroidered table cloths.

'A cup of lemonade please,' he stated.

'Why, if it isn't young Alastair. How are you, dear one? How is your father? Not drinking as much, I hope. My, I do excuse myself. I shouldn't say such things to you.' Mrs. Musty tried to brighten her face even though the underlining concern for her husband was always there under the surface. The vicar had lost his happy-go-lucky ways, had become humourless and short-tempered. But worse was his obsessive behaviour of storing food and clothing and she had sometimes found him tying brown paper parcels with these things inside. He would never explain his actions or loss of happy temperament.

'How old are you now, Alastair? You must be thirteen. How time flies. Here is your lemonade. That will be one of your smallest coins please.' Mrs. Musty held out a slender hand. Alastair extracted the coin in question and placed it in the lady's palm. 'Hallo, Mr. Fippet. You are looking well. How is your dear mother? I hope...'

Alastair took his filled paper cup and wandered from the tent. 'How is your dear mother?' he whispered.

He walked from stall to stall admiring the leather work and woodcarving, gazing wistfully at the pottery and craft trappings whilst fingering the other coins in his pocket.

He stared absentmindedly back over to the crowd which hemmed the main arena. Then casting his eye along the line of people his attention was drawn to a stout man, dressed in a tweed suit and a mauve cravat, holding a large cigar, who stared back at him. Alastair felt embarrassed. He was sure he had seen him somewhere before but could not remember where or when. The unusual man smiled pleasantly from below his greying moustache and gave a short wave. Alastair waved back.

The boy's attention was distracted. 'Get off my toe, you big oaf. Those are my best shoes,' pronounced a plump lady to a short gentleman. Alastair grinned and looked over to the arena again. The smiling man had gone.

The afternoon finally grew old; skylarks had completed their clever skylarking and pheasants no longer trilled through brushwood. Schoolgirls from The Smudge Academy had danced, the horses had paraded and raced, the archers had shown their skills. Mr. Tittering had lost another pair of false teeth; the temporary structures were being prepared for collapse. And as the sun grew red and plump, streaked with yellow and gold,

Thimriddy Fair drew to a close for another twelve months. Men clutching beer tankards, women with silver spoons or potted plants, children laughing in delight or crying in disappointment, or blowing whistles and waving flags, all left the grassed field.

Even before the last clutch of families had departed, Sammy Solomon was pulling up tent pegs while others began to manhandle the canvas of the marquees and Mrs. Goodwithin limped from the pottery stall to a wooden box, packing away her wares.

Alastair thought that he would run away; he would go to Grinding to seek his fortune or to Limpington to become a pig farmer. Then his stomach grumbled and he felt tired and so decided to go home.

CHAPTER 23

The Question

A NOTHER BROWNISH DROPLET of water fell from the tap. Another fly scribbled invisible lines in the air and came to rest on the lightbulb which dangled naked from the ceiling. Another snore thundered into the small kitchen from the front room. Another bead of water fell from the rusting tap.

Alastair slouched at the table in the kitchen. His finger created meandering patterns from the pile of salt that lay amidst the aftermath of dinner. The digit furrowed the crystals of its own accord though, for his young features were carved in concentration and his mind tumbled with stormy thoughts. He sighed and wished for summer again; climbing tree branches and collecting conkers and net-fishing for guppies and chasing cats, finding birds eggs and Thimriddy Fair.

Mrs. Battlespoke called to her Golden Duck Wings and Bantams to tell them of her imminent departure to the butcher's shop which overlooked the green. The Reverend Musty was washing dishes, pronouncing serious prayers to his congregation of crockery but Alastair was not to know or hear these things nor indeed the sobbing wind that rattled the windowpanes.

In his perfunctory manner, Dr. Snippet was attempting to calm his shaking hands to enable him to prepare medicines and lotions, while Miss Crouch strode into The Bulldog Fish Tavern for her weekend stint behind the bar. Alastair was not to know or see these happenings nor indeed the paper bag that scuttled up the path in chase of the fallen leaves which danced and curtsied.

Though his eyes and ears were unaware of the characters who played out their lives in Muchmarsh, his thoughts were of them. There was a stifling of his faculties from their suffocating influences and yet, as though in contradiction, he felt isolated and apart from their community. A familiar despondency swept through him.

Perhaps he could tend the vicarage garden or feed Mrs. Battlespoke's chickens again or bake bread in Mr. Spittle's bakery.

As Alastair considered ways to integrate himself more into the lives of the villagers, the ideas were sucked into a vortex by a depression which whirled inside him. His head felt filled with cotton wool and a light nausea curled in his stomach. The tap still dripped, flies still scratched their imperceptible patterns and another obscene snore crawled from the front room.

He tried to unravel his vortical thoughts into separate ideas but not one scheme wished for an identity of its own. He was lonely; if only there was someone in whom he could confide and trust. The more he had been imprisoning his fears the larger they had become. Was there someone to whom he could talk about his nightmares that seemed more real than reality itself? Someone that he could need and love and be loved in return, someone who would listen to him in sympathy and understanding? The question which he had asked many times came to him again but he knew the answer would always be a growling snarl and for his father to ignore him for the rest of the day.

He heard William Stubb awaken from his drunken doze, a hoarse cough and a flurry of a newspaper as it was flung to the floor.

Having accomplished the majority of the chores from the

day before, Alastair assumed that his father might be responsive to conversation this time. He was determined to rid himself for always of his fundamental question which tormented him; the answer had to be found. He heard the wireless set – given by Dr. Snippet – crackle into life.

He walked into the front room and stood patiently with hands held behind his back. His father slouched in an armchair, staring at the dismal wallpaper and crumbling cornice along the wall.

Now is the time, Alastair told himself. 'Please, where is mother?' he whispered rapidly.

He fidgeted on the spot from apprehension that made his throat dry. Despite never being told, he still held an excited speculation of the answer as he perched on the edge of the battered settee.

Stubb replied with a grunt pursued by a groan that rose in pitch to burst into a bellowing cheer of praise for the six that had been hit, enthusiastically commented on by the radio presenter. Whooping with excitement, he leant forward with an avid interest at the continuation of the game, quite unaware that he held the bottle of beer flat along the arm of the chair in which he sat. The liquid trickled to the threadbare carpet and formed a puddle. Alastair fixed his gaze onto the pool while it seeped into the balding material though his thoughts were still on the dire need for an answer. His confidence had begun to melt the more from the insinuations and tauntings of the other children at school; if he did not have a mother, was he really born from an animal?

Stubb bent forward with his arms outstretched as though in apparent readiness to dive into the radio, in sympathy with the wicket keeper who might have held a similar stance. The bottle swung in a grip of two fingers, until he roared with satisfaction at the commentator's babble and the rounds of tinny heckling and clapping. He began to sup the remainder of his ale much like a baby would while suckling its milk.

'Where's my mother?' Alastair timidly said a second time yet somewhat louder than the first occasion.

A sudden lapse of noise from the wireless set caused the question to become too distinct and lacking in subtlety. Stubb had been engaged upon draining the last of his beer as though attempting to balance the bottle on the end of his nose; his unshaven sideburned face thrown back exposing the skin that hung about his neck with the texture of a plucked turkey and the black hairs which tufted from his nostrils. Upon hearing the question he flung his arms and round head forward so violently that the bottle escaped from his grasp and flew over towards Alastair. It shattered when it struck the wall behind him.

Alastair flinched and cradled his head for protection from any glass shards and he threw an expression of pained surprise to the man he called father.

Stubb was caught unawares and he wore a face of regret. He told himself that it would not do to allow his son to see such a mild expression in place of his practiced snarling visage. He moulded a sneer to his features and thus his saddened eyes acted to his advantage as they glimmered with mock concern.

Alastair clasped his quivering hands together. He knew that he must demand an answer. He was in no mood to choose the appropriate tone with a muttered question.

'Where is she? Tell me,' he said and he flushed from the experience of raising his voice to Stubb but then felt vulnerable in front of the large man and worry took hold of him. 'Tell me, please tell me,' he whispered humbly. 'You said you would tell.'

Stubb hunched forward, the sneer still haunting his face. With a mock admiration at Alastair's boldness he chortled, then cocking his head to the side he clapped his hands together. They made the sound of wet fish slapping onto a fishmonger's slab. He rose to his feet, rubbing his belly which had grown larger over the years. His mind had become a mass of scratching thorns. This boy was asking him, once again, to sift through the memories that he had so many times tried to destroy. He dared not reminisce for fear that they lay intact and harsh inside the prisons to which he had condemned them. Though he desperately tried to communicate the idea that his curling lip was a mere external covering for a superiority lying beneath, he equally tried to hide his true feelings of remorse. And a growing sense of emptiness, gripping him more each year Eleanor was apart from his life. He bowed and placed his hands on his knees. His face twitched into a forced smile and his double chin trembled from flat laughter which vibrated from his stomach. Something would have to be said once and for all, to put an end to the constantly repeated question.

'I have never told you before, boy – the full story – because it isn't important, and it's not really your concern. However, seeing as you still wish to know, I will tell you finally. She is... in hospital. Way over in Grangeling's Sanatorium, near Smudge. She's been there for years,' he said and then murmured, 'and she won't be out for a long time. A very long time.' He had stumbled on the words: if when he had lied to his son at other times without conscience, why was it that this falsehood brushed his mind with guilt? He turned his back to Alastair with the pretence of a renewed interest in the wireless set.

Without his father's face to contend with Alastair felt a surge of confidence and he could not contain his excitement any longer. 'Mother's in hospital. Can I go? When? When can I visit her? Please let me see her...'

Stubb was tormented by this outburst and the walls to the

dam of his memories burst apart and he was unaware that he had thrown his short arms into the air, attempting to grip a part of it for support as though it were solid. Nor did he realize that he was shouting high above the voices from the wireless set, 'Never – you will never see her for as long as you live.'

Alastair heard his mouth say, 'You take life too seriously, William.' Stubb did not hear. He urgently scratched his head as though to impede the onrush of memory impressions that had begun to activate dormant emotions into being, all of which he had hoped were drowned by ale long ago. He twisted on his heels, bustled through the doorway and down the hall. 'Never!' he shrieked again as he jerked open the front door, and slammed it behind him.

Alastair's face was drained of colour and a numbness pervaded him. The aching for maternal comfort returned and though he knew that crying was too insufficient an emotion to rid himself of a mental anguish that was becoming part of his life, he allowed the tears to flow. A part of his distress would be dismissed for a time. Not caring about the shards of glass which lay about him, he fell to the settee and sobbed; not in loneliness or self-pity but in the realization that he would never see his mother. He felt a juvenile hatred for his father lurch inside. It blocked his torrent of emotion for a moment whereupon the aching welled up again and he resumed his outpouring of grief.

Stubb stood outside, immobile for a second only, then, through years of practice, all thoughts of the occurrence that had taken place were swept away. His anxious face faded and was replaced by his usual one of disgust with the world. Wiping a tear with the back of his hand he tutted and walked the few paces to the wooden gate.

As though waiting for an opportunity to cause havoc, a robust wind sprang from hiding, and after running cold fingers through the hedges of the terraced houses, it leapt along the pavement and swung impishly on unlatched gates, leaves running circles in its wake. The large oak tree which had stood for more than a century at the end of Pepper Lane clung to the last of the foliage as its stark branches swayed gently in the wind. The occasional leaf would flutter to the ground to join those already lying dead, there in a profusion of colours. Autumn had descended upon the village.

On feeling the skipping wind playing with the modicum of hair from the nape of his neck, Stubb mused on the idea of retrieving his raincoat from the house but dismissed the idea. The Bulldog Fish Tavern had already been open for more than twenty minutes.

He noticed her the moment he had stepped out into the street. Unsure as to what to do he gaped stupidly and as contrivances wormed slowly through his mind, the figure shuffled closer. She peered intently through the monocle that snuggled beside the bridge of her nose. Her other eye bulged blindly from its socket at a most obscure angle. Stubb gulped down a pool of saliva that had collected.

'Afternoon, Mrs. Battlespoke,' he said reluctantly, 'I can't talk today. I've got an important job to do.'

'Why if it isn't Mr. Stubb; you are looking well, as fit as a fiddler.' The last of her sentence was stressed with an agitation of her withered hand. 'I was saying to Mrs. Stick this morning...' Her croaking voice ceased as she paused for breath and Stubb saw his opportunity.

'Well, I really must go.'

'I said, ignore your daily constitutional and you ignore a longer life, because you know Mrs. Stick. Doesn't wash but it's understandable what with her lumbago and those very cosy veins. Have you heard, Mr. Stick pulled a cartridge in his ankle?

Rub olive oil into his joint bone, I told her. My mother swore by it; she worked at the old cotton mill over at Grinding. With all that standing up and having to come home, do the washing and scrubbing and put us six children to bed and then back at the mill by six o'clock the next morning, well, you might imagine. It was like our Mrs. Crowpack before she passed on. Did you know she left me her card table and commode in her will? And that reminds me: poor Edith – that will be Edith Clocks, not the other Edith – got trouble with her drains again. It's all of that cotton wool I tell her...'

Stubb impatiently huffed through his nose as he towered above the frail shrunken woman who gabbled incessantly before him. He folded his arms across his chest and glared at her. Mrs. Battlespoke had looked after Alastair very well in the past; often supplied brown eggs from her brood; and for those reasons he found it difficult to ignore the old lady. The words emanating from the chattering mouth seemed to curl and be whisked away by the wind that still played in the street. Stubb found himself staring intently at her blind eye which was involuntarily circling and twitching in its socket.

'How is our young Alastair? I hope he found what he wanted, to make up his collection the other day.'

'His collection? What's he up to now?'

'Why Mr. Stubb, his collection of insects of course. I let him have a good look around the coop; plenty there if the chickens don't eat them. Oh my yes, he has a good show already, striped beetles, snail shells...'

Stubb shuddered. He would have to put a stop to that.

Mrs. Battlespoke clucked and tutted, sighed and complained, all the while swaying gently on her slight body while she added to her monologue. 'Of course, you can't be expected to, what with the price of meat nowadays...'

Stubb noticed that her poor sight was elsewhere. It was wandering through the factory in Grinding or skipping through the fields of her childhood in Stillstone or ranging over the price of bread at Spittle's bakery, chasing her dusty memories from their nooks and crannies of her over-active mind. The irrelevances of the past and the mundane happenings of the village clouded her sight of the singing gate, the parade of terraced houses and William Stubb. This he saw in a second and he scuttled up the road to leave Mrs. Battlespoke swaying and gesticulating as she told her reminiscences to the wind.

CHAPTER 24

A Fight

A LASTAIR SIGHED AND rubbed his nose. How anyone could muster enthusiasm for Colonel Crotchet's Poems of Life was beyond his understanding. For a third time he scanned the page but being in no mood to read he deliberately skipped the paragraph that he was next to digest. Telling himself he could not find his place he looked dreamily about the classroom. All of the other children were quiet and intent upon reading.

Through the window, on the playground, stood a beech tree with its branches swaying gently. He mused on what it could be like to be a tree. 'Fancy not doing anything but stand around all day,' he thought. 'A bit boring I suppose, but better than reading this rubbish.' He tapped the book with contempt. Upon his sight returning to his desk he saw a tiny spider.

His mouth twitched and his eyes fluttered involuntarily and an image of a large and dark room flickered before him; then the vision was gone.

He was fascinated by the patient labours of the spider as it journeyed along a deep furrow that had been carved into the lid of his desk meant for his pencil. Several times it climbed the walls of the wooden corridor only to return to the bottom. 'The poor thing must be confused,' Alastair thought. He mentally nudged it along for he felt its claustrophobia. His face creased in concentration but then he grinned as it reached the end of its confinement. It scuttled rapidly across the desk. Happy in the knowledge of the creature's escape, he was quite prepared to resume reading his book until a shadow passed over the spider and a fist ground it into the wood.

Alfred Gristle, the gravedigger's son, had turned in his seat from the desk in front of Alastair's and was stabbing a finger and jeering in animated mime. Alastair glared for a moment at the boy's wide nose then looking down at the crushed body of his intrepid climber, its hair-fine legs scattered like eyelashes. He was filled with rage. For a peculiar moment the face of Gristle became the face of William Stubb. Alastair brought his fist to his cheek as though pulling on a bow. To avenge the pointless death of the creature he knew that he must retaliate.

Unknown to Alastair, young Sidney Pump, the son of the manor house ex-butler, had been watching the proceedings with obvious glee from the school desk behind him. As Alastair's hand touched his own jaw in preparation for its flight towards Gristle, Pump seized it and pulled it down over Alastair's shoulder while tugging the hair on the nape of his neck. The victim crumpled his face in pain as a muscle was pulled in his armpit and the back of his neck began to sting. All thought processes were curtailed by the torment and his aching arm did not care to ease its pain for the time necessary to imagine a just retribution for the instigator of his agony. Anger and discomfort were a burning molten core. Gristle chuckled quietly as a tear rolled down Alastair's cheek. Pump pulled viciously on Alastair's fingers with both hands. There was no alternative but for him to scream in the hope of lessening the pain that shot through him like a shock from electricity.

Save for the occasional muttering as a child whispered the words from a book or perhaps conversing in conspiring tones with their neighbour, the classroom had been silent. The yelp of a beaten dog caused a few gasps and enquiring looks and it dispersed the intellectual rambling of Miss Crouch who sat at the head of the class with her back as stiff as a new shirt collar. Her cultured head jolted away from the papers which lay in front of her on her large leather-covered desk and darted from side to side as she attempted to ascertain the whereabouts of the animal which had made such a dreadful noise. She was bemused by the fact that all heads were away from her and she followed the lines of sight of the children. They converged onto one point.

Gristle and Pump were scanning the books before them; although Pump was trying to read the few words printed on his closed volume and Gristle attempted to examine his copy which lay upside down.

Miss Crouch watched Alastair as he tenderly massaged his sore arm and fingers. The shuffling of feet and interested chatter that had occurred upon hearing Alastair's shout had evaporated. A silence spread itself thickly over the classroom. The wind outside weaved through the poplars along School Lane. Miss Crouch rose majestically from her seat, her back never faltering from its straightness. Her long arms stretched their full length downward and she placed her fingertips onto her desk as if it were her pulpit and she was preparing to deliver a sermon. Though instead of speaking, she navigated around the bulky desk that was also littered with books new and old and the ragged exercise pads of her class. Her long legs were covered by yards of pea green material, (which was quite content to drag upon the dusty floor,) and as though floating she made her way to Alastair. Pump and Gristle tired of their pretence of reading and they smiled at the nearing of the schoolmistress, foremost for the apparent act of gliding across the floorboards as though propelled on wheels but also in the possibility that Alastair could receive a severe reprimand.

Miss Crouch reached the boy. She stood with her hands

planted firmly on her hips and a wry expression on her plain face. 'What on earth do you think you are doing, Alastair,' she demanded and before he could answer, continued, 'disturbing the class with this outburst? It will not do, you know. I'm sure it was you, wasn't it? Unless you have a dog tied up in your desk.' The classroom pupils reacted with laughter. 'Children, quiet,' she spoke loudly above the noise. She had not meant to say anything amusing. 'What have you got to say?' Alastair could only groan in reply. He rubbed his burning arm. 'Hmm? What is the meaning of it when you should be reading your poems?'

Alastair drew breath to answer but then expelled the air and winced as Pump gave him a sly jab in the back. He remained silent until animosity overcame his fear and to Miss Crouch's 'Well?' he simply replied, 'Sidney, miss.' He still burned inside. Pump cast his eyes with innocence and looked enquiringly to the schoolmistress who folded her arms and expelled a puff of air as impatience. Gristle turned his back to Alastair.

'Sidney, is this true? Do you have anything to do with this terrible outburst?'

A look of surprise masked Pump's face and he gasped, 'No miss, honest. I dunno why he should say such, honest I don't.' Slowly his eyelids dropped and he looked sullen. Miss Crouch watched him suspiciously.

'Now look,' she said, 'I am not sure who is telling the truth so you will both stay in later: half hour detention.' She raised her head and addressed the class after glancing to the clock on the back wall. 'Right children, it is time to go now, anyway.'

Suddenly there was a cacophony of noise; of books cracking shut and desks banging and coughs and laughter and raised voices of "Goodnight, miss"; the scraping of heels on the floorboards and squeaking on the square of linoleum; the clatter of wooden chairs and clomping of feet that gradually diminished as the class filtered through the doorway. Hoots of delight echoed from outside the room and the clamour of voices became the sound of a solitary pair of feet running down the corridor. A door slammed with a reverberation and all was quiet again.

'I have to ring the bell for the other two classes, so you will both wait here and don't get up to any mischief. I will be back soon.' With that said she glided to the front of the classroom and opened a cupboard beside the blackboard to produce a brass bell. Apparently floating from the room and down the corridor, she swung the bell violently in front of her, the echoing peals resounding through the small school.

Pump grimaced at Alastair. To catch him unprepared he would have to act fast. Realizing that his body had stiffened he relaxed and grinned. He held out a hand and beckoned with a finger. 'Come on then mate, Alastair,' he said, stressing the inflexions in the name unnaturally. 'Let's be friends,' he hissed. 'Shake.'

Alastair quivered in a moment of indecision. Was he to trust this character? He looked at Pump's clenched fist and he held out his own hand to shake. Pump opened his fist to an outstretched palm and Alastair gazed in horror at the contents of the hand. A blood-matted mouse lay on its back with its paws drawn tightly to its skinny body. Pump sneered and Alastair recoiled from him but was too surprised to guard against attack. Like a coiled spring that had been released, Pump lunged forward. He took hold of Alastair's head and held it under his arm in a tight grip. Alastair gasped for breath while he was smothered and his ear stung as it was pressed into a button on Pump's jacket. A tear was squeezed from between his eyelids. With his face reddening and his teeth clamped together, his breathing rasped hoarsely.

'Hit my mate, would you,' yelled Pump, 'tried to hit my mate?

Have a bite of this.' He wiped the tiny corpse around Alastair's mouth; Alastair choked as the cold bloodied fur smeared his face. A stark terror gripped him, his muscles had contracted so much that he ached. He began to grunt rhythmically, becoming louder until he could not contain himself any longer.

The being who clawed at Pump and tried to bite him was not Alastair but the unsophisticated animal within driven out. Pump let go his hold and he shouted in surprise. Alastair pulled repeatedly on the coarse black hair on Pump's head with all of his strength, a glint in his eye as scratches on Pump's face began to show beads of blood. As Pump wailed, Alastair glared and snarled, 'You idiot, you are nothing but a cowardly drunkard. You should have been thrown out years ago. So you would tell William of Eleanor and me?'

Pump gaped and licked his hand. 'What are you talking about?'

'What am I saying?' Alastair muttered and then without any control of his mouth he spoke the words, 'You will pay for that as will all the others. Frightened of water, are you?'

'Are you talking about my dad?' demanded the frightened Sidney Pump and, before he could speak further, Alastair punched his face; Pump's lip split and began to bleed. He howled in pain, his mouth open wide, showing his untidy rows of teeth.

The sight of blood and screaming brought Alastair back into control. He saw that he still had a firm grip of Pump's hair and he relaxed his grip. The boy's head fell forward with his eyes closed. Alastair stared in horror at the sight which filled his mind only. He held a decapitated head dripping with blood; and death, second by second, was remoulding the face to suit the grave, making it waxen and drawn. With a screech, he let go and ran.

Miss Crouch stepped back into the corridor from another

classroom in time to see Alastair pulling open the school entrance door. Blinded with fright, the boy did not see or hear her. 'Alastair, what mischief are you up to? Come back.'

Alastair gasped and greedily gulped the air that was beginning to chill as the sun prepared to sink below the horizon. He lay on his back on the coarse stubble of one of farmer Solomon's fields and stared upwards. He followed the flight of a crow as it raced with the ragged clouds which daubed the sky like paint. Slowly, his senses, his breath and the stupidity of his actions returned. He looked at the tight fist that lay beside him as though it was not a part of himself. His mouth curled in disgust and he shuddered and slowly uncoiled his fingers, holding his sweating palm out flat.

A clump of thick matted hair lay upon it.

CHAPTER 25

Mr Badger

MIST HAD TAKEN refuge in the hills and a nebulosity crawled over the horizon towards the abandoned canal. The clock on the green gave its slow chimes; a hush lay over the land then, scratched only by the harsh caw of a crow or broken to a whisper as the stream trickled from the hills, making its way under the stone bridge.

A scruffy outhouse snuggled up to one of the barns which stood in farmer Solomon's yard, slouching in the sun's dying rays. Its rain-battered wooden door had swollen and like a stubborn mule which needed more than gentle persuasion from a brutish type, it received several hefty kicks. It shuddered, loosening more of its paint before casually opening.

A thin man wearing spectacles and with ringlets of white hair stepped out onto the yard, trailing a broom behind him over the scattered straw stems, horse droppings and clumps of mud. He shuffled over to another outhouse which faced the straw bales stacked to the eaves of an open-sided construction. Beside that stood ploughs and a steam-powered threshing machine.

A long shadow was cast behind Mr. Badger from the last of the light filtering from the darkening sky. His nose began to run in sympathy with his weak eyes; he drew the grubby cuff of his waistcoated shirt across it. Not content to let his thoughts run silently through his mind, he allowed them to slaver from his tongue; a stream of sibilant muttering, a barrage of curses and blasphemies; idle perverse and obscene statements thrown to the moon which had now taken a sketched residence in the evening sky. By vocalizing such meandering, interspersed with wordless parrot noises, he was able to clear his mind for a while of the queer erotic thoughts that insisted on coming to him at the most unexpected of times. The mumbled monotone was lost to the outhouse as he entered, the broom skipping over the step like a puppy in playful chase of the farm hand.

Mr. Badger heaved the door shut behind him. The scene was static again save for the mist that was creeping furtively up to the farmyard.

CHAPTER 26

Shocking News

STALK WIPED THE blood from his fingers onto his stained apron and smiled to himself. Pulling the cleaver from the tree stump which lay beside him hatched and cross hatched, he playfully slammed it into the flesh which lay on the counter. He winked slowly as to make it appear he was simply closing an eye then gave a contented sniff as the cleaver struck a rib. He rubbed his bearded chin and then the back of his hand and said, 'I will cut you up after tea.' He snorted and made his way to the door, saying as he went, 'The day's going too quick for my liking.' He spoke the words crisply though the only ears for his remarks to reach were his own. After he had turned a sign around on the door of his butcher's shop from "open" to "closed", it tired of its grip by the rubber sucker and fell silently to the mat. He tutted and casually bent his back to retrieve it and, as he did so, he looked through the door pane to scan the village green. Small birds pecked frantically at the earth; wooden benches and a horse trough, the village clock there; the oak trees huddled together as if from the wind. The omnibus stop shelter waited patiently for occupation; and, as Stalk swung his head back to the left, he saw William Stubb ambling across the green towards the public house. The Bulldog Fish Tavern, tucked neatly at a corner of the green with its door open, stood beside Martha May's Wool Store and Miss Dripping's confectionery shop.

The public house seemed to glare at Stubb's approach with shuttered eyes and a gaping, toothless mouth. Stubb was licking his dry lips in anticipation and attempting to lengthen his stride towards his objective. Stalk allowed the half-smile to drop from his face. He mumbled an obscenity under his breath and waited until Stubb was no more than three yards from The Bulldog Fish Tavern whereupon the butcher opened his door. The bell rang nervously above him. He remembered that he had forgotten to put the sign up but waved the thought away with a twirl of his hand whilst the other hand produced a family of keys from his apron. He selected the appropriate one and locked the shop.

He turned into the next doorway. A gaudy sign spread itself across the small wattle and daub building declaring it to be Nuckle's Tea House. With stained hands shoved deep into the pockets of his apron, Stalk pushed on the door with his elbow. The door creaked as if with annoyance at being disturbed.

The tops of the tables were rarely cleaned; the tables stood haphazardly about the room, covered with scraps of mouldering food and dust and distemper from the ceiling. Cigarette ends and scraps of paper littered the floor, as did petals and plant stems. Arrangements of dead and dried flowers stood in containers where space allowed. The wallpaper was dirty blue stripes and streaked with damp.

Stalk strolled to the counter which lay at the back of the room. A glass cabinet before him contained three bread rolls, green with mould, and an object Stalk guessed might once have been a cake. He coughed twice and placed his elbows on the counter thus spoiling a perfect layer of dust there. A daily ritual had grown over many years and though Stalk was aware that it would not produce Mr. Nuckle, he coughed once more and stood scratching his beard for a full minute.

He turned away from the counter and stepped lightly over to his chair which sat by the window. The seat was devoid of varnish through his unintentional backside polishing every day.

❧

As Stubb moved across the sticky and stained carpet in the public bar of The Bulldog Fish Tavern, all heads and eyes turned to him. There was a sudden ceasing of conversation apart from Sammy Solomon who was enthralled with the sound of his own voice. A sharp jab in the ribs curtailed his waffling save for an urgent whisper of 'What was that for?'

Stubb rubbed his chin thoughtfully. He was perplexed as to why he should have such an attentive audience. They sat with dark beer-filled jugs in their hands about the hefty barrels serving as tables, stony expressions and without movement as though posing for a photograph. Stubb finally rested his sight onto Chess the publican who stood behind the bar with his usual posture of arms folded tightly about him as though embracing himself.

Miss Crouch, engaged upon her lunch-time duty of washing the glassware, stood pondering the question of the validity of classical authors on modern-day literature and seemingly oblivious to the strange event of silence in the public bar of The Bulldog Fish Tavern.

As if he could not make a decision as to who needed the sight of his perplexed expression the most, Stubb swung his attention from Chess to the hushed members of the room and back again. Still no one moved. He fumbled in his pocket for a packet of cigarettes and cast his perturbed eyes across the beamed bar. Then, like a disappointed child, he stamped his foot on the carpet.

'What's the matter with you lot?' he shouted.

Hearing no answer from the brewery congregation who sat as stiffly as mannequins in a fine clothes shop, he whipped his bulk around, away from their unblinking stares. He flushed with anger when his nose met the yellow face of Chess who still appeared to be cuddling himself.

'What's wrong? I've got it. You've run out of beer. That's it, isn't it?' Still no one moved or spoke. 'I've got something, food stuff in my teeth? Or my whiskers?' Stubb's balding crown turned lobster pink and a shade of red washed into his cheeks. He threw his head back in a lordly manner, ironing out some of the loose skin about his neck. 'What is the problem with you bunch?' he questioned loudly but apparently to Chess.

The publican behind the mahogany carved bar, a line of pewter and glass tankards at his back, placed his elbows down upon the top with his arms crossed, hands still determined to meet around his back. 'Queenie's returned; been seen in Muchmarsh,' he stated matter-of-factly. Without moving his sallow hands he slowly wiped a scratch from his ear onto his shoulder.

Stubb's torso twitched the once and his mouth fell open. He groaned and sighed and gasped and his eyes were rendered dark by his own exclamations. He appeared suddenly exhausted and he seemed to subside when his shoulders fell lower. He stared sightlessly past Chess's left arm and he mumbled to himself. Chess dropped his head closer to Stubb's downturned mouth. 'What's that?' he asked, seemingly to the beermat.

'When?' squeaked Stubb, his voice jumping an octave. He gazed dreamily through a whitewashed wall and then to a ceiling beam covered with dried green hops.

'Can't rightly say, William. Young Solomon says when he was out herding the cows this morning, he sees her running across Scripping's Field as though the Devil himself was after her. Isn't that so, Sammy? But still, it don't seem right, does it? I mean, she's not been seen for two year or more, as well you know. Even the food parcels weren't collected this last year, were they? Begging in Smudge, we all reckon. But see, two days ago our Isaac swears he's seen her along Daisytrail Lane, sitting there, crouched on the ground like, laughing to herself. Though you know Isaac, what with his eyesight and all.'

Chess smiled over to the old man in question who sat in his special chair in the corner of the saloon bar next to the open log fire. The farmer moved his fingers through his grey beard and said, 'I ain't lying neither. I did see the woman as I see all you now and by the by, I'll be having another tankard full, Chess.' The silent crowd exploded into laughter and they raised their ale to the old farmer, some patting him on the back.

'Don't you be worrying yourself, my old friend. I'll be pouring in a minute as soon as our lady is ready,' Chess replied with a chuckle. Glancing over to Miss Crouch, he raised an eyebrow and winked. The locals laughed heartily again and loud enough to jolt Miss Crouch from her reverie. Chess cuddled himself the more. Stubb twisted his mouth into an obscure expression.

The school teacher turned away from the soapy water in the stone sink and blinked. She saw a quivering Stubb and reached him with two strides.

'Mr. Stubb, do forgive me please. I didn't see you standing there. The usual?' She cocked her head to one side as though listening for a faraway sound and a becoming smile lit her plain face.

Stubb did not hear. He turned abruptly to the silence behind that had once more descended. As though his turning was a cue, the group of locals began to laugh and chatter in a most unnatural way. He held onto the edge of the bar to steady himself as if he might drop to the floor. Wiping his mouth with the back of his hand, then holding the stiffened tendons in the back of his neck, he strode regimentally to the entrance, swung it open and departed. The door thudded behind him and rattled the latch, and the villagers immediately ceased their affected babble in preference to muted tones.

Miss Crouch was concerned and she said, 'What is the matter? Did I say something wrong?'

❧

'Well, well, well,' said Stalk to himself when he saw Stubb appear from the doorway of The Bulldog Fish Tavern and hurry across the village green. Through the years that he had spent his lunch hour in Nuckle's Tea Shop, he had acquired the habit of staring through the smeared window to watch for any signs of life which might occur in the sleepy village so that he would occupy himself until Nuckle appeared. The butcher hissed through his teeth. 'Very unusual,' he murmured. Flicking a fly away that had landed confidently on his cheek, he rose to his feet. He wiped invisible blood onto his apron and walked a pace closer to the window to gain a better view of the most uncommon sight of William Stubb leaving The Bulldog Fish Tavern before closing time. 'Go on then, Stubb. Clear off and get out of it,' he jeered. 'Nothing but a lazy fat slob.'

'You are talking to yourself again,' came a gruff voice. Stalk had not noticed Nuckle behind the counter, the curls of his white hair seeming tighter than usual. 'Something to no one, as it were. If one was to listen to one's self, one wouldn't talk when there is no one there to listen. I distinctly heard you talk to yourself. Muttering your usual rubbish no doubt. That is typical of you, did you know that?' Nuckle's eyes never left the magazine spread out in front of him. He peered intently at the matt pages and carefully turned them while stroking hair coils.

'Where is my tea, you?' demanded Stalk and then, changing

his tone of voice, in the same breath stated, 'I have this minute seen Stubb,' seemingly proud of the statement.

Nuckle looked up, as always his large eyes possessing an expression of sadness, as though constantly weary with calamitous thoughts. 'So what,' he growled. His grumbling voice was no match for his wide, innocent eyes. He removed his spectacles to wipe the lenses on his filthy apron.

'You're born and bred and lived in Muchmarsh...'

'I was born in Staffingham.'

'...lived in Muchmarsh for as long as I have and you say so what?' answered Stalk irritably. 'It's very queer, that's what,' and he added precisely as an afterthought, 'most strange.' Musing on his own remarks he stared to the yellow and brown mottled ceiling while Nuckle continued to peruse his magazine. 'Still reading them dirty books, you,' said Stalk quickly. 'Don't know what you see in it. A grown man reading that rubbish. It's smutty.' He looked down his nose at Nuckle. 'Are you listening to me?'

'Do you want your tea? Perhaps you don't because it seems your time is taken up with shouting. So do you or don't you want your blooming tea?' Nuckle raised his head and stared into Stalk's eyes, his own brimming with sadness. He replaced his spectacles. 'And anyway, these aren't rubbish or smutty. They are nature magazines. It is the anatomical study of the alive and beautiful female form, free from caskets; what's more it's for the serious application of science to art.'

'Dirty books.'

Nuckle sighed. 'Do you want your tea, I asked you.'

Stalk marched up to the counter. 'Where's my tea then, you?' he said starchily.

Nuckle took a step backwards and without averting his glistening eyes from the magazine, put his hand around the doorframe and produced a chipped china cup filled with tea. Through years of habit, he said, 'The usual price,' and through years of habit, Stalk replied, 'Put it on the slate, you,' and through years of habit, there was not to be another word spoken between them until the next day.

CHAPTER 27

Fog

'PLEASE DO SOMETHING,' Alastair had pleaded to the person he looked to as his father, after awakening from another bad dream, terror-stricken and trembling.

'What can I do about it? Go back to your bed and stop your thinking; that's half the trouble boy, you think these stupid things then you wonder why you have nightmares. Go on, do as I say,' demanded Stubb as he turned his back on the young teenage boy. Alastair sobbed and walked slowly from Stubb's bedroom to his own, shivering with fear and cold. He fetched a woollen blanket and crept downstairs. He would spend another night on the settee.

Stubb was concerned; Alastair had been saying some strange things. The night before he had been kept from sleep while Alastair had screamed and raved. Upon investigation he was found cowering in a corner. Yet the situation was changing: that very night he had looked white-faced and frightened and told of somebody trying to get into his head until he had slept but only to have had nightmares which seemed – he had insisted – too real. Stubb decided he would take him to see Dr. Snippet before the situation became worse. With that conclusion made, he relaxed, cleared his mind and fell asleep.

Alastair sat on the settee in the front room with the blanket held up to his neck, not daring to close his eyes. But upon hearing the clopping of a horse's hooves, chinking bottles and the dry whistle of the milkman, then Mrs. Battlespoke calling to her chickens, he realized he had slept after all. He yawned and scratched himself and climbed the stairs to his bedroom. The rattling snores of his father reached his ears. He dressed and slipped out of the house.

A cold, whispering Wednesday morning. He walked along Stutter Lane deep in his own thoughts. There was not much to see; he could barely make out the grass verge on the other side of the lane for a thick fog impeded his vision to no more than a few feet. The whiteness hung in the air to form a canvas to paint his thoughts onto. After the incident with Sidney three days before he was expecting some form of retaliation soon and he had begun to wonder how and when.

As insubstantial forms loomed from the fog he would shudder for they would become a vague impression of the head of Sydney Pump, with a mouth curled into a vicious expression. The shapes would turn out to be trees holding their branches in grotesque contortions or bushes, weighed with frost, wild and straggly.

Delicate cobwebs sprinkled with dew adorned the hedgerows. All was a hush save for the muffled sound of his own footsteps and the occasional bleating of a sheep from one of the silvered fields. Alastair opened his mouth wide to feel the refreshing taste as he took in the air, icy and cold, but after a few minutes his teeth began to ache and his tongue was numbed. He was forced to breathe through his nose that was already blocked with rheum from the onset of a cold. His exposed ears, deprived of sensation by the chilliness, had begun to glow red. He was increasingly convinced that his eyelids had been frozen open. The feeling conjured up reminiscences of two summers ago when he had explored the shallow bottom of Laughing Pond, the gentle pressure of water upon his features.

Quaint houses and cottages loomed out of the whiteness.

There was the vague outline of farmer Solomon's farmhouse to the left of the farm yard. Further on, a thatched cottage hiding in an overgrown small garden, a sign on its gate with the words: "close cup mushrooms for sale" and "best quality horse manure". A pious hush still pervaded the countryside. Alastair felt that somehow it would have been wrong to make any sound; for worry perhaps of a disturbance to the praying bushes that huddled together along the verge. The moisture and frost had rendered them flexible and drooping and they hung their heads in worship.

The fog began to thin. He decided to trot the remainder of the way along the lane.

After taking five steps only, a piercing scream broke the silence. He froze in his tracks; the shriek plunged an octave in a second and there began a trill like some demented bird, quavering with a passionate energy. Alastair was transfixed with fear. The alien tremulation warbled for so long he convinced himself that its source was mechanical. Though the slow-shifting fog was beginning to dilute to a mist it was still difficult to define any object other than in his immediate vicinity. He attempted to thrust his sight through the glowing haze to find the origin of the unusual ululation.

In spite of the initial shock that had reduced him to immobility so successfully he found it easy to laugh for the noise was indeed amusing but no sooner had he begun to chuckle, the odd utterance plummeted another octave to become a guttural and emotionless growl. The sudden transformation in the quality of the sound extinguished his derision. He was greedy for air and gulped spasmodically.

Alastair had become quickly frightened and walked with swift steps, all the while suspiciously glancing about. When it seemed that the originator of the sound was following he whimpered and broke into a trot. Then, as quickly as it had started, the noise ceased. Now it was the absence of sound that shivered his spine; he was ignorant of the whereabouts of the strange being. His thoughts spiralled and entwined into strange images as he wondered what the creature might be.

Pieces of a strange puzzle began to slot together in his imaginative head: the resulting mythical creature filled his thoughts and so, with his sight turned inward, he didn't see the hole in the compacted earth and rubble which served as a road for the lane. He would normally have skirted around it; he tripped and toppled to the ground. He lay sprawled and he resigned himself to his fate from the fantastical carnivorous beast which he was convinced was stalking him. In response to the tingling from his grazed elbow and knees he gave a cry. He wondered what it felt like to be savaged; maybe his body would be found that evening. Mrs. Battlespoke might discover him while out for a slow stroll. He gave another shout as his limbs began to sting. In reply, a horse whinnied, a sheep bleated mournfully in the mist and someone giggled close by. Alastair clenched his fists and flinched.

All hope of saving his own life had fled and he calculated that nothing more could be lost by catching sight of his attacker before the inevitable mutilation. There would surely be bloodshot eyes staring, the creature hungrily licking its jowls with its tongue dripping with saliva, flicking across a dark brown mouth.

CHAPTER 28

Queenie

E ROSE SLOWLY TO crouch on his haunches then turned to take a glimpse of the beast. But, upon catching sight of the origin of his alarm, was so surprised that he fell to the stony ground again. The intensity of relief that surged through him left him undecided whether the stupidity of the occasion warranted blushes or laughter. He chose the former and muttered in embarrassment, 'I'm so silly.' Miss Crouch had told him often that he possessed an over-active imagination.

'Sorry if I worried you but I've had a lot on my mind lately and well I...' Alastair tried to explain. The woman giggled again. 'Yes, I suppose it is funny,' he said. She grinned and he found himself smiling in return. 'Did you hear that strange noise not long ago?' He waited for a response but the woman remained silent. Alastair wondered if she was a gypsy; she had swarthy skin, rough and dry, and her large unblinking eyes were set deeply into her face making them the more penetrating. Wisps of hair had escaped from their confines of a headscarf which looked to have been tied hurriedly around her neck. There was a pungent, earthy odour about her. She wore a long pink dress and thick knee-high socks and a cardigan, all matted with mud and darkly stained, and torn in several places. Was the dress a nightgown? Alastair could not suppress a titter of amusement at this thought and even more so; he looked to her feet and saw that she wore green carpet slippers, the soles lined with leather.

The woman seemed surprised all at once and she acquired

a quizzical expression, though this was broken by a strange laugh; then the jocularity shown upon her wind-swept features was replaced with a scowl. It was such a contrast that it caused Alastair to take a pace away.

'Anything the matter?' he enquired.

With this she raised both arms in the chill and fogged air and upon tilting her scarved head back, her arms returned to her sides, only to start flapping furiously as if attempting to fly. She began to croon like some demented bird and Alastair recognized the sound as the one he had heard which had caused his fright. He watched in amusement when her hands began to slap her thighs with each downward stroke of her arms.

Is she an actress? he wondered. She began to bounce up and down, crooning with each jump, with her arms flaying and whipping her legs. Alastair was happy and enjoying himself; all thoughts of ferocious animals and school had left him. He was having fun playing games with a funny actress.

Was there no end to the woman's stamina? Her flights upwards, her crowing and thigh-slapping and landing firmly onto the ground in her green slippers was repeated again and again. He held a growing admiration for her as he watched in fascination and he realized that the woman's strenuous activity had begun to have a ritualistic quality about it. Before he could think he found himself bouncing and crowing with all his might and slapping the sides of his thin legs. 'Hooray!' he shouted alternately with his chicken impersonations.

There was the clomping of his boots and the flapping of her slippers on the flat stones; the crooning woman bouncing with determination and Alastair trying his best to copy her antics, laughing when not crowing or shouting; both of them slap, slapping their thighs.

His legs wobbled from the fatiguing exercise. His knees gave way and he collapsed to the ground, panting and coughing. Waiting to recover, he sat watching the woman, then thought that it was right to introduce himself. He looked doe-eyed up to her and said, 'Hallo, my name is Alastair. This is a tiring game, isn't it?'

The reaction to his remark was sudden. She landed onto her feet and ceased the ludicrous noise and crossed her beautiful but haunted hazel eyes. Alastair giggled.

'I'm the queen,' she announced haughtily and she stuck her nose higher.

Alastair had been taught by Miss Crouch not to carry a game too far and yet the lady was still playing. She was indeed the strangest adult he had ever met. 'Don't be silly, you can't be the queen; the king isn't married anymore,' he remarked with suspicion, considering this must be a particularly artful adult game. She bowed her head slightly but then returned her precise nose to its oblique position. 'If you are the queen, then where is your crown?' In spite of the appeal that pretence held for him, he was becoming impatient. The woman stroked her dirty headscarf. 'Are you mad?' he asked, becoming worried. She tilted her head back as far as it would go and her tongue protruded from between her greying teeth.

Alastair twisted a finger into his ear. He wanted to shock her, to break her silence. He was also enjoying the feeling that nestled within him; it was not often he had the opportunity to be rude to his elders without the fear of a reprimand. 'You must be crackers. Totally round the bend,' he added with increased confidence. He stood and pressed the palms of his hands to his sides.

'Crackers round the bend,' was the certain reply and the woman leant forward in mime to Alastair's bold posture, placing her hands upon her hips.

A familiar sensation tingled the back of his neck and burned his cheeks. With his head held low, he muttered under his breath, 'Perhaps I'm the one going round the bend, jumping up and down like I've lost my marbles.' He looked up to the woman and was annoyed to see her standing with her head lowered as she also mumbled to herself. 'Are you copying me?' he shouted angrily, the words catching in his throat.

'Copying me?' replied the woman.

'Go away. Leave me alone. I think there is something wrong with you.'

'Leave me alone, leave my baby, leave my baby!' shrieked the woman as she clutched the hem of her muddy nightdress, her mouth twisted into a snarl. Alastair shuddered while the woman gabbled insanely then gave a pitiful cry that transformed itself into a scream with her whole body trembling. Still holding the hem of her dress she turned to run along Stutter Lane and her eyes met Alastair's for the last time. For a moment only he caught a spark of sanity, then it was gone, and so was she as she hopped and jumped and ran, yelping and crooning and wailing. Alastair stood motionless. 'My baby,' she cried out pitifully as she disappeared into a gap in the hedge which stood at the perimeter of one of the ploughed fields, hazy in the muted pastel of the fog.

There was a soft glint as something which had fallen from her caught the light. It lay on pebbles in the rough road. Alastair ran over to the item and picked it up. It was a pocket watch, caked with dried mud. He opened the cover to reveal the watch glass smeared with dirt so he wiped it clean with his sleeve. Ants were trapped between the glass and the cogs and gears, and they scuttled clockwise about their prison, as if racing the second hand. What an unusual possession, he thought. But it was not his; he should return it to its peculiar owner. But she was gone for good; only the fog and sad trees were there about him.

He retrieved a piece of string from a pocket and tied one end onto the ring, for the watch had no fob chain. Once he had placed the find into his jacket pocket he watched the silence of the lane and though he smiled, he felt an immense sadness inside. In a strange way he wished that the odd lady hadn't gone.

The last of the fog clung for existence as it thinned the more to mist. A crow cawed and flew lazily overhead to its nest.

'School,' Alastair gasped. He spun on his heels and ran as fast as he was able, past the dry stone wall that guarded the poplars and into School Lane. There would be trouble in store from Miss Crouch for being late, he knew.

CHAPTER 29

The Breakdown

FOR ALASTAIR, THE day at school seemed to drag. Several times he had closed his eyes and nearly fallen into sleep. As the confident voice of his schoolmistress broke the silence in the classroom, he stifled a yawn. Finally, he heard the words: 'Time to go, children.'

He stood as though to attention and looked behind him to Pump and then over to Gristle. They both returned malevolent stares. Alastair broke into a trot, heading for the classroom door.

'Come back, young man. You must put your history book away,' Miss Crouch called after him.

Alastair froze with fright at the thought of returning anywhere near Sydney Pump. He nervously sucked his cheek. He would have to be quick. Turning then, he hurried back to his desk but collided with Rose Gupper. She was sent spinning along the classroom between the rows of desks and her head struck the back wall with a sickening thud, and she flopped to the floor. A drawing pin fell, followed by a child's painting fluttering down from the wall. The children stood open-mouthed but none moved. Miss Crouch's voice had left her and her legs had taken root. She looked at Rose who lay motionless on the floorboards and after to Alastair who had also been knocked to the ground by the collision.

The spell was broken; the young girl groaned and rubbed her head and appeared confused and frightened while the children congregated around her, some offering to lift her to her feet, others speaking words of sympathy. She was helped up and she swayed gently, her eyes brimming with tears. Pump and Gristle smirked and Alastair rose to his feet and his lip twitched. Miss Crouch found that the roots of her feet had retracted and her voice had taken residence again. 'It could have been serious,' she shouted. 'She could have been badly hurt.'

Alastair put his hands behind his back and hung his head low. It was then he heard a voice in his ear, quite distinctly. It was tutting.

Rose had finished her fitful crying and was shaking her little head in a daze.

'Thank you everyone but you can all go home now. I will look after Rose,' announced Miss Crouch. The children filed out through the doorway into the school corridor, sending sympathetic glances over their shoulder or glaring and shaking their heads at Alastair. The teacher accompanied the sniffing girl to the door with an arm around her shoulders. 'You are a brave girl now, aren't you?' she cooed and she squeezed Rose firmly to her side.

The teacher whipped her tall body about so quickly that Alastair jumped back in surprise. He heard chuckling inside his head. He was dumbfounded: there was the school mistress with fiery eyes, her mouth twisted into a cruel surliness. The demon spoke, flame spurting from its mouth and nostrils. 'You had better pull yourself together. And I think you must apologize.'

Alastair felt his throat tightening and he stared at the vision before him, stricken with an acute horror: the strange woman he had met that morning stood framed within the doorway by the blackboard with her hands slapping her thighs and screaming, 'Are you mad?'

'No!' Alastair bellowed, desperation taking his voice to the heights of a shriek. He beat his hands on the nearest desk and ran towards Miss Crouch who stepped nimbly out of the way as though parrying a bull.

Once out of the school he fled to the corner of School Lane and staggered past the poplars into Stutter Lane and ran its full length. He was wrought with anger and fatigue, his mind a jangling, shouting disorder, the events of the past week chattering through his brain. Why did words glue themselves to his mouth so that he was incapable of answering the simplest of questions asked of him? What barrier walled him away? Why did he hear voices in his head and see things that were not really there? The words of Miss Crouch echoed through his mind. 'Am I stupid?' he moaned. He was irritated by his own whining voice, a familiar sense of unreality beginning to overtake. He eyed the ground and the toes of his boots scuffed the pavement as he dawdled along.

So engrossed was he in his morbidity, he had not realized that his legs had turned him into Thrush Avenue and from there, between two stout houses.

He was awakened from his reverie of self-examination, so suddenly was he plunged into the corridor of stone which was shunned by the neutral afternoon light. Baffled, he pressed his hands to the walls of the alley which were declaring their intention to crush him. But slowly, as his arms quivered from exertion, his eyes grew accustomed to the shadows. And upon realizing his whereabouts, he felt a sticky foolishness clump in his throat. His body shuddered with hysterical laughter and he beat himself with his fists, his sight distorted by tears. Then, staggering with his arms swinging apishly about him, he sobbed and laughed until his midriff ached, moving in an ungainly fashion to the entrance of the alley.

The street gas lamps were already lit and the moon was

becoming more distinct with every heartbeat as he ran along Pepper Lane towards home.

He stopped abruptly. There were two figures. They seemed oblivious to his presence even though he had crossed the road and was walking towards them. Alastair sent a stone clattering along the pavement and two heads, previously bowed in consultation, turned to his direction. They acknowledged him with snorts of mirth. The sneer which spread across Pump's face was contagious for Gristle caught it a second later.

Peculiar thoughts ran through Alastair's brain. This was surely one of his dreams.

'If it isn't Stubb,' said Pump contemptuously. 'We've been waiting for you, Stubb the mug, Stubb the worm. His royal highness slimy worm.' Pleased with his tauntings he broke into laughter, his skinny body agitated into motion.

Gristle caught the cue and began to giggle, and squeak like a piglet. 'Belt little girls would you?' he cried out.

'Shut up a minute, Alf,' complained Pump. 'Hit girls, would you?' he echoed. 'Can't hit back, that's why, can they, you big baby. And look what you bloody well did to me.' He tipped his head to show Alastair a small patch there, the pink of his scalp showing through. 'You are gonna pay for that.' He took two steps towards Alastair who stood looking with interest at Pump's skull. 'I'm going to smash your head in and it's going to take a lot to put it together again,' the ex-butler's son threatened. He leered and waved a fist; Alastair stood unconcerned, he knew he dreamt. Sidney Pump heaved a sigh of impatience. His threats were not creating the desired effect.

Gristle screwed up his nose and belatedly repeated, 'Yeah, we're gonna smash your head in.'

Smiling benignly, Alastair took a pace towards Pump, who recoiled in surprise at the unexpected reaction.

Thinking he was about to be attacked, Pump lowered his head in defence and charged at Alastair like a maddened cow, slamming into his stomach. Alastair doubled over from the blow and was pushed to the ground. 'Take that, worm,' called Pump and he glared at the writhing figure on the pavement, Alastair floundering on the same spot like a goldfish twitching out of its water.

He was not so much concerned with his shortened breath and bruised stomach muscles as the accumulation of his strained emotions and an alien voice laughing within him. Like a careless alchemist who adds this liquid to that chemical, who pours this preparation to that solution, so he had opened gates to his young mind, creating an abnormal concoction of memories, thoughts and emotions. Ringing in his ears changed in quality to become a saw-edged noise buzzing loudly like a trapped bluebottle.

Alastair cried out inanities and, amidst those unintelligible noises, shrieked, 'Let go – poison me, would you – all will pay – leave…'

'He's gone potty,' Pump said, 'he's lost his brains.' Both he and Gristle ran up the road without looking behind them.

Lights appeared. Mrs. Battlespoke opened her front door. Her blind eye revolved in its socket as she fiddled with the monocle to the other. Still only vague shapes swam before her. 'Who's there?' she cried out in a cracked voice. 'Alright dears, don't be frightened,' she said, directing her words through the terraced house to her backyard. Her chickens were too busy warming their eggs or asleep to take note of her comforting assurance. She slipped back inside and closed the door.

William Stubb opened the front sash window of his house and thrust his head out. He stared in disbelief at the tormented form of Alastair, flopping and shouting on the pavement outside.

CHAPTER 30

A Dream

HE SCREAMED, 'YOU'RE MAD!' and he jumped up and down and bellowed obscenities that were transformed into a vile crooning which came from a woman wearing green carpet slippers. Holding her head tightly, he began to pull out strands of hair as though plucking a chicken. The hairless pate belonged to William Stubb but Miss Crouch appeared and announced, 'Time to go, children,' and then he was on Grinding station platform.

He threw a clump of hair onto the track and it landed in a bathtub and arranged itself like a bunch of flowers. An important decision: should he have a bath or not? He pondered and wondered, all the while observing the tub from obscure angles, until he was high and hovering above it. His stomach heaved and he was sick with fright.

He was on the station platform again. In front of him stood a porter, smiling and leaning on a broom. He felt afraid. The porter persisted with a steady gaze and from this he felt naked at being watched: not an absence of clothing but an absence of his physical self. It was as though the man was seeing his essence. 'I need to borrow your spirit, my boy,' the porter whispered but then he was gone.

Alastair looked to the bath and laughed at a bald Sidney Pump who lay contentedly within it, water slopping onto the track as he sang, 'Stubb the scum, Stubb the germ, Stubb the mug, Stubb the worm.' There was a whistling in the distance.

It increased in volume until a steam train thundered through the station, a clamorous noise rising high above the screams of Pump.

He started to run. The bathtub had been knocked into a deranged sky and it was falling rapidly until it landed on top of him and showered him with soapy water. Engulfed in blackness, save for a conglomerate mass which rushed towards him, spinning and whirling and becoming larger, driving the blackness away and swamping him with a myriad of colours. Colours which flumed and swirled and convulsed until finally congealing into reality as Alastair awoke from his dream, clammy from a fever which had soaked his body with sweat during sleep.

His eyes flickered open and focused, dispersing the imagery that clung obstinately to his vision. It was half a minute more before he realized that he was not soaking from any dirty water from the sky, but from perspiration. A pain seared across his brow which corrugated in response; his puffed eyelids covered his sight. Isolated thoughts wriggled into mind only to be stifled by a pressure above his eyebrows.

He ignored his thumping head, blinking sleep from his eyes, and fixed his attention above him onto a lightbulb dressed in a frilly shade. The army of events of days before clattered into mind, though before he could think any further, his headache reminded him of its continuing existence. The ceiling was blemished as shadows flicked over it with diluted red.

Alastair had the distinct impression there was someone else in the room. He could feel their presence; could feel he was being watched.

A weariness had secreted itself into his torso so successfully that he hardly possessed the strength to lift his head. He managed to see in front of himself with a measure of success however. He saw a mauve counterpane covering him. Then, looking beyond, he saw the flames of a dying fire licking the embers of wood surrounded by ash and smouldering remains, blinking in the grate.

He was in no rush to determine the identity of the person who cast a wavering shadow across the fireplace. He rested for a time until his headache subsided. Then he turned to the right, taking in the rose-patterned wallpaper, a crouching chair that seemed ready to pounce and a grandmother clock which stood anonymously in the corner, acting as sentry to the door that stood ajar beside it.

In the corridor that lay beyond was a table. An oil lamp was upon it, emitting a dull light enough to cast the shadow from the silhouetted figure who stood framed by the doorway.

'Leave me alone,' Alastair wanted to say but silly trivialities ran circles in his brain. A composite smell of disinfectant and coffee, ammonia and leather reached his nose.

He attempted to speak and the words became a croaking whisper: 'Who is it there?' He licked his dried lips and tasted salt from his sweat.

Dr. Snippet walked into the room and closed the door behind him, shutting out the light from the lamp. He stepped lightly over to the bedside with a stethoscope twitching in his shaking hand. Alastair could see his horse-like face from dying embers of the fire. The glow cast strange colours under the doctor's eyes and nose; it accentuated his grinning mouth into a grotesque expression. The boy gasped in terror. The poor light was playing tricks: standing before him was Sidney Pump holding a knife. 'No, please don't. Leave me, don't touch me,' Alastair raved, finding an inner strength to toss and turn.

'It's alright young man, I am here. Snippet is the name. You know me,' said the doctor soothingly. He saw that he was having no effect upon Alastair's delirium. Under the circumstances he felt the situation warranted the use of the new electrification system recently installed into the manor house, despite the expense of the electricity. He stood and walked over to the switch and upon flicking it, the bulb flashed twice before settling to emit an even yellow light.

Alastair ceased his ravings and flopped back down onto his pillows, recognising the doctor immediately. He felt exhausted. 'Where am I?' he croaked.

'Why, you are in my house Alastair, getting better.'

'I'm thirsty.' Dr. Snippet turned to the bedside table and poured a glass of water. The panting Alastair was helped up to a sitting position and with a trembling hand, he took the tumbler and drank greedily, pausing only to gasp for a breath before consuming the next draught. The glass was handed back to the doctor who had been studying him the while. 'Why am I here?' Alastair said. 'I can't remember.'

Dr. Snippet pushed silver hair behind his ears and replied, 'I will not beat around the tree. You have been ill and you need a lot of rest. You won't be dashing around yet awhile because you have had what we call a nervous episode, an unfortunate fugue. I consider also that you have slow blood. Your father tells me of the nightmares and voices and the such. This is all due to strain on your gentle mentality; and with a physical low this was the unfortunate result. Do you understand? Still, with time, patience and medicine, you will be up and about again.' He smiled. 'There is nothing to worry about, nothing at all. You are making fine progress.' His smile widened to a generous grin.

'When can I leave?'

'When you are better,' was the reply, the grin still plastered onto his compassionate face.

'Oh,' replied Alastair, sounding disappointed, 'and when will that be?'

'As soon as you are better,' repeated the doctor, not so much as avoiding the question as forgetting his replies the moment he had made them. 'Well, time is pressing and prodding me to action. I must leave now and you should have more sleep. If you need anything though, ring the bell.' He walked to the door, opened it with a shaking hand and turned to say, 'Ah yes, and if you need anything, ring the bell.' He paused and looked thoughtful. 'Have I said that? Heavens, I will be forgetting my own name next. Or even worse, forgetting that I am forgetful.' Acknowledging the grandmother clock with a wave of his hand, he flicked off the light switch and left the room.

Alastair stared with suspicion at the stethoscope curled like a snake on the seat at his bedside then threw his sight about the darkened room for the bell. It was not to be seen. Sighing, he snuggled down into the warm protection of the bed. He did not care to look through the flesh moulded to his aching bones into the harsh world of reality, but into the silence of dreamless sleep. His consciousness evaporated as he slipped into the quietness.

CHAPTER 31

Possession

H E AWOKE WITH A start. His name had been called, softly but distinctly. He wondered what the time was. Early morning, he guessed, for though it was still dark he saw, through a gap between the curtains, the blackness of night had been diluted to warm grey and there was the occasional bird practising for the dawn chorus.

He sat himself up and felt surprisingly refreshed and alert. His name called again. He did not feel alarmed, only curious. The voice became more insistent and he tried to recognize its whereabouts, though as soon as he thought he knew, it would appear to come from another place. It came from downstairs, then from outside of his door, then from above, and then from the middle of his head. The voice changed in quality and he recognized it. He stiffened and paled: the voice was his own; he had been calling his own name. Feeling uneasy and confused he lay back down but pulled himself up with a start as the repeated word spoken began again. Alastair found that he could still hear it even with a hand clasped over his mouth. He sat and thought and tried to reason. It was useless to concentrate on the sound as it would only change its place of origin.

Who would be calling him in the early hours of the morning? He swung his legs over the edge of the bed and stood but, no sooner had he done that, he fell back with his head reeling. He felt uncomfortably hot. For several minutes he sat, every now and then experimenting to see if he was stable enough to walk.

Eventually he felt strong enough, though the mild headache still pressed upon his forehead. Once he had pulled on his dressing gown over his pyjamas he stepped over to the door, swaying as he went, and opened it.

He stood and listened intently. The wide corridor was empty and as he walked past the suit of armour, there was a muted snoring from one of the other bedrooms it seemed to be guarding. When by the banister rail at the head of the stairs he peered cautiously down into the hallway. There was no one to be seen.

Without warning, his name was called again, insistent and continuous, and it came from anywhere and everywhere, as if it were the stones and the tiles and timbers of the manor house speaking – 'Alastair…Alastair…Alastair…' – from his bedroom at the end of the corridor, from the hallway, from under the house, from between the walls; and his heartbeat galloped faster and his lip twitched involuntarily and he felt cold and frightened. His name echoed and reverberated from one wall to the other, from one room to the next and all the while he possessed an irritating sharp and harsh sonority within his dazed mind.

While he was wondering why the noise had not roused any of the other occupants of the house, it stopped again and the whine in his ears receded to leave his own rasping breath and the dull, blunted ticks of the grandmother clock from his bedroom and those from the clock in the hall.

It was another dream, surely. He felt surprisingly weary for someone so young; he sat upon a small padded chair that was conveniently beside him. He was attentive to the quietness and the dull thump of his heart, and the posed figures in their gilded frames inspecting him; until he drifted into a light sleep. He told himself even then to go back to bed but, with his weariness, could not move.

His name had been whispered into his ear and his head whipped around. Now the murmuring voice came from the end of the corridor and Alastair stood and stretched, yawned and walked slowly towards it. There were no feelings of fright for him now; he knew he was definitely dreaming this time. While walking past a bedroom he heard the muffled snores of its occupant. He told himself he would remember to tell Dr. Snippet that he had featured in his fascinating dream.

Upon reaching the end of the corridor and turning to his left he saw the beginning of a spiral staircase before it corkscrewed out of view. His name was being called from the top. He began to tread up the stairs. After reaching halfway, he stopped to gaze from an oval window which looked out from the side of the house, seeing a small church painted a ghostly white by the moon, but the voice commanded, 'Hurry, hurry!'

At the top of the staircase he felt tired again and leant against the door to get his breath back. He turned and tried the door. It was locked so he retrieved a cast iron key hanging from a hook on the wall and unlocked it. Pushing the door inward, he entered the attic.

There was the smell of fresh wood and dampness. Alastair walked into the centre of the room and looked about him at the emptiness and stillness. He decided that he would go back and began to walk out but stopped abruptly. He was startled. 'Who are you?' he demanded to the form shrouded in darkness. Alastair took a step towards it and wondered why the figure seemed blacker, denser than the poor light in the room. He walked confidently towards the person but then froze in horror. The stout man was covered in soot and dust and his clothes were singed and ripped and he was badly burned on one side of his face. Alastair was startled and cried out.

'My son,' the man stated almost casually. Alastair had heard that same voice many times before. He had not heard the man move: he wheeled around and back again but the figure was gone.

Then, to his astonishment, flames appeared around him, tongues of pale yellow spikes, dancing frantically. The burnt figure, there once more, writhing in agony within that phantom fire as it licked and tormented him. Alastair tried to make out the words emanating from the blistering lips. 'Help me,' the man appeared to be saying. Alastair instinctively ran forward and found that he could move through the flames without harm and he held out an arm to the convulsing figure, the man grasping Alastair's hand with both of his. Alastair felt a pulling sensation as though being irresistibly drawn by a magnet.

The manifestation and the flames vanished in an instant. The whining ceased and he heard, spoken softly, 'You will not remember any of this. I own you now, my son. They will pay.'

Alastair curled up into a ball in the middle of the attic floor and fell into a chasm of sleep.

CHAPTER 32

The Nurse

'WHAT IS THE day today?' Alastair asked when the nurse brought him his breakfast.

'Friday, boy. Now you get on with your food, and less of the idle chat. I don't want you leaving any either.' She walked to the end of the bed and proceeded to tuck the sheets further under the feather mattress.

'That's too tight,' he complained when he tried to move his feet.

'You are always complaining, boy, did you know that? Now you shut up and eat or else.'

Alastair pulled a face at her and began his meal. He was very hungry. It was not every day he ate food that was not prepared by himself nor, indeed, so delicious. Content to eat, he forgot the presence of the nurse until he looked up and saw that she was seated on a chair by the fireplace and was staring blankly at him. Alastair stopped chewing, his cheeks bulging. Tired of returning an expressionless gaze while waiting for her to speak, he concentrated on eating the piece of meat and attempted to ignore her presence as best he could.

'The doctor wants to tell you off,' she said quickly. Alastair shrugged. 'He's very angry,' she added as ominously as she could.

'Why? I haven't done anything wrong.'

'Don't be cheeky. You know very well what I'm talking about. What was you trying to do, sleeping up in the draughty attic last night? Are you trying to get pneumonic lungs? It was stupid. You must be very stupid, boy.'

'I am not stupid,' Alastair shouted in return, flushed with annoyance.

The nurse ignored him and pretended that she found a great deal of interest with a book which stood on the fireplace mantlepiece. She turned quickly and glared through her small, weasel eyes. 'You said some very strange things in your sleep this morning,' she whined. Alastair gulped. 'Rambling you was. Talking about voices and rubbish like that.' Alastair looked at the nurse, unconcerned. 'Then you was babbling on about Pumps, or something similar.' Her eyes glinted. Alastair paled. 'Then something about a queen.'

Alastair had a coughing fit, choking on the food that was in the back of his mouth.

The nurse seemed pleased by the effect she had produced by her remark. 'You have heard about her?' she said. Alastair ignored her, managing to swallow. 'You have heard about her then?' repeated the nurse with a note of agitation in her voice. 'You know who I'm talking about.'

Alastair nodded slowly and replied, 'I think I know who you are talking about. I have met a lady who thinks she is the queen.'

The nurse smiled. 'Oh, yes,' she said with interest.

'Yes, and I can tell you it was not nice, if you really want to know. I am sure she is mad. A bit funny in the head.' His voice trembled.

'Do you know who she is?'

Alastair's eyes became slits. 'No,' he whispered.

The nurse dropped her smile and as though in a trance, she walked over to the bedside with both arms outstretched. 'Let me tell you,' she cooed in a sickly sweet tone, and she took hold of Alastair's quivering hands in her own.

He pulled them away, with a shudder. He felt miserable. 'Please, leave me alone. I'm not sure I like you very much. I don't want to know.'

'Oh, but you do. You will be most interested to know.' Alastair gazed at her twisted mouth and she pulled back her top lip from crooked teeth and spat out the words: 'She's your mother.'

Alastair gasped and moaned, 'No, you're lying, it's all lies! Go away,' and he beat his hands on the bed covering and began to weep.

The door opened. 'Nurse Pump,' said Dr. Snippet firmly. 'What in heaven is the matter?' He looked across to a sobbing Alastair and back to the nurse.

'Tell her to go away, please Mr. Snippet. She tells lies.'

'What is this about lies?' he demanded to know.

'I am sure I don't know what the boy is talking about,' nurse Pump said stiffly. 'I think he's been having a delirium again. In fact I was on my way to find you.'

The doctor was perplexed as he walked further into the room. He looked at Alastair for a moment then sat on the side of the bed and held his hand up to the boy's brow.

'Mr. Snippet, she tells awful lies,' said Alastair, sniffing. He looked to the nurse who stared stonily back.

'What has she been saying, young man?'

'She said I was sleeping in the attic and then she said my mother is the mad lady.'

The doctor put a finger to his lip and stood. He winked at Alastair and grinned. Alastair did not see this for he felt an irresistible tiredness sweep over him and he heard a voice mumbling incoherently and then he remembered no more.

'Mrs. Pump is it? So it's you who has the unfortunate task of scurrying around to the whims of a drunken fool. That idiot should have drowned in drink long ago; still he's a lucky rat. Remember the time he almost killed himself by pulling one of the wine racks over? The useless cretin laughed at the smashed bottles of one hundred year old port and wine. He will pay though – you will both pay – for letting me burn while he sat in the cellar and drank himself stupid.'

Both the nurse and Dr. Snippet stood immobile. 'Dear boy,' said the doctor finally, 'what on earth are you talking about?'

Alastair did not answer. His face lost its tautness and the expression of hate vanished. His eyelids fluttered and he fell back onto his pillows. The doctor went over to him and after checking his pulse and listening to his heart, he turned slowly to the nurse with a shrug.

'Well?' said nurse Pump.

The doctor sighed. 'He is asleep.'

A bicycle bell was heard to ring from somewhere in the lane outside. A dove landed onto the bedroom window sill and flew off shortly after. The doctor took nurse Pump by the arm and led her to the door. 'I want a word with you,' he said.

'And I want a word with you,' was the reply.

They sat in the kitchen. Dr. Snippet took a sip of his tea. 'Mrs. Pump, I did not employ you to upset my patients. What on earth is the matter?'

She blushed and twiddled with the rings on her fingers. 'You know the reason.'

'Yes, I most certainly do. But you still went against my wishes. I told you that your boy's head and scratches will heal in time. I hope, by the way, you are rubbing them twice a day with the cream I prescribed.' She nodded. 'But to tell Alastair about his mother, that was quite unnecessary. Physically, your boy will heal but mentally, you could scar Alastair's mind for life.' The doctor looked grim and took another sip of his beverage. 'As for asking him why he was in the attic in the early hours of the morning, I specifically told you to leave that to me.'

Nurse Pump became serious. 'Perhaps I do owe you an apology. I was a bit nasty. But Sidney wakes up in the middle of the night and can't get back to sleep again worrying about his bald patch; he gets all of the other kids at school pointing and laughing behind his back. Underneath it all he is sensitive. Half our problems would go tomorrow if only my husband would pull himself together and not live in public houses for hours on end. I don't see him from one day to the next sometimes. I'm sorry, you know all that.' Blinking and sniffing, she rubbed her smarting eyes but then her face became hard again. 'Alright, I'll apologize to you and Alastair, if you apologize to me.'

Dr. Snippet replaced the cup which he had been holding to his lips and looked surprised. 'Apologize? For what?'

'For talking behind my back. What have you said to Alastair about my husband?'

The doctor raised his generous eyebrows and leant on the table with his arms crossed. He spoke quietly. 'I can assure you Mrs. Pump, I have not said anything to anyone on any such topic concerning you or your husband. I am sure it was a symptom of Alastair's serious breakdown. After all, he spoke of being burned which is, of course, quite ridiculous. And then you saw for yourself how quickly he fell into a deep trance of a sleep. He has had a severe mental bludgeoning, and in confidence I am not sure as to all of the reasons. There are still many things puzzling me.'

'I accept that then. But how did he know about my husband's accident? That happened years ago, before Theodore Stubb went off and even before I was married. Anyway, it wasn't so much what he said as how he said it. There was hatred; it didn't sound like Alastair at all; and what did he mean by saying that me and my husband would pay?'

The doctor shook his head slowly. 'He has had a severe trauma to his mentality, Mrs. Pump. You must try to understand. Most unusual that it should happen to one so young. There is a long way to full recovery, even when he leaves here.'

'I still don't think it's any excuse to be so rude about my husband, specially that sort of language from a thirteen year old. I think his father has got a lot to answer for, filling Alastair's head with rubbish.'

'I will have a word with Mr. Stubb the next time I see him,' answered Dr. Snippet, though knowing he was sure to forget.

She seemed satisfied and nodded and they both sat sipping their drinks. The conversation thus punctured remained so until Mrs. Pump remarked, 'And while we are talking, there is something else. I've changed the sheets on Alastair's bed every day for almost a week.'

'That is one of the tasks for which I employ you.'

'Of course. But do I have to have the sheets soiled in that way?'

'I didn't know Alastair had bowel trouble as well,' the doctor answered in surprise.

With a shake of her head, nurse Pump replied, 'I'm not talking about his bowels.'

'But you have told me that the sheets are soiled. Soiled with what then?'

'With insects, doctor; squashed, dead insects.'

CHAPTER 33

Departure

A SKY, DIRTY AND dismal, scowled from above. Rain began to spot the ground and tap the window; it steadily increased to a snare drum roll. The wet spots were quickly joined and the sound outside became alive with dancing droplets. All colours seemed to have been washed away in the rain to leave endless variations of grey.

The fast-moving clouds took a more definite form. There was nurse Pump sitting on a broomstick, crying out: 'She's your mother, your mother, your mother!'

Alastair felt his lip twitch twice so he put his hand to his mouth and snorted; tension bound in his stomach as the depression which he had become acquainted with took possession of him again. When his lip twitched once more he stamped his foot in annoyance. He heard the click of the door and turned from the window in time to see it open.

Dr. Snippet did not enter but stood on the threshold in conversation with somebody in the lobby. 'But everybody has to pay their way I am afraid. Oh indeed, everyone. Even Mrs. Battlespoke. Yes, even her.' He gave a ridiculous grin.

'Do me a favour, I've—' Stubb was promptly interrupted.

'Mr. Stubb, if I did a favour to everybody in Muchmallow, where would I be then? Hmm?' Dr. Snippet backed through the doorway into the sitting room followed by Stubb.

'Look here, I've already told you three times that I am going into Grinding tomorrow to get my money from the building society. And it's Muchmarsh, you old fool.'

'Very poetic I'm sure, Mr. Stubb,' remarked the doctor, procuring a wider grin.

'What is?'

'What is what?' replied Dr. Snippet for it was at that moment that he had forgotten what they were talking about. He looked enquiringly to Stubb who grunted impatiently.

'Let me remind you, Snippet, what we were discussing. You seem to be under the impression that I am trying to avoid paying, when I have attempted several times to get it through your thick skull that I am asking for a reduction in the price. A favour; if you would only remember, I did a favour by selling this house to you at a considerably smaller sum than it's worth. It's a stupid place to have a practice anyway. And what's more you should have retired years ago.' In preparation for a verbal retaliation Stubb half-closed his eyes with a distorted nose and mouth but it was well proven that slander or rudeness did not have the slightest influence upon the doctor's temperament.

'I will consider your words carefully, Mr. Stubb. I cannot be fairer than that can I?' is all that Dr. Snippet said in reply. Then, both Stubb and the doctor, realizing they were not the only occupants of the room, looked to Alastair; and Alastair, not wishing to meet either pair of eyes which were scrutinizing him, threw his sight to the intricately patterned carpet. He felt trapped and helpless.

Stubb stepped closer to his half-brother he thought of as his son, and ordered, 'You're coming home. You are better.' Alastair turned his back to look through the window again, unable to stop the nervous twitching of his lip he had acquired. Clouds still obscured the sun and sobbed rain.

The doctor parted his lips to give an airing to his teeth. He tittered and spoke: 'Well young man, it is time for you to go home. You have made an excellent recovery. Indeed you are better and you will stay that way as long as you take life steadily and do not get excited. And take the herbal preparations. So, come along now.'

Alastair bit firmly onto his lip and passed a hand across his brow. He wished they would both leave him in peace. He watched bubbling water outside the window as it flowed into a drain.

'Come on then, boy,' shouted Stubb. His patience was rapidly evaporating. 'Get a move on.' He strode across to Alastair and stood before him with his arms folded across his belly, about to speak again. Alastair turned without warning. With his eyes glowing with enmity, he glared at the father figure and their sights locked together. Dr. Snippet smiled gleefully at what he saw as a happy reunion.

Being so taken aback by the disturbing expression from Alastair, Stubb lost the words he had wanted to say. Those narrowed eyes filled him with a sense of foreboding and fear. The chilling look upon Alastair's face was alien to the boy, yet it seemed somehow familiar. Stubb dismissed the incident with a shake of the head.

Alastair became aware of his surroundings again – the hissing rain and the occupants of the room and the swirling patterns on the carpet.

All three moved at once. Dr. Snippet shuffled towards Stubb with a question quivering on his lips while Stubb turned to face him, then Alastair turned away from them both and headed for the door. He walked through from the lobby to the hallway, followed closely by a scowling Stubb who, in turn, was followed by the beaming doctor.

Alastair took his jacket from the peg of a coat hanger in one deft movement and then, ignoring his collected belongings, he opened the door and walked into the rain, pulling his jacket on as he went. Stubb angrily tore an umbrella from the stand and picked up the valise.

'Oh yes,' said the doctor looking smug with himself as he had remembered what he had wanted to say, 'about the payment.'

Stubb gave a fretful sigh.' You idiot,' he said as he opened the umbrella.

The raindrops bounced off the umbrella and onto Dr. Snippet's trouser legs. His smile did not falter. As Stubb walked briskly over the gravel to the open gates, the doctor closed the door. He chuckled and muttered, 'Now, I wonder how the lad is getting on,' while strolling through to the study.

Alastair had walked half the length of Daisytrail Lane with William Stubb trotting after him, panting and cursing. The rain began to ease to a fine drizzle. Stubb was irritable and tired of the small suitcase hitting his legs as he jogged along. He placed the offending article down and gave it a hefty kick. He felt better after that, picked it up and began to trot again. Once he had caught up with Alastair – at the end of the lane where it widened out onto the village green – he placed a hand onto his shoulder. Quite out of breath, he whispered, 'Wait a minute.'

Alastair did as he was told, waiting at the side of The Bulldog Fish Tavern. Stubb paused to catch his breath. 'What has got into you, young whelp?' he scolded. 'Running off like that. There was no cause. Now you take your case and get on home. Do you hear? If you're not careful you'll be getting another of those breakups.' Alastair looked to his feet. 'Answer me, will you. I didn't give up my drinking time to collect you from the doctor's to be ignored.' After letting go of the valise and umbrella for them to fall onto the lane, Stubb clipped Alastair's ear with a swipe of the hand. 'That'll teach you. Now get on home before you get wetter.'

Alastair yelped and clutched his stinging ear and threw a hateful glance. 'I'm the queen, the queen,' he shouted at the top of his voice and running across the village green, stopped occasionally to bounce up and down and croon as loudly as he was able.

Stubb stood still, horrified and stricken. All that he had strived for to keep the tragedy a secret was lost; it had all been for nothing. Alastair knew and was using the knowledge as a weapon against him. Within a matter of seconds, the boy had slashed open the already raw and bleeding wounds of the past. As the raindrops ran down Stubb's crumpled face, he picked up the case and the umbrella before turning the corner to the entrance of The Bulldog Fish Tavern. He was going to get drunk again.

CHAPTER 34

Abergail

K NITTING LAY ON an armchair with the needles sticking up, the bundle thrown in frustration and annoyance. The antique sideboard had been polished so that once more Abergail could almost see her face reflected. Her mother would not be taking her through the next chapter of English Grammar for Young Ladies until the next day. Because her watercolour painting bore scant resemblance to any real scene, Abergail decided she had painted enough and it would remain an unfinished sketch only. So all she had to occupy herself with was to sit near her bedroom window and look out onto the village green.

In case she might be seen by a villager outside – which would surely not do – she sat well back from the window. Many times her mother had told her that she was different from other people. At one time, Abergail had believed she looked like her mother, possessing the same infliction. But why did the reflection in the windows tell her differently? If a mirror was to be found she would be certain.

There was a boy: he was sitting on a bench by the horse trough and the trees on the far side of the green. Despite the distance, Abergail could see that he held the end of a piece of string and swinging freely from the other end was a round, shining object. If only she could speak with him for a while, she wished. As much as she liked to talk with her mother and aunt, she could not recall ever conversing with anyone else.

Abergail was tiring of her observation and so turned into her room; and anyway, she remembered that her needlepoint needed to be finished so went down to the sitting room to do exactly that.

CHAPTER 35

Pump and Gristle

THE RAIN HAD stopped, leaving the bushes drooping and dripping with the cobwebs glistening and Mrs. Battlespoke's washing looking sorry for itself. The sky was not rid of all the storm clouds though eventually the last of them was dismissed by a zealous wind.

Sidney Pump's hair was sent splaying in all directions like a sea anemone while the cropped style that had residence on Gristle's head stood prickled. They dawdled aimlessly along Cinnamon Street, neither caring to speak, both engulfed in their own thoughts.

'…Alastair has lost his brains, though what with his mum round the twist, it must run in the family. Wait till I see him again. He'll know it…' Such were the thoughts of Pump. He did not consider a butt in the stomach as revenge for the pain he had felt from the hands of Alastair. He gently rubbed the sore patch on his head. 'Bloody boring,' he finally spoke out loud and he kicked a pebble, sending it skipping along the road. It landed in a rain puddle with a plop.

'Pork chops with loads of spuds. Covered in gravy. I'm so hungry. A cream cake. That's it, I'll buy a cream cake dolloped with thick cream…' and such was the rumination dominating Gristle's mind. He was sure he was wasting away. 'I'm hungry,' he complained dolefully and, to keep his mouth occupied he sucked his fist.

'That's all you think about isn't it? Your fat belly.' The

offending part of Gristle's anatomy received a prod from Pump's finger. 'Let's do something. I didn't come out to listen to you moaning. Think of something.' Fixing his gaze onto Gristle's stomach he added scornfully, 'Apart from anything to do with food.'

They walked in silence again. Gristle pouted thoughtfully but then abruptly stood still with a look of revelation on his chubby features.

As though petting a cat, Pump stroked his bald patch and asked, 'Well, what's your bright idea?'

After a deep breath Gristle gasped, 'Let's go to Spittle's. I want to buy an apple pie.'

'Shut up, will you,' replied Pump. 'you make me sick,' and he tried his best to look so.

They reached the end of Cinnamon Street for it turned the corner to become the bottom of Pepper Lane. Pump walked briskly past the lane and along a muddy track which was an extension of Cinnamon Street for he did not wish to be reminded of the incident outside Alastair's house. Lagging behind, Gristle called out loudly, 'What about Alastair, then? Coming out today, isn't he.'

Pump's face lost its colour. 'Shut your mouth. Belt up.'

'He's probably after you. Do you reckon? In fact he's—' Pump wheeled around and ran the few paces between them. He clouted Gristle around the head and Gristle buried his neck into his shoulders. 'What was that for, mate?' Offended, he shuffled around in circles, kicking at invisible stones. 'I was only telling you...' He became quiet, then suddenly brightened and in an attempt to calm Pump's agitation continued, 'Still, he's a real softy anyway. A raving nut. I tell you...'

With as much force as he could muster, Pump projected his foot into Gristle's backside and Gristle let out a sharp cry as he was pushed to the ground. 'Shut your stupid mouth for five minutes,' Pump shouted. 'And you had better not mention his name again until I do, or else.' He strode swiftly along the track.

His companion rose to his feet and ignoring the clumps of mud soiling his clothing, massaged one of his buttocks. It was a mystery to him as to what had upset his best friend Sidney Pump, and he was agitated with the idea that he had lost the friendship with his blustering comrade. But then he shrugged his shoulders and followed Pump, calling after him, 'Sorry Sidney, sorry mate. Won't mention Alastair's name again. Where are you going?'

'To the canal,' was the stern reply.

In an awkward fashion, Gristle ran after him along the track that was thick with grey-black mud. Though his boots were breached by the mud which oozed into his socks, he did not notice for food began to take control of his thoughts once more.

CHAPTER 36

The Confectionery Shop

LASTAIR HAD MOVED from the bench and now sat on the stone base of the clock tower at one corner of the village green. After replacing the watch into his pocket he glared at The Bulldog Fish Tavern and willed the building to collapse. Failing in that he protruded his tongue. The shuttered windows became blinkered, sorrowful eyes, the rain canopy over its entrance a wet nose and the outer door that gaped open acquired two rows of fine pointed teeth. The chimney became a fin; the vertical sides of the public house began to sag until they slipped into heavy curves, moulding the drooping jaws of the bulldog fish which stared blankly at the poking tongue of Alastair.

With a twitch of his mouth at the apparition, the bulldog fish became The Bulldog Fish Tavern again.

Mrs. Battlespoke stepped out of the butcher's shop onto the cobbles, thoughtfully fingering the items in her wicker basket. Birds spotted the green in search of worms and slugs which the rain had produced while PC Flute rode past on his rickety bicycle.

Alastair stood, his mind filled with gloom. After gaining an odd comfort from feeling the watch through his jacket, he toyed with money that sat in his pocket, the weight of coins heavy against his thigh. He decided to buy something, anything, to console himself. The cake shop could provide an opportunity to do that but Spittle's bakery was too far for him to want to walk.

There was the trinket shop along the Grinding Road although the same reticence to walk such a distance ruled that out as a possibility. He looked over to the confectionery shop which stood next to the tavern.

William Stubb had insisted that Alastair must never visit that shop and he thought perhaps it was not such a good idea. But then his loneliness and boredom swept aside all inhibitions and although he had avoided the shop on so many occasions, this time he decided to go.

He passed Mrs. Battlespoke who was quite ignorant of his presence as he made his way across the green. She rectified the placement of her monocle and muttered to her basket.

When he reached the shop he stood spellbound by the bow windows which lay either side of the oak panelled door. How anyone could view the sweets through the dusty dimpled glass of the window was beyond him though he could make out the neat rows of glass jars, coloured with their various unknown contents.

He heard someone whistling above him. He thought that maybe it was the person from the upstairs window he had seen earlier. Though, upon raising his head, he saw that the noise came from a sign blown by the wind, swinging on two rings of metal which hung from an iron decoration projecting from the shop. It presented itself to be "Confectionery and other Delights" and then, in italics, "Proprietor: Miss F. Dripping".

'It's only a sweet shop after all,' he told himself repeatedly but upon noticing the large door knocker, the comforting thought evaporated. It was a gargoyle; its tongue lolled over the metal ring from between cracked lips, a twisted face contorted with sinister eyes.

Alastair looked about him, then, grasping the handle, he opened the door to enter. His head twitched once in response to the tinkling chimes that announced a new customer.

He felt as if there were a hundred pairs of eyes upon him as he walked to the counter. To his left stood rows of jars and porcelain pots containing bonbons and lemon sherbets and nut chocolate, on darkened pine shelves. In front was a sturdy block of mahogany on two pillars of wood, holding up printed boxes containing perfumed tablets and mint lozenges, and a chrome-plated till.

Was he doomed? No matter how hard he studied the windows, the curious refractions and deflections of the misty bottlegreen glass prevented him from gaining a view as to his whereabouts. Would he ever see Muchmarsh again? There must have been a sincere reason for his father insisting that he never went there. Could it be that the owner who sold the confectionery was much like the mad woman pretending to be his mother he had met in School Lane? He did not dwell on the theory.

The door that lay behind the counter opened. He stared at the figure before him – ignoring his own twitching lip – the sight underlining his feelings of unease.

న్

'Cheers, dad,' called Pump cheerfully to his father who was entering The Canal Bargehook Inn.

Ignoring his son's greeting, Mr. Pump queried, 'And where do you think you're going? Not getting into mischief I hope. You be home for tea, you hear? And tell your mother... tell her I won't be back till late. I've got a meeting, tell her.'

'Alright dad, bye; I'll see you sometime.'

'Where did you say you was off to?'

'Alf and me are walking to the canal.'

His father let out a short cry and held his son's arm. 'No! You're not going there, I won't allow it. It's dangerous with all that water. You keep away, you listening to me?' He became red-faced as he broke into a sweat and put his fingers into his collar to loosen it.

'Come on, Bazil, we're waiting for you,' yelled a fellow who was looking out from the entrance of the public house. Letting go of his son, Bazil Pump turned his head.

'What? Oh, right'o Henry. I'll be in.' He turned back and ordered harshly: 'Now you hear me, Sidney. Stay away from that canal.' With a worried look upon him, he went into The Canal Bargehook Inn.

Gristle looked enquiringly at Sidney. 'What's your angry dad got against the canal, Sid? He was getting quite hot under the collar about it.'

Pump grimaced. 'The doctor says he's got a fibia or something.'

'What's that? Is it dangerous?'

'It's a fear. He's afraid of water. But don't you mind that. You forget I told you, see? Let's go.'

'Go where?'

'The canal, where else,' answered Pump and he turned in the direction of the stile that stood only thirty feet away.

CHAPTER 37

The Canal

FTER CLIMBING OVER the stile, Pump called out, 'Come on then.' He galloped across the scrubland, slapping his thigh and shouting at the top of his voice, 'giddyup, giddyup.' Gristle climbed over in a clumsy fashion. On reaching the rough ground he cantered off in a playful chase, copying his friend's antics.

The canal stretched for two hundred yards or so before it reached rotting lock gates, one of six along its length, until it came to an abrupt end. The remainder had been filled many years before. Reverend Musty's church lay ahead in the distance, alone near the top of the valley. The stagnant water of the canal smelled of oil and filth with the stench of rotten timber and refuse which floated on its stillness. Some of the old railway sleepers which had been used to bank the sides lay in the slimy water and those that had remained intact stood rotting and disintegrating, a green mould grown over them. There were even some of the diseased apples still floating there, dumped into the canal a few years before. The rare bulldog fish and red snapper eels, as well as the thriving trade of the canal boat owners, had all long since gone.

A rodent scurried from amongst piles of rubbish, metal implements and discarded clothing that lay on the farside, disturbed by Pump who waved and shouted excitedly. 'Come on, you fatty! What a slowcoach.'

He picked up a stone and threw it into the black, still water and disturbed it, ripples racing to the sides. He threw pebbles over the canal at the bottles and wooden crates and twisted metal, red and powdery with rust.

Gristle was moving the best he could on his stumpy legs, meandering a course around the profusion of weeds that grew to extraordinary heights on the scrubland.

Puffing and panting from the effort of keeping up with Pump, Gristle finally reached his companion. He pulled burrs from his woollen jumper.

Pump stood eyeing him. 'What a slowcoach,' he said again and gave Gristle a playful push then ran off beside the canal. Gristle followed in chase. Pump threw glances behind him, laughing all the while; after tripping over a clump of tangled bindweed, he stood, ready to start off again, but seeing that Gristle had tired and was strolling behind him at a distance, he turned and walked back towards him. 'Alright then,' he said breathlessly, 'quits?'

Gristle nodded, red-faced and snorting. Pump sat on the ground. He leant on one elbow and produced from his pocket a crumpled packet of cigarettes. Gristle sat beside him. 'Blimey, I'm whacked,' he said. 'Oi, this ground is wet,' he added then and he brushed himself.

'Sit down sissy. A bit of damp won't do any harm.'

Gristle shrugged and, as he did so, noticed the cigarettes. He looked worried. 'You're not going to smoke those, are you?' he questioned.

'No, I'm going to stick them up your nose, what do you think?'

'But you don't smoke. I've never seen you smoke before.'

'What am I doing now?' replied Pump curtly. After placing a filterless slim tube into his mouth he waved another under Gristle's nose. 'Want one?' Not content with a negative reply he fumbled in a pocket for a box of matches and threw the cigarette into Gristle's lap.

'Does your dad know you smoke?'

'Course not. He'd bloomin' kill me if he knew.' Pump struck a match and putting it to his cigarette, lit it and filled his lungs with fumes from the burning tobacco. The smoke burned his throat but he tried to conceal it by laughing. He could hold out no longer. Wheezing hoarsely and with streaming tears, his face burned red. He recovered after gulping and rubbing his stinging eyes then lit Gristle's cigarette. It stuck out at an obtuse angle from his mouth. Gristle inhaled deeply and with a deft flick of his finger he knocked the ash from its end and blew a column of smoke.

'You're meant to inhale it. Take it down,' explained Pump, rather hurt that his friend had succeeded without choking.

'But I did,' replied Gristle, inhaling a second time.

Pump looked hatefully at his own cigarette, the smoke curling and corkscrewing about him. He threw it away in disgust. 'I'm going to the other side,' he said abruptly and stood to walk to the lock gates. Failing to impress his friend with the cigarettes he felt sure that Gristle's respect for him would be lost if he did not somehow prove himself.

He passed the gate mechanism, rusted into a solid mass of metal. Then, like a tightrope walker, he began to step across the top of the lock by placing one foot in front of the other. He wobbled dangerously and stared down at his feet. There was the width of eighteen inches to walk upon and he therefore decided that the exercise was not dangerous enough to warrant admiration. Both of them had run across to the other side many times before: certainly, he thought, to impress Gristle he would have to make the exercise difficult. Not content with his progress as a tightrope walker he decided to introduce some acrobatics into the act. He stood on one of his scrawny legs sticking from his short trousers and he swayed from side to side. 'Are you watching me, mate? Are you looking?' he shouted. Gristle didn't seem interested. He sat on the ground with his legs crossed, smoking and contemplating his cigarette, savouring each fill of his lungs like a connoisseur.

Pump sighed in annoyance: determined to gain his audience he began to jump, first on both legs, then on one. Gristle ignored him still and he giggled softly when he stopped himself in time from biting the end from the cigarette, for his thoughts never strayed far from food.

'I said are you—' Pump's arms seesawed and waved haphazardly as he tried to regain his balance. He brought his other foot down to stabilize himself but misjudged it for his attention was drawn away by a man with a grey-flecked moustache who stood before the smoking Gristle, smiling and puffing on a cigar. Gristle did not seem to see him. Pump's foot landed on the edge of the decaying wood which splintered away; his leg dangled over the side for a second before it pulled his body out of balance and with a shout he fell into the stinking water of the canal.

The oily film was broken, the surface like black glass destroyed with a splash. His head had hit one of the floating railway sleepers with a sickening clunk. Filthy water rained down upon Gristle, who awoke from his daydreaming in time to see Pump slip into the liquid murkiness.

⁂

Some children called her Dismal Dripping. The lady stood behind the counter, her nimble fingers pushing a hairclip back into place into her fair hair. The palsy which had befallen her five years before had paralyzed her face, pulling her cheek and mouth downward and her eyelid with it, leaving the left side frozen into a permanent frown. Alastair could not understand this; the obscure sight of a woman continually frowning on one side of her face while the other side contradicting the expression was odd to him and it began to make him uncomfortable. He became convinced that she wore a mask and underneath lay a face of true ugliness and malevolence. She looked straight into his eyes without blinking.

The spell was broken. 'Um, two ounces of those please.' Alastair pointed to the first jar of sweets that his sight fell upon. The lady nodded, the half-grimace etched upon her. She walked to the shelf and stretching her arms to their fullest extent, retrieved the appropriate container, and then returned to behind the counter. She spun the lid from the jar with a deft twist of her left hand and poured the bullseyes into the scales, taking her sight from Alastair only to check the weight. He felt troubled and played nervously with the money in his pocket.

Abergail had sat back from her needlepoint after hearing the chimes on the shop door and, as was her habit, she began to imagine what sort of person had entered.

Even before the sound of muted voices she could often tell whether the customer was male or female; the manner in which the door had been opened, the way that the chimes had sounded and the footsteps to the counter. She would open the sitting room door a fraction without her mother knowing, to check the correctness of her assumptions, and would find that, more often than not, she had been correct.

Firstly, she would rule out some possibilities. This time she was certain it was not the butcher nor Mr. Fishcake and possibly not the old lady with the monocle. Indeed, she believed that it was somebody whom she had never seen. When she had heard the handle rattling and the door singing open slowly, the chimes becoming silent after a shorter time than was usual, then the furtive steps across the wooden floorboards to the counter, she guessed that the person had never visited the shop before. The footsteps had sounded light and Abergail was sure they belonged to a child.

Though she stared intently at the piano stool, she did not see it: her mind had started to construct a picture. But then the picture began to paint itself. She no longer consciously aided its development with ideas or notions. An image easily formed within her of a balding man with a moustache and a paunch, and he held a cigar.

It was then that something peculiar happened. The man composed from her mind, standing by the memory of the counter in the shop, beckoned to her. Abergail tried to erase the picture but it would not be dismissed; still the portly gentleman motioned and, though he did not speak, his intense eyes seemed to call out, demanding that she come to him.

It was not as though her will had been taken but rather that she had never possessed a will in the first place. The man with the cigar was calling silently, namelessly, and Abergail knew that she had no choice but to go to him.

It happened quickly: Abergail opened the door from the sitting room and walked decisively through into the shop. She looked at Alastair and was surprised to find the boy whom she had seen sitting by the trees on the green, instead of the man she had envisaged.

Alastair blushed at the sight of her. He did not understand the sentiment which took possession of him. He felt that she was beautiful; and a new feeling, that of some connection, a spiritual bonding, a sympathetic ambience, collected. She was not much older than himself, he supposed, perhaps sixteen or seventeen.

She had large brown eyes though they seemed to hold a sadness within them. Her well-proportioned nose had a slight upturn at its end and her lips were full and held slightly apart. He knew this girl, as though they had met many times, though he could not recollect ever meeting her. 'Hello,' he found himself saying. Abergail's face did not change its expression nor her eyes leave his, her sight upon him as intense as those of her mother.

Because she had not spoken to another living soul, except her mother and aunt, she found that she could not speak. The boy did not seem at all frightened by her appearance, indeed quite the opposite. Instantly happy with the knowledge that she did not appear as repulsive to him as she had imagined – surely the reason that her mother had kept her away from all others – she smiled pleasantly and Alastair could do nothing else but smile in return.

Miss Dripping cried out and turned on her heels to confront her daughter. 'Abergail, get back in,' she screamed and stood panting and licking her lips as though hunted. Her eyes glistened and the right side of her face matched the left, worry and panic over her. 'How did you know she was here? Who told you? If you tell anyone that you've seen her, I'll...' she coughed spasmodically and thumped her chest. 'I'm telling you, Alastair, you will tell no one. Promise me.'

Alastair shook his head and then nodded. He did not understand. 'How do you know my name?' he said finally.

'Never you mind. Pay heed to what I say,' Miss Dripping's speech becoming agitated. 'Abergail, get back in,' she demanded.

Alastair, quite without warning, felt dizzy and numb. The jars of confectionery behind the counter seemed to recede from him along with Miss Dripping and her illegitimate daughter.

'Shut up, Florence,' he heard himself say, 'you always did talk too much.'

'How dare you be so familiar,' he heard as though from afar.

There was the sound of somebody chortling before a stern reply, 'Familiar? You're the one to talk.'

'Get out! Get out, Alastair.'

'Am I not entitled to see my own daughter?' he said.

Florence Dripping clutched the paralyzed side of her face as though attempting to push it into its original shape. She was cold with shock. Somehow Alastair was confirming the conclusion of her constant analysis over the past seventeen years concerning her miraculous impregnation despite never having been with a man. Even kind-hearted Archie String had told her, once Florence had explained about the child, that no such miracle could occur, and that his heart was broken and that they could no longer see each other. And more, her eventual understanding that Theodore's game of swinging a pocket watch had somehow taken control, for her to have become submissive and to have succumbed against her will, was not enough to convince the barrister's clerk. They were not to see or hear from each other again.

As Alastair produced the pocket watch from his jacket and held it high by the string, she almost collapsed to the floor. 'The watch,' she shrieked, 'the hypnotizing watch! Where did you get it? What are you doing with it – what are you doing?'

Both at the same time, Alastair saw the watch, huge and shining, and Abergail minute, flung into the distance. Then the world proportioned itself once more. Miss Dripping stood wailing and swaying. 'Abergail, please get in to the living room,' she pleaded through tears, and then, 'Alastair, what are you trying to do to me?'

'I think you're mad,' Alastair replied. He backed to the door of the shop, leaving Florence Dripping and his half-sister swaying as though on a boat; wrenched open the door and ran out onto the cobblestones. The wind ran to him and ruffled his hair and instantly cooled his brow.

He heard Florence cry out, distraught; weakly: 'Alastair, wait! You have forgotten your bullseyes. I mean, I must talk with you.'

❦

Dazed from striking his head on the wooden sleeper, Pump surfaced, sodden hair about a veil of horror covering his face. His arms scythed wildly and flayed the water. 'I can't swim,' was his plaintive cry. 'Help me mate, I can't swim.'

Gristle was struck with indecision and he stood moaning and pulling at his jumper. 'What do you want me to do?'

'Get me out,' Pump shouted but then his words were lost as he sank below the rippling dark surface again.

Gristle's features moulded into a mournful expression and he moaned; twisting his neck, he cast his sight to the right and left over the weedy scrubland in the hope of seeing somebody.

He gasped. There was someone. A man: he was waving. 'Over here, quickly, we're here,' yelled Gristle so loudly that it made his throat sore. The figure in the distance still waved. Gristle looked down into the canal. Pump had surfaced again, hair still plastered across his contorted face, and Gristle stuttered, 'Don't worry m-mate, I'll get h-help I will.'

A thought clicked into his slow mind and it felt to him like utter inspiration. 'Hold onto that piece of wood,' he shouted. Pump had his eyes closed. 'There – next to you,' he bellowed as he poked holes in the air with a finger.

Pump couldn't hear him. He slipped into the cold, murky darkness and tried to scream but felt instead the filthy liquid sucked into him and he tried to breathe through heavy water-filled lungs. He almost smiled at the weightlessness and coolness of his body suspended in time and space: living under water for an eternity that was a handful of seconds, breathing the muddy blackness until he knew no more. The canal had devoured him.

The waving man had gone. Gristle was convinced that his friend would hold on until rescue was brought. He ran shouting and screaming across the windswept scrubland, weeds trying to trip him and thistles whipping his plump body.

᪥

Alastair was confused and elated at the same moment. Confused because of Miss Dripping's strange behaviour and elated at meeting the girl. He mouthed her name. He said it out loud. He dismissed all thoughts of the woman with the twisted face. His depression had been lifted: Pump; the mad woman; his father; none of these mattered. He had met a true friend of the soul. His mind seemed as clear as the stream where he used to catch minnows.

Upon reaching the clock tower on the green he saluted it and ran into Stutter Lane. He pranced over the stone bridge that arched the brook, skipping and laughing until he had reached School Lane. Breathless but exhilarated, he whooped with joy at the sight of the humble school which waited patiently to be filled with life again once the weekend was over.

Shafts of light played through the trees and dappled the cobblestones upon which Alastair stood panting for breath. The whiteness spotted the flint wall that braced itself against advancing poplars. Crows cawed to their companions, or squabbled noisily as they flew from their scruffy nests perched precariously amongst the top branches.

Alastair turned to face the village green but bushes and trees obscured any sight of Florence Dripping's confectionery shop; but still he waved to his vision.

There was someone returning his wave. A figure stood on the bridge; immobile, save an arm which slowly described an arc. In an attempt to identify the person, Alastair strained his head forward. Could it be Abergail who was acknowledging him?

The figure had come closer and Alastair realized that it was a man who walked casually towards him. There was an annoying insect-like buzzing in the shells of his ears. A starling flew by. The man was waving now with more agitation. It seemed that the nearer he came, the louder the buzzing and humming of tiny wings became. The idea of responding to the stranger appealed to Alastair. As he raised an arm in readiness to wave, all of the crows took to the air as one with a raucous noise and they flew in circles. The sudden evacuation from the trees caused twigs and dirt to topple from the branches, showering Alastair beneath. He rubbed the dust from his eyes and from his shoulders, before looking to the sky, and wondered what could have startled the crows into flight. Blinded for no longer than a few seconds, with an equally short time looking away from the lane, he looked back there. The waving man had gone.

There was the sound of chuckling behind him, low but distinct. He wheeled around; still the sound trailed from his back. He looked nervously about, trying to locate the source of the subdued laughter.

He moved one way, then another; even spinning on his heels like a dancer, but it was useless. It was as though the sounds of mirth were attached to his back by an invisible rod, for every way he turned, the sound was always behind him.

Then, distinctly, inside his head…

The buzzing and the laughter, the laughter and the buzzing;

Alastair cried out and held his ears tightly. Slowly, the maddening noise of a million flies with their vibrating wings receded, and it felt to him like the ending of toothache; but still the drowsy chuckling went on within...

And then returned to outside of him. Alastair realized where the source of merriment came from. He listened to himself laughing.

CHAPTER 38

The Pistol

'AND WHERE THE blazes have you been?' shouted William Stubb, a spot of saliva ejected from the corner of his morose mouth. 'I've been looking all over for you, everywhere.' He threw his free arm wildly about him, his other hand occupied with his beer. He knocked himself off-balance and staggered backwards for a few paces. 'You blinking pup,' he bellowed, bringing the empty bottle high into the air. It fell onto the carpet behind him. 'Look what you nearly made me do, you good for nothing... think you can skimper off and get away scotchfree? Far from it.' Alastair shivered and sat meekly on the settee, blinking at his ravings.

Stubb belched while lurching and reeling in a circle, and reached across to the small cupboard of a sideboard and produced a jug of ale. He pulled out its cork stopper. 'Where've you been, you whelp, do you hear me? That quack of a doctor told you to rest, not go gallivanting around. Do you want another breakup?' He screwed a finger into a ruddy cheek. He gulped greedily from his jug, the skin about his neck rising and falling with each mouthful.

Alastair found that his lip had begun to twitch again and the memory of his new friend Abergail was becoming unreal. He felt panic rise. He whispered urgently to himself, 'Please be real.'

'Stop mumbling when I'm speaking,' responded Stubb, his words slurring. Then he stood motionless for a moment as a thought took root in his drunken mind. 'The stick,' he shouted gleefully. He smirked, proud of himself. 'What you need is a good beating, boy.' His doped thought: A good hiding, so you'll forget Queenie, I'll forget Eleanor.

Alastair cringed, terror taking hold of him. 'No please don't,' he shrieked imploringly. Stubb's face creased in amusement while the boy whimpered; then suddenly he seemed to lose interest. 'Clear off. Go and get the dishes out of the way before I thrash your hide. There's three days' worth there.' He was pleased with himself for being so merciful and he slumped into the armchair, his head lolling from side to side. His belly quivered from a giggle that erupted from the pit of his beer-bloated stomach. Tossing more liquid into the back of his throat, he let the jug drop from his deadened fingers, his arms swinging apishly over the sides of the chair and his head sunk into his chest. He fell into an alcoholic stupor.

Alastair ran through to the kitchen, relieved at the reprieve. He glanced abstractedly at the dirty plates with the grimy cups and cutlery that sat precariously piled in the sink. Upon hearing his father's snores he relaxed and decided that the washing up was a mountain he was not prepared to climb yet.

As all he saw were the grease-spotted walls, animosity swarmed freely through him. His father had destroyed his elation; he was the cause of the return of confusion and depression. Accompanying that was a tenseness returning; it was a gnawing, a power that he dare not fight against. He would have to release the energy that clawed him before it turned inward to destroy.

His arm flinched: his hand darted to the pistol that lay inconspicuously amongst more dinner plates and cups on the table. He took the weapon from its holster. The shining object lay flat on his palm and he stared in wide-eyed astonishment. Soaring over his woolly thoughts, a signal, subtle and without source, was given: the time had come. He let his fingers engulf the metal handle with his mouth set firm.

A chaffinch landed on the window ledge and began to tap at crumbs. Finished with its hasty snack it prepared to preen itself but startled by a sound that came from the kitchen, it leapt up and flew over the garden fence – Alastair's face crumpled and he caught his breath when he accidentally kicked a small coal bucket. It was sent clattering across the floor and it tottered on its base before coming to rest by the stove.

He turned to rock. Upon hearing the steady snores from the front room he breathed again and walked to the kitchen door. The gnawing sensation was growing in intensity. He ignored the high pitched buzz in his ears. 'Quickly, quickly, quickly,' a voice in his head urged. Alastair looked down to the metal in his hand. The pistol was sweating, he was certain. He slid into the hall, gripping the weapon tighter. He listened again but a snore supplemented by a grunt dispelled any idle worry that he had awoken Stubb. The hostility had not let go its grip but sat firmly in the back of his brain, as did a distant voice, both forces willing him on to his task. He afforded a smile and stepped boldly into the living room.

Alastair tried to ignore the faded and torn wallpaper; the settee partially hidden from view behind the door; the patchy carpet scattered with newspapers, and a huddle of beer bottles and jugs, some covered by the drab curtains; boxes of cigars and cigarettes on the sideboard: he tried to ignore these, but all seemed too real; surreal. The recognized buzzing became insistent. He watched the rise and fall of Stubb's belly in time with clamorous snoring, his cheeks flushed and nose twitching. Alastair was reassured by the weapon in his hand.

The voice became closer and demanding: 'Now... now...' and he banished all thought when lifting up the pistol, the handle in both hands, pointing the barrel towards Stubb's open mouth. Alastair's body trembled; he squeezed his eyes shut and pulled the trigger. The concentrated juvenile contempt which had been pounding through him was ejected from the gun in one climactic moment. The pistol spat flame and jumped in a spasm in his hands.

The pistol tutted. Stubb groaned and Alastair felt faint.

He saw his father, crimson fluid pumping and spurting from a gurgling throat, weird blasting notes of anguish crawling from his blood-smeared mouth, wide and agonized. His whole body was jerking in an ugly fashion, like an ungainly marionette, until finally his thrashing form became still as his whorled eyes lost their sight.

The vision which Alastair beheld splintered into a myriad of pieces before him, to reveal Stubb sprawled in his armchair, snuffling and snoring.

Alastair let go of the pistol, an item taken years before by Stubb from Theodore's trunk in the box room. It bounced once and lay dead on the carpet. The granular buzzing within became mocking laughter: somebody in his head thought it most amusing. He ran trembling fingers through his mop of hair and willed his legs to move.

He scampered through to the hall and up the plain stairs to his bedroom, where he would try to heal his ruptured mind.

And a lazy, taunting voice whispered, 'Not yet, my son; not yet.'

CHAPTER 39

Discovery

BERGAIL STEPPED OUT through the door entrance of the confectionery shop. She scanned the village green, and shivered with excitement and fright, her thoughts pitching and keeling in a storm of confusion. She reminded herself that perhaps dangers beyond were as great as her mother had warned but then remembering the boy who lived freely outside without worry or care gave her courage.

She stood as though in a trance with her head thrown back and her hands held to her heaving breast. Everything looked and felt so different without windows between her and the unknown world. So many times had she sat in her chair and watched the slow changes of the seasons. She had no memory of wind playing through her hair or the summer sun on her back or rain splashing her face.

The wind buffeted about her. She breathed rapidly. It was as though she was to be reborn. A ripple of warmth scurried up her spine. With a sharp inward breathe, she stepped out onto the cobblestones. She walked stiffly to the edge of the green and waved her arms; and like a delicate sea plant, her fingers wavered. The new sphere of discovery stretched on and on – her new, soon to be cherished, domain.

The ecstacy evaporated. 'Abergail!' Miss Dripping screamed. 'Come in, please come here, now. Quickly, before anyone sees you,' she wailed. She stood by the door clutching at her dress.

'Leave me alone, go away. I never want to see you again,'

shouted Abergail defiantly. Her head whipped around as though she were trying to find a place to hide. Florence ran over to her daughter, who flung her fists at her and pulled at her hair but her mother would not let go as she tearfully dragged the struggling Abergail inside, then slammed the oak door shut.

They sat in the poky living room. 'Never leave this house ever again, you silly, stupid girl. After all that I have told you, warned you about.' Florence began to sob and clutched a handkerchief to her mouth. 'Now, get up to your room,' she ordered, with her distorted face supporting the command. She explained, 'I love you too much for you to go out in broad daylight like that.' She continued with her original understanding of the virgin birth. 'You have no earthly father; people cannot understand; you would be hounded, chased or worse. Promise you will never go out again. You have no reason to. I open the windows for you, we play cards, I teach you from books.' Her bottom lip quivered. Abergail cast a rebellious look. Florence Dripping howled, 'Promise me, please.'

Abergail left without a word and went upstairs. Her mother felt the curves of her paralyzed features with a shaking hand.

The inclination for a stronger surveillance of her daughter's whereabouts was renewed but still Abergail slipped out to her new province. Each time her confidence grew which allowed her to walk further from the confectionery shop. Her visits were best conducted during the early evening when her mother slept.

The season changed. It became winter and a white sheet was dragged across the village. A small battalion of lopsided snowmen stood haphazardly to attention on the green, as though awaiting inspection. Snowball fights were the order of the afternoon for the children. A biting chill of a day. It was on such a late afternoon when Miss Dripping took a nap, having had a busy morning checking her stocks.

Abergail stood in the middle of the village green, now without colour. The whiteness stretched around her; she was the orb, the centre, the ruler of the purity about her. She bent and picked up snow. She licked it and crystals made the tip of her tongue cold. She did not see Nuckle nor his squashed nose pressed to the tea shop window like a mollusc stuck on glass.

'What are you looking at? You've been at that window for the past ten minutes.' Stalk strode over to Nuckle, pushing wooden chairs aside as he went.

'Beautiful,' Nuckle said simply. His jaw hung slack as he stared at the young female who stood like an apparition in the middle of the green. The wind moulded her dress to her lithe body, every contour graceful and distinct.

'Here, don't you look like that, you.'

Nuckle had been biting his lip and when it retracted from behind his crooked teeth it showed white marks. He breathed rapidly, emitting a squeak with every exhalation.

'She's not for your eyes. Who is she anyway? Come away, I want my tea.' Stalk heaved a sigh and turned to trace his steps back to the counter, hoping to promote the same action in Nuckle, but the tea shop proprietor did not move. 'She's not worth looking at. Come away, before anyone sees you gloating,' Stalk said worriedly.

Nuckle's large eyes moistened. 'Beautiful, exquisite, alive,' he breathed. 'Perfection.'

Abergail waved her fingers, feeling and caressing the air. She longed to see more, to see the lanes and streets which lay beyond the green, to explore the whole village, perhaps even to meet again the boy called Alastair.

'I quite love her,' stated Nuckle in the same tone that he would use to ask for a pound of potatoes. 'I think she is the most attractive creature on this earth,' he continued melodramatically.

Stalk curled his lip in distaste. 'It's all those smutty magazines you've been reading, you,' was all he could think of in reply.

CHAPTER 40

Molestation

THE SILENCE OF the night. The powdered stars winked at the snow wrapped over Muchmarsh. It had become bitterly cold: Mrs. Battlespoke's washing – put outside for some reason known only to herself – hung like cardboard from her line. Mr. Fishcake scraped ice from the windscreen of his new motor car and Badger braved the cold again and stepped from his cottage by the farm yard to sweep the path to his shed clear of snow. The moon was full. She peered shyly from behind a bank of cloud, occasionally gaining the courage to scamper from behind her covering, sending a mellow light to stain the ivory landscape.

A beetle scurried across the floorboards from a hole in the skirting and disappeared under the bed. Alastair heard the clock on the green strike eleven. He lay down. He always wondered at the voices in his head and the strange images that had become part of his waking life. He stood and kicking balls of newspaper at his feet, walked to the blotched mirror which hung on the wall beside the door of his bedroom. He studied the face: holding his breath, he started to trace his features with an index finger. It began on his forehead, nestled within his forelock. The digit slid to the tip of his nose which was too much of a scoop, he decided. He pondered on this anatomical deficiency until the finger reached his lips. 'Fat lips,' he yelled suddenly to his reflection. He bit the end of his finger with such force that his teeth made a mark as clear as a white elastic band. He saw a dazzling flash of light and an image of Queenie, fingerless, licking the stubs on her palm like a dog contentedly licking bones.

The image faded. He pulled faces; he twisted his mouth and closed an eye and swivelled his eyeballs in their sockets. His reflection seemed larger than himself. But all at once it was not his reflection at all: it was an elderly man with twinkling eyes and a bristly greying moustache, who laughed silently at him. Alastair's hands were on his hips and he craned his head forward. His own reflection appeared again and he gazed at his visage in outraged fascination.

You're so ugly,' he shouted with glee, 'ugly, ugly, ugly, ugly, ugly.' The repeated word began to sound strange and then to lose all meaning. 'What does it mean?' he demanded and he expected an answer. He grew impatient. The reflection changed again to the man with a moustache. 'Who are you anyway? Why are you always in my room?' His voice rose to a fevered pitch. 'Out, out!' His own reflection returned once more and mocked him, mouthing the same words. His tight fists were pushed to the wall and his nose was numbed as he flattened it against the cold glass of the mirror. His mouth twitched spasmodically.

'They will all pay. Pump has paid the price; the rest will pay for destroying me. Who are you?' Alastair laughed. His throat was dry and he looked around the bedroom. He felt confused and ill; all about him began to spin. He staggered to his bed and collapsed onto it but it was as though he fell with a slow motion, seeming to take an age for his head to reach the pillow. The left side of his face jumped with the spasms of his mouth and his legs began to shake. He crawled underneath dirty sheets and lay there huddled, holding his knees to his chest.

Like a flare, the absence of light was dispelled by another brightness exploding before him. There was Abergail calling and Queenie crying out, both as mournfully as ships' horns sounding in a night fog. They were searching; they were near. Mustering a mental pressure he willed Abergail to find him.

He dared not sleep with the fright of his dreams nor did he wish to stay awake for fear of a dread question quivering upon his lips. The strain of the day had taken its toll and he lost both battles. As he drifted into fearful unconsciousness, a question dribbled from his tongue. 'Who am I?'

෯

Abergail had come out of the shop and was running away, occasionally sliding on ice patches as she made her way across the green to Stutter Lane. The uncharted village had become an addiction, with every visit making her the more determined to go again. Unsure as to whether she ought to have gone at night, she had slipped out all the same – opportunities were rare, and too valuable to waste.

She wanted to find Alastair for she believed that he could protect her and help her understand this new life. He would surely accompany her to find new wonders. Though despite these wishes, the further she ran from the shop, the more worried she became. Where would she look for him?

If only she had borrowed her mother's overcoat instead of the woollen jumper which covered her blouse and part of her long skirt.

She stopped for a while. There had been somebody walking across the yard of a farm – and for a moment only, the poor light from the street lamps had convinced her that it was Alastair.

Realizing it was a man holding a broom she began to run again. Badger's obsession to sweep the yard every evening had been interrupted by the sound of running feet and he had looked back to her as she stood illuminated by a lamp on the corner of School Lane.

When Abergail reached the oak tree which stood at the top of Pepper Lane she slumped to the ground, out of breath and frightened. She was cradled by the large, twisted roots of the tree and felt chilled to the bone in the freezing night. Everything looked so different without the light of the sun. If only she had not left the warmth and security of her home. She was about to stand when she became immobile: she was certain there had been a voice. The weight of darkness leant heavily upon her. The wind played with her hair and flapped her skirt. As though trying to draw heat from the frozen bark, she huddled closer to the grasping roots of the tree.

The voice again. The wind quietened to a whisper.

Abergail stood quickly and tried to pierce the darkness. Without warning, Queenie leapt from a bifurcation of the tree and landing with her slippered feet in a snow drift. The woman pointed a bony finger, her head almost resting on a shoulder. 'Child,' she crooned. As though to dispel dust from her eyes she blinked rapidly. 'Come child, castles in the lair, castles don't care. Rabbits and feathers.' She tottered towards Abergail and with her long dirt-rimmed fingernails digging into the girl's flesh, grasped her waist in a firm embrace. Abergail struggled and whimpered and tried to push Queenie away but she clung on. The stench of her breath and the smell of her body filled Abergail's nostrils and she felt nauseous.

'Leave me alone, let go,' she demanded.

Queenie cackled. 'Tree be damned,' she barked.

'I want to go home. Please let me go,' Abergail begged. Queenie sprang away with the agility of a cat but no sooner had she landed on the icy ground she jumped forward and pushed her. The girl lost her balance and fell heavily onto the base of the tree. Her mother's warnings sounded in her head.

'Mummy,' she said.

Queenie had been scratching herself and staring without expression but then with outstretched arms she pointed both index fingers at Abergail. 'Mummy, baby mine,' she growled. She came closer, her panting breath becoming more rapid as she advanced.

Abergail cowered and blinked at the accusing fingers held a few inches from her face. Instinctively, she clamped her teeth around one of the digits and bit. Queenie let out a piercing howl, her eyes revolving in their sockets before turning to white. She grinned and held out both hands – streaked with candle wax – as though for inspection. Blood dripped from a severed scab on the finger and fell onto Abergail's skirt. 'Bitching soles,' she hissed and stuffing the digit into her mouth she ran rapidly along Stutter Lane and disappeared into the night. Her howl of surprise and pain began again and it could be heard crawling across the snow-covered fields, her maddened soul crying out in desolation, until all was silent.

Abergail stood again, shakily and startled, crushing the crimson spots which had stained the snow with her shoes. She must get home to warmth and safety: she began to run back along Stutter Lane but because Queenie had gone this same way before her, she would stop now and then to listen.

Although the attempt to find Alastair had been unsuccessful, still she held his image within her mind as she ran. It gave her a hope and comfort. She gasped and slowed to a trot, for a bat had swooped past and brushed her hair. She shuddered and lengthened her stride once more.

Tiredness began to eat the strength from the muscles in her legs. Panic had taken hold; the distance between the gas lamps along the lane seemed longer than before so that, while plunged into darkness in between, trees and bushes loomed threateningly, blocking light from the moon and preventing escape to the left or right. It was a nightmare tunnel leading to nowhere, seemingly without end. This thought, that she would travel for ever under a network of dark branches, encouraged a deep trepidation. The extremities of her body had been rendered lifeless with the cold and from delayed shock at her previous encounter and she began to cry.

Still she trotted on, miserable and frightened and tired. If only she had listened to her mother. The outside seemed worse even than had been described. She would promise that never again would she leave the shop. She ran into a soft mass.

'Portside; my lost beauty ... *squeeerk.*'

As she struggled to release herself from the grip of a man's arms she let out a scream. It was a long, terrified scream which was cut in flight by a greasy hand over her mouth.

'Quieten, loved one, the other sailors will hear.'

The moon dipped behind a cloud. Abergail's terror-stricken eyes tried to identify the black shape before her. The man clasped her hand in his and dragged her across the lane and moved her gently against the wall.

'Give us more – *quarrrk* – kisses, my pretty girl, come on...' Badger's elbows padded at his sides, and his neck slid and writhed as he preened invisible feathers, 'then I'll sing you a sailor's song.' Abergail lashed out and her hand caught him. His spectacles flew from his curly-haired head and landed by the verge of the lane. He squeaked and went to pick them up and Abergail fled from him.

She saw the bridge, and further on the clock tower on the green lit by a gas lamp but, as she ran towards them, Badger had followed and reached her, holding Abergail from going further by grasping both wrists and planting slobbering kisses across her cheek and onto her throat.

Abergail shuddered as she felt his hot breath. On impulse, she brought her knee sharply upwards and it hit him hard in the groin. The man backed away with a groan and Abergail ran shouting and howling like Queenie had done before her.

Badger cursed, limping back to his cottage at the side of the farm yard.

He awoke as if from a vivid hallucination and took his broom, pushing and pulling it over the concrete, curses and illogical sentences flowing, created like bubbles from under water. And as like a bubble would pop, so he forgot his previous insult, replaced with the next, and another after that. To lull his mind into some form of calmness, he began to mumble, 'Left, right, left, right, *squawk*, left, right…'; and for a time he was able to concentrate his full attention on the act of sweeping with his horse hair yard broom.

CHAPTER 41

Aŋ Arrest

L IKE SOME ARCHAIC pageant, a carnival which had lost
all meaning, several members of the village walked one
behind the other across the green. Their shoes made new
indentations in the fresh snow of the morning. Police Constable
Flute strutted as their leader with his helmeted head held high
and his firm jaw set firmer.

Florence Dripping clutched a cotton handkerchief to her
mouth and wailed and along with Stalk, was left behind the
main procession. She tried to cull sympathy from the butcher
who did not understand what she was talking about and indeed
was unaware of the reason for the exodus, but all the same had
gone to the end of the line. Seeing the villagers by the clock tower
in an apparent state of excitement had been enough to cause
him to leave tying pork crowns to join the group; though as it
became obvious that their destination was the tea shop, Stalk
realized he could have tamed his inquisitiveness and waited in
his butcher's shop for their arrival next door.

It was Constable Flute who pushed his forehead to the
smudged window of Nuckle's small establishment. All eight
members of the entourage then filed into the dingy, albeit flower-
perfumed place and most of them sat at tables more as though
for an informal chat than the formal arrest of Mr. Nuckle for the
attempted assault of Abergail.

Stalk whispered, 'Why are you all here, then? Old Nuckle is
going to like this,' and he smiled, surprisingly almost pleasantly,

although it was lost when he received a mixture of blank expressions and aggressive looks. Only Constable Flute had remained standing and he placed the bottom of his arms on the counter beside the glass display case, as though expecting to be served. 'Are you somewhere there, Mr. Nuckle?' he called out harshly.

No time was wasted. The condemned man seemed only too eager to appear. 'Customers!' he shouted with glee, his eyes brimming with tears of happiness behind his round spectacles. A particularly grubby cloth was produced from his equally grubby apron and he darted from table to table, wiping the dirty and scratched surfaces. 'Tea? Coffee? Cakes? Yes, anything you wish. Strips of fried pork back between two chunks of wholemeal? And best butter. My own invention. Who's first? '

He looked to those assembled with his wide eyes. They all turned away and began to speak in confidential whispers except the constable who remained silent. He narrowed his eyes and looked hard at Nuckle and was surprised at the man's calmness given the situation (save for his excitement at so many customers).

࿔

Perhaps after all he was losing his mind, for in the silence of his bedroom Alastair began to hallucinate. He was not dreaming nor asleep; neither was he really awake but suspended in some vague mental state. The village was spread before him and some great calamity had befallen it. The remains lay smouldering and blackened, homes and shops charred or burned beyond recognition. Leafless trees stood contorted or lay unceremoniously in mud, uprooted and tossed aside as if by a monstrous hand.

Cries of suffering and torment: a herd of gesturing people ran amok across the village green which had been turned to black, and they tore at each other's clothing or clawed at faces, shouting blasphemies to the conceited heavens for the destruction which had consumed their houses and gardens. The clock tower toppled to the ground and its mainspring coiled up from an untidy heap of rubble. It stood quivering like some giant spiral flatworm.

Mother.

Angry screams of trauma; howls of pain and guttural wails, shouts of anger and confusion. Mrs. Battlespoke ran from the main pack with an idiotic grin upon her tired face. She sat on a clump of house bricks and then, like the top of a moneybag with the drawstring pulled tight, her lips puckered and she blew kisses about her. Alastair's stomach heaved with a sudden nausea.

Is this real?

Her hand rested on her cheek and she stroked it as though to brush aside stray hairs. Quickly, without effort, Mrs. Battlespoke took hold of her eyeball between finger and thumb – her monocle having dropped to the ground – and she extracted it, accompanied by the sound of a suction pad being lifted from a pane of glass. The diminutive globe dangled from the end of the clock mainspring by its optic nerve. The old lady wept while hunting on all fours with desperation for the organ. The crowds laughed, rocking backwards and forwards, some jumping up and down, slapping their thighs, others rubbing their bellies or pointing to Dr. Snippet's manor house, the only property which had remained intact.

As though these visions had, in some peculiar way, been encapsulated within a watery film covering Alastair's sight, upon simply rubbing his eyes, he dismissed all to leave his bedroom before him.

He was left shaken by what he had seen and he found it difficult to shift thoughts which insisted upon morbidity. They were as fine as cobwebs and to brush them aside meant another nauseous heave to his stomach. He lay in bed for a while and after mulling over echoes of the vision which had passed, he finally got up and dressed.

Upon reaching the bottom of the stairs he passed the entrance of the front room. There was Stubb – usual pose and position – slumped in the armchair. The boy's lip twitched; a tooth hooked: the voice had convinced him that William Stubb must see the emptiness, hear the quietness, feel the deadness. Alastair was reminded of the extraordinary awakened dream of the burning attic; his father must visit there.

Alastair walked past the oak tree towards the village green, talking quietly to himself as he went. 'He has to learn, doesn't he? He has to know pain and anger, smell death; it's only right.' When he heard himself speak he laughed aloud for all he had to do was move his mouth and the words were placed there without any effort on his part. He felt a different person but how and why? The question which had tormented him for the past few days came to mind again. 'Who am I?' There was no pause in his jumbled thoughts, no time or inclination to consider the answer. It was simple. 'I am Theodore,' he said proudly and he skipped along the lane.

Upon reaching the clock tower, he sat on the bench under the bare trees and ice crackled about his feet. From between the broken shards of ice crawled a host of cockroaches and they quickly scattered, scuttling away under the bench and into holes in the trees. He looked up to see a group of villagers standing on the snow-covered green. One of them was a policeman who was holding onto somebody as though to prevent him from falling. Alastair found the activity interesting and it became more so when all in the group began to walk towards him.

He smacked his lips. He was thirsty. Perhaps water then a distinct voice suggested port – as though the suggestion had been whispered from within the inner ear.

The villagers had stopped, congregating a couple of yards in front of Alastair, and were so busy arguing that none of them seemed to notice he was there.

'Look here, this is a terrible mistake. You have got the wrong person,' moaned Nuckle. 'Will anyone tell me what I am supposed to have done? I've done nothing – I am innocent. The opposite of guilty.'

Stalk spoke. 'Constable Flute, what is Nuckle's crime? Look you, is it anything to do with what I said this morning?' He pulled the belt of his overcoat tighter about him and lifted the lapels to his neck.

'What did you tell him, Stalk? If you told him anything about anything, then you've seen your last cup of tea,' shouted Nuckle angrily.

'If so, you've got it all wrong,' continued Stalk to the policeman. 'They are nature magazines.'

Before the constable could answer, all attention was drawn away from him towards Alastair, for he had a cigar hanging from his mouth; and the flare of a lit match had dispersed the gloom made by the overhanging branches of the trees.

In a show of authority and importance, the constable puffed out his chest and commanded, 'Move along there sonny, there's nothing to watch.'

Alastair chuckled knowingly and stood. He plodded across the snow to the policeman and stared unblinkingly, as an animal would, with his mouth in a twisted grin. With a glint in his eye he turned to Nuckle before speaking.

'Body snatcher,' he declaimed coarsely. Nuckle put a finger

vertically over his lips and look alarmed. 'Body snatcher,' Alastair repeated. You are paying your price. So you would have taken my body and disposed of it on some rubbish heap? Isn't that what you were going to do?'

Nuckle shivered and the villagers began to talk in low whispers. This was not the Alastair that they knew.

Stalk the butcher pushed his way through the group and confronted the boy. He had been standing at the back to complain to Reverend Musty of a possible misunderstanding and of the coldness of the weather and had not heard what had been said. A young boy had been holding up the proceedings of the arrest of Nuckle was all he knew and he was impatient to learn of the unlawful act which his shop neighbour might have committed. 'Go home, Alastair. Clear off, you,' he said curtly and Stalk turned to go, presuming that his remarks had the necessary effect.

His coat sleeve was taken in a tight grip and he turned back and was surprised to find that the strong grasp belonged to the boy.

'You always were a pompous ass, Brood,' Alastair murmured in a low voice. 'Fit only to weed lawns and water rose bushes. Even that not good enough.'

Brood Stalk gasped in amazement as Alastair let go of his arm. 'How did you know that? How did you know I was a gardener? What's that miserable slob of a father of yours been saying? Now clear off before I box your ears, you.'

Alastair ignored his threat and gave a wicked smile. 'Poor Eleanor. Did you really think you would get anywhere with your pathetic smutty notes? And as for the rat poison,' he chuckled, 'well, of course I knew everything, after the arm-twisting. Remember? But you are going to pay, Brood, for wanting to murder me.'

The butcher was filled with rage. 'Stubb has gone too far this time. I'll teach him a lesson that he won't forget in a hurry.' He strode across the snow towards Stutter Lane. 'I'm going to pay, am I? I'll make that idiot pay.'

'Brood,' Alastair called out, in a deeper voice than was usual.

Upon hearing his name, the butcher stopped walking. Alastair ran towards him, taking out the pocket watch as he did so. The villagers ignored them both in preference to another interesting argument which had developed between Mr. Nuckle and the policeman.

Brood Stalk kicked snow towards the advancing boy. 'Buzz off,' he yelled. Alastair reached him and gripping the end of the string, he raised his hand as high as it would go so that the opened timepiece could swing close to the butcher's chill-whitened face. Alastair's arm had numbed and he wondered why he felt the need to show the butcher the watch.

'What's all this then, you?' Brood asked mockingly, rubbing his beard, though once his sight had rested upon the intricacies within the swinging watch, he found it difficult to look away. He became fascinated; the numbers had become alive and were milling about beneath the glass. He heard a low voice and he felt tired and uneasy. 'Buzz off kid, I told you,' he said in a lazy manner, unable to wrench his eyes from the timepiece. He stared at it all the more, following its movements before him, wondering about the strange phenomenon upon its face, the precise cogs seeming to spin fast then slowly. Still the voice was heard, surely still too low for a boy. It snuffed out his anger. 'If you...' he began but his voice trailed away. The monotone, which seemed spoken so near had the power to draw energy from his limbs, to pull his eyelids down. The snow seemed too bright as it reflected and magnified the winter sun's rays. A warm lethargy gripped him. He passed a hand across his brow.

'I feel dizzy,' he said. With a flicker, like a candle flame going out, his eyelids finally closed, though before this resignation his mind registered two things. Alastair standing before him had vanished and Theodore – the long dead Theodore – was there in his place. Then, through watering and stinging eyes, he had realized that the dancing numbers upon the watch face had not been numbers at all, but ants.

Brood stumbled forward as though in a trance while Alastair stood on his toes and wrapped his arms about the butcher's neck. He pulled the head down to his own and began to whisper. After ten seconds of this Alastair retrieved the half-smoked cigar from his top pocket, lit it and chuckled at the somnambulant butcher swaying in front of him. And with a click of his fingers, Brood's eyes were quickly open. He looked dazed. Then, as though nothing had passed between Alastair and himself, he said loudly, 'If you don't clear off, I'll give you a dratted good hiding, you,' and with his hands shoved into his overcoat pockets he marched across the white green in the opposite direction to that of Stutter Lane. The butcher's shop awaited his arrival.

The village entourage had moved off and were nearing the stone bridge. Some turned to look back and they saw Alastair walking quickly towards them, waving slowly, having added another set of footprints to those already intersecting along the whiteness of the lane. Constable Flute was becoming annoyed. He waited for Alastair to reach him before he demanded, 'Look here sonny, you are obstructing police duty and if you don't go away, I shall be forced to take you to the station and you wouldn't want that, would you?' He paused to speak more but, before he could, Alastair spat out the cigar butt that had been clamped between his teeth, and he ran from them. He darted occasionally to his right like some crab to avoid ice patches in his path. Tears streamed down his cheeks as he wondered where his legs were taking him. He had a crazy smirk upon his face and spoke calmly. 'He must pay. They will all pay and suffer because I suffered.'

The villagers continued on their way to the police station, Nuckle still held in the firm grip of the policeman and still protesting his innocence; though not as vehemently as before – the encounter with Alastair had shaken him.

As they turned the curved corner of Stutter Lane into School Lane bound for the police station, Badger the caretaker came out from his shed. Upon seeing them all, he waved his broom and gave them one of his best smiles while spitting out exclamations of an avian nature.

CHAPTER 42

Insects

STUBB AWOKE WITH a start. Hurriedly, he pulled on a jacket and left the terraced house. He was already late for the opening of The Bulldog Fish.

Upon reaching the top of Pepper Lane and gazing along Stutter Lane, he was surprised to see Stalk trotting towards him. 'I wonder what the old sod wants?' he asked himself aloud and he began to walk towards the advancing butcher. Stalk stopped ten feet from Stubb and his chest was heaving as he gasped for breath but then he recommenced walking. He shivered strangely. 'What's this all about, Brood? After all these years, you of all miseries decide to talk to me again. Want to apologize, is that it?' Stalk did not answer but stepped nimbly to the side and Stubb twisted and yelled with fright.

The butcher had quickly unbuttoned his coat and produced a meat cleaver from his stained apron underneath. He seemed confused then for he gazed at the instrument as though without recognition. He looked up, his eyes burning with a fierce passion. 'Miserable monster, you, wanting to kill my master,' he said as he raised the cleaver. Beads of perspiration trickled suddenly from his brow despite the low temperature and his sensitivity to it.

Stubb moaned and cringed away. He was transfixed for a short time until he cried out, 'No!'

The meat cleaver quivered in the air as Stalk began to babble. Ideas of escape percolated through William Stubb's mind in an idiotic muddle. In the face of death with the cleaver still hanging above, tears formed, as memories which the butcher had dislodged rose to a conscious level; and they taunted and floated like bubbles. For a moment, he dismissed the danger and looked with sadness inward but then, wiping the mist from his sight, he heaved his fist into the butcher's stomach. Brood Stalk's voice, which had risen to a strangled screech of blasphemy, was cut short. He bent double from the blow. His arm and the cleaver were brought down with him. The tool buried into Stubb's arm: he screamed at the burning pain when the cleaver went easily through his coat and shirt and seared through the flesh. It had made a deep cut to the bone; blood leapt crimson and in a second had soaked his left side and spattered the snow. Stalk retched from the punch as Stubb reeled in agony. A thought scratched him: he must get to the doctor or he would bleed to death. He steadied himself and putting a hand over his dreadful wound, ran up the lane as fast as he was able.

Stalk straightened up. Fresh blood had splashed the old stains on his apron. This observation spurred him into action. Retrieving the cleaver from the snow-covered ground he brandished it high above him in pursuit of William Stubb.

⁂

Alastair stood on the threshold of the doctor's house. He knocked and waited in a daze. Dr. Snippet opened the door. 'Dear lad, what a surprise. How are you? No worries I hope? But do come in.'

Alastair muttered and followed the doctor into the manor house. His lip twitched. 'We are expecting visitors, Pump. Fetch me my port, will you,' he heard himself say.

'Come and sit down,' said the doctor. 'Are you feeling unwell?' He guided the boy into the drawing room, ignoring the front door which Alastair had left ajar despite the cold chill entering the manor house. 'Now you sit there while I make a nice cup of tea and then we can talk. I won't be long.' He went to the kitchen.

❦

Stubb was on the verge of collapse from exhaustion and the loss of blood. Sweat produced from the effort of running had made his armpits damp. His arm burned and hung limply down. As he passed The Bulldog Fish Tavern he threw agitated glances behind him. Stalk was gaining ground. Stubb stopped for a moment to gulp draughts of air, a hissing of breath issuing from between clenched teeth like asthmatic bellows. He felt a blackness descending but he willed his hollowed legs to move. A dread had drained his face of colour and paralyzed his features into a mask of terror. He whimpered and staggered on, skidding and sliding on iced snow along Daisytrail Lane.

Upon reaching the open gates of the manor house he turned to see the butcher running casually towards him, the cleaver slicing and slashing. Stubb crawled the final yards over the short gravel drive to the front door before falling to his knees in the porch. He leant on the door and it opened inward. A dark curtain began to draw across his mind as he fell forward and groaned with the searing pain. With much difficulty, he stood up to dismiss the oncoming veil of death. He staggered blindly into the hallway, disorientated and half insane with agony and weakness. 'Doctor, losing blood,' he tried to shout but his voice was a whispered croak. Stalk appeared on the doorstep and gave a hoarse battle cry. 'Please, no,' whispered Stubb, trapped like a chicken running circles in a barn unable to escape the wrath of the farmer.

For an instant, Stalk looked puzzled again as though he did not know his whereabouts. Stubb cried fitfully, petrified and weary beyond measure. He began to pull himself up the staircase, clinging onto the banister, every movement costing him dearly from his depleted energy. He heard Stalk behind laughing lazily as though drugged. Stubb, sobbing and gasping, cried out; he reached the top of the stairs and heard the slow padding of feet. 'Do it now. Get it over and done with,' he moaned, for if he was to be murdered he would rather die now than with the maddening agony of living a moment longer. He grunted like an animal as he crawled on his hands and knees along the carpeted corridor with Stalk so close behind that the soles of his shoes were kicked.

He reached the foot of the winding staircase to the attic and Stalk pushed him to herd him up, a smile of satisfaction quivering on his lips.

The doctor lay slumped across the kitchen table, deep in a hypnosis-induced sleep. The water in the kettle spat spitefully and rattled the lid. Alastair had left the kitchen and had gone to the hallway. He stood at the foot of the stairs and his eyes glowered. Another cigar stuck rudely from the corner of his mouth. He held a glass of port.

Stubb lay on his back on the new floorboards of the attic. His chest heaved and every breath was painful, his arm still bleeding profusely. His face was ashen, with his life dribbling from the gashed limb, already his heart losing beats and rhythm. A dark pool of blood formed beside him. Stalk stood framed in the doorway of the empty attic. 'Brood,' whispered Stubb with the last of his strength. 'You don't know what you are doing.' He coughed. 'Brood, do you hear me?'

Brood Stalk shook his head as though to dismiss some morbid thought. His expression changed from a lunatic grin to bewilderment as he looked to the bloody cleaver which he held. He gave a shout as though he had been bitten. His sight had fallen upon the grotesque form lying at his feet. Blood, sweat and dirt were smeared across Stubb's face and his hair was wild and matted. His white shirt had turned red, his open coat a darker brown.

'Brood,' mumbled Stubb. 'Fetch Dr. Snippet.'

Stalk did not move.

He gave a long groan that rose in pitch to a howl.

Stubb turned his sight to Brood Stalk's eyes and he saw them bolting from his head, filled with abject terror...

There had been the odd one at first, here and there, wandering aimlessly as though waiting, until more came from holes in the floorboards and the skirting, and dropping from the rafters, multiplying, slowly growing in number and type. They came flying through the open window at the end of the attic and from cracks in the roof, slitting the space with black lines; and they crawled and hopped out of the fire grate and the packing cases which stood in the middle of the room.

The butcher stood with feet frozen to the floor, gaping with morbid fascination at the floorboards and bare walls and beams that were now covered with insects of every description and the air filled with multi-coloured points, becoming thick as though forming a solid wall of living particles. Insects that buzzed and hummed and rattled and whistled and cracked and ticked. Insects with rainbow wings, opalescent bodies, and striped, speckled or stippled heads. Dense with butterflies, moths and bluebottles and stag beetles, dragonflies and wasps and bees; the floor a writhing layer of ants and snails, woodlice and worms and centipedes, slugs and beetles of every type and colour. The stench in the attic was a fetid odour of the earth and of darkness and deadness.

This mass of creatures seemed suspended in time as though awaiting a signal, until they flew, crawled and slithered onto the prostrate figure of Stubb. They squirmed over his body and wriggled into his ears and nose and into his clothing and bit him and stung him and sucked his blood. He was the epicentre, totally covered by the abundance of writhing creations.

Stalk was stricken with horror and he stumbled screaming down the staircase, but even above his voice he heard an inhuman cry which petrified him. It was part pain and part insanity and part animal, and it ripped and buried itself throughout the house, seeping into the floors and wood and stone, into the essence of the structure, creating an electric hatred and revulsion that slashed at Stalk's nerves to be instilled forever.

He sobbed and ran down the last of the steps from the attic to the landing then on to the top of the stairs and upon realizing that he still held onto the cleaver he let it go. It clattered down the main staircase and landed with a crack upon the ceramic tiles of the hallway. He began his descent but stopped suddenly when Alastair stepped into the hallway from the drawing room. He bent and picked up the cleaver and cradled it in two hands. The butcher edged down the stairs with his back flattened to the wall, his heart thumping a fast drumbeat in his chest. 'Get out of my way. Put that cleaver down before you cut yourself, you,' he demanded. Alastair laughed heartily. 'Alastair, you vandal, do as I tell you.'

'Alastair cannot hear, Brood. It's you and I.'

'What are you talking about? Get out of my way, your father has been…is…dead. He's dead, you.'

Alastair nodded, 'Yes, I do know. He has paid my price. You must pay yours, you shortsighted buffoon. Can you not see who this is? I am Theodore.' Stalk gasped. Had the boy lost his mind? 'And I have come back to take my revenge.' Alastair flicked ash from the cigar end and gripped tighter on the handle of the cleaver with the other hand.

It happened swiftly; Alastair had raised the weapon and ran forward, and brought it down onto Stalk, but the butcher was too quick. He had leapt out of the way and through the open doorway. The cleaver gave a thud as it was embedded into the wooden carving of the stag beetle. Alastair cursed, but with a smile still frozen to him he walked back through to the kitchen. He clicked his fingers. Dr. Snippet's eyes flickered open and he pulled himself up from the table that was strewn with small glass phials and medical papers.

'My dear boy,' the doctor said, 'I am becoming more forgetful every day. I had quite forgotten you were here.'

≈

The boy had to be stopped; the police would have to be told. Alastair had become insane. Brood Stalk's head reeled and he wanted to be sick when he remembered the vile fate of Stubb. He had hated the fool but would not have wished that upon him. He shuddered; the situation smacked of witchcraft, he thought, devilry even. He began his journey to the police station when he changed his mind. He would go to his shop first to warm himself, to calm his juddering nerves and, more importantly, to fetch a crucifix. He felt foolish at the thought until he felt the vomit rising up to his throat again. He sensed that there was more to what was happening than Alastair losing his mind, something he could not define but which all the same made his flesh creep. He couldn't even remember why he had wielded a meat cleaver and chased William Stubb.

❧

'There we are, Alastair. There is nothing quite like Mr. Pikesquallor's unequaled mint and camomile tea to soothe the nerves, I always say,' said Dr. Snippet kindly. He placed the cup on the table.

'You old crow,' Alastair growled. He brought his arm down and swept it aside and it smashed onto the floor, the contents leaping from the cup and spilling over the tiles.

'Now what on earth possessed you to do that?' said the doctor in a hurt voice. He opened a drawer to take out a cloth to clean up the mess.

'Leave it,' snapped Alastair.

The doctor looked up enquiringly. 'But the tea—'

Alastair spoke through clenched teeth. 'You heard what I said, you stupid crank.'

'Well really, Alastair. That is not the sort of language I expect to hear. You must behave yourself or I shall be forced to tell your father.' He wagged his finger in reprimand.

Alastair's eyes glinted and, upon seeing the stern face of the doctor, he gave a hearty guffaw. Then as though a tap had been turned, his face lost its mirth and he said, 'You won't be talking to William. No one will.'

'What do you mean? My dear boy, I don't think' – he stepped lightly over to Alastair and placed a comforting arm around his shoulder – 'that you have yet fully recovered from your small illness.'

Theodore as Alastair shrugged the doctor off. He barked, 'Leave me be. You're fit for nothing but retirement, something you should have done fifteen years ago.' With a scowl, he left the kitchen.

In the hallway, he paused by the cleaver embedded in the

banister finial. It was alive with leeches. He stroked the blade and departed.

Dr. Snippet fell onto a chair, feeling miserable and not quite sure what to do next.

CHAPTER 43

The Butcher

THERE HAD BEEN a time when Florence Dripping had felt an inner peace within or an excitement through some small change for the better in her fortunes. It was occasions like these when she would exude a sense of well-being, giving happiness to her eyes and putting a fresh accent upon her palsied features. Though her mouth would be as ever paralyzed it would project a hint of a smile; her cheeks as taught as ever, the promise of a cheerful expression. But when her life had taken a wrong turning, the distorted visage would be exaggerated the more. A minor upset only was enough to affect her; her face would project a melancholic and forbidding dejection, robbing her of years, forcing the judgement upon others of believing she was much older than she was.

She thought of her daughter and missed her so. At least the girl was safe, recuperating with her Aunt Beatrice in Grinding. It had taken an hour or more before Abergail had ceased her hysterical shedding of tears to be able to give her lamentations. She had been confused as to the exact whereabouts of the man's attack though she remembered it was not too far from the village green clock tower; and that he wore round glasses and had white curly hair. The brute! The swine! Much willpower had been required to prevent Florence from attacking Mr. Nuckle. His self-righteous denials did not fool her. She saw his ranting upon the village green in her mind's eye and then remembered Alastair sitting upon the ice-covered bench smoking a cigar. A nagging feeling was telling her that something was amiss; that he was somehow connected. He had acted in a most peculiar way, quite unlike the actions of a boy. And what could he have spoken about to the butcher which had been so important as to cause Brood Stalk to walk to his shop?

She put her worries into words. The constable sympathized but could not find any reason to search for Alastair although after some inducement and seeing Florence's dismal expression he agreed that they should find him. He felt it would lead to nothing but was willing to try if there was a chance it could throw some light on the Nuckle affair.

Four of the local youths had followed the determined couple from the police station. Although their eagerness to help had satisfied the policeman, Florence was not so convinced. They lagged behind, dressed more for summer than for the biting day and they chatted and laughed as though on a country ramble.

❧

Alastair was blinkered, his sight constricted, or so he felt; the perception of the snow-smothered green before him hampered as though seen through a tube. The voice within had become more demanding; his lips were numbed and yet he heard himself say words which he had no intention of speaking. Even the control of his own body had been lost: he would go to places where he had not wanted to be. Reality was transforming into a real nightmare. Objects appeared insubstantial, mere abstractions of their original selves. He had difficulty in concentrating to remember the events of the day before or indeed, even the events of that very day. Why he was walking towards the butcher's shop, he did not know; the knowledge of where he had been, impossible to find. It was as though he had awakened from a long slumber only to find he was more tired that before he had slept. His eyelids felt heavy again; the irresistible tugging of sleep, producing a delicious languor, a drowsy submission. He tried to speak but his tongue had lost all feeling and it flopped about his mouth. Then, with a whispered, smooth tone dispelling any last remnants of consciousness, he knew no more.

He walked unhurriedly, though now he spoke with an urgency. 'The fool thinks he has escaped me.' He paused on the cobblestones outside the butcher's shop before peering through the window. A few lumps of meat, hacked without consideration, sat quietly rotting upon the marble slab; battered weighing scales stood on the counter and behind that was the tree stump with cuts and slits gathered over an age. The cleaver was not at home. An iron rail ran the length of two sides of the shop with meat hooks hanging from them, all bare save for one which held a shrunken side of pork.

Receipts, pen tops, bent keys, unpaid bills, chewed pencils, buttons, waste paper and bits of metal and wood lay in a heap on the floor while Stalk scrabbled about in the depths of the drawer of his sideboard. Panic clung to his throat. He could not find a crucifix and he cursed. He told himself to hurry; he imagined that Alastair had murdered Dr. Snippet and was on his way to murder him. A boy all the same, though puffing on a fat cigar and for all the world sounding like Theodore. He shuddered and yawned to stifle his churning stomach; he had seen Stubb in his mind's eye with the multitude of insects burrowing and squirming into him. The cry still echoed through his head. He was more convinced than ever that it was supernatural. Creatures in their millions do not appear from nowhere and boys do not take on the mannerisms and voice of a long dead man. Where was that crucifix?

Unable to find it in the drawer he went from his sitting room into the store room of the shop and heard the bell make its sound.

With the noise of shuffling feet reaching his ears, he flinched and the back of his neck stiffened. Valuable time had been wasted. His hand shook as he clasped it over his mouth. Alastair knew where he was, he was convinced. He would have to hide.

⁂

Florence cried out, 'Look!' and with her arm outstretched, she pointed a finger. The policeman and the self-appointed entourage turned their heads. There, between the winter-ravaged branches of the trees along Stutter Lane could be seen the white rooftops of houses and shops on the two sides of the green. Billows of dark smoke rose from them into the wintry air, twisting and turning like kite tails.

'My house; my shop!' Florence screeched and she broke into a run, her scarf dropping from about her neck, the ends swinging wildly with every step she took. Her five companions followed in chase.

Once Florence had reached the end of the lane at the perimeter of the green, she stopped running and stood in a stunned amazement. The policeman and the four young men reached her and all fell silent at the bizarre sight which confronted them.

The snow, previously a stretch of a pure whiteness, blemished only by indentations from boots and shoes, was peppered liberally with flies. They crawled over each other or hovered in puffs over its surface. They flew in grey and black patches and tumbling columns; what Florence had thought to be smoke from the buildings were clouds of houseflies and horseflies. Bluebottles lay their eggs amongst pupating larvae, four-winged mayflies mingled with thrips while flat stoneflies vied with alder flies for position on the ground. Snakeflies crawled over the large, membranous wings of lacewing flies and pincered scorpion flies fought and maimed any opponent. With their long, thread-like antennae, caddis flies sought out nesting places, oblivious to the absence of heat. There was a dull, low drone from the abundance of tiny wings. Large areas of snow were being furrowed and sculpted to form holes for egg laying. The cold air was slashed with black lines and it vibrated with their vast number.

A woman flung open the door of her cottage and marched out onto the cobbles to join other villagers there. She held an old net stocking to her face and wielded a fly swat as though a sword. She bid good day to Mr. Fishcake who, being so engrossed in looking to his feet and stamping the ground in an attempt to crush the invaders, did not reply. Over on the other side, upstairs window shutters of The Bulldog Fish Tavern were opened with a violence and a yelling Chess let out a myriad of mosquitoes from his bedroom. His customers stood about outside on the cobbles, shouting encouragement and advice up to him, waving their hands before their faces as though to cool themselves before a hot sun to distract any flying creature.

Chess was in a dilemma. His habit of cuddling himself was being severely affected: once he had wrapped his arms about him, midges would become tangled in his hair and crawl into his clothing. He paddled the two limbs and with shudders coursing down his spine, wriggled about and slapped his chest and legs. Any attempt to replace his arms to their usual position resulted in a repeat of the ridiculous performance. His hands and face were spotted with stinging bites. He cried out to the saloon bar for Miss Crouch to help but she ignored his call from upstairs, too busy with sweeping away strings of beetles emerging from the skirting boards.

The clock tower began to strike the hour of twelve; though the full quota of tolls was not supplied. Upon the fifth peal, the clock glass shattered and the hour hand fell to the stone plinth, followed by the minute hand which impaled the frozen ground. With the weight of numberless insects behind it, the clock face was pushed from its spindle. It fell away and hit the tower base with a clatter. The interior – usually a private and solemn domain – was rudely exposed, and it teemed with spiders of all types, jamming the cogs and blocking the bells.

Dr. Snippet ran screaming and half-blind, (for he had had no time to put on his spectacles,) pursued along Daisytrail Lane by a squadron of wasps.

Florence looked disconcertedly at the ruined monument and the invasion. 'This is impossibly unusual,' she said. 'Can we find Mr. Stalk now?' she asked. 'I would feel better if he was here.'

The constable took mild offence and a step back at this remark and replied, 'I am sure that my special training and expertise in all forms of crime and civil situations would be more than enough for any contingency, Miss Dripping. I really should be alerting the station to this dire insect problem.'

Florence was insistent. 'I want to find him. I feel we really must. He went to his butcher shop.'

'I don't think you know what you want,' Constable Flute stated. Florence stared back at him and her distorted features hardened. 'All the same,' the policeman added with a long sigh. Ignoring the phenomenon taking place on the village green he pointed a finger at random to the youths. 'Alastair was last seen heading for the doctor's house,' he explained. 'You go. See if he's there.' The appointed youth trotted off, glad that he didn't have to cross the infested green. 'Let's see if we can find Stalk then,' the constable said to Florence. 'I must admit, something's not quite right here.'

The understatement made, Florence and the four men began the trek across to Brood Stalk's butcher's shop, angry insects flying in swathes.

৯১

Alastair smiled. Reaching into the top pocket of his jacket he extracted his half-smoked cigar and ran it through his fingers. He was in no rush.

Stalk was in a hurry. With every muscle taut, he tiptoed back into the modest sitting room and wondered where to hide. He would feel insecure behind the settee and, as if to prove it, he crouched on all fours and immediately stood up again. He looked through the window to the small garden. There was surely no escape. The insects knew where he was. His breathing began to rasp hoarsely as he took in the ravaged evergreens, the light brown brick wall turned to a mass of black, the garden shed quivering with insects as though alive. He looked about him within the grip of a stark terror and ran to the narrow, steep stairs but even as he reached the top of his staircase he knew that there would be nowhere to hide. Even if there were, he could be enclosed and easy prey for the mad boy. He felt the hairs rise on the back of his neck.

He was trapped.

There was a clattering noise from the shop and it fanned the flame of panic. He remembered his cupboard in the store room.

If he could reach there to hide before Alastair came through from the shop, he might have a chance. He would lock himself in until the crazed boy had gone. Then the butcher flushed with relief as a thought unfolded. It might not be Alastair after all. It could be Mrs. Battlespoke waiting for her quarter of mince.

He ran back down the stairs to the sitting room and stuck

his head around the doorframe which led to the store room. There was the scratchy wheezing of his breath. He rubbed his hands together briskly. He was sure it was getting colder. How he hated the cold. If only he could have found his gloves.

He stared hard at the closed door which opened onto the shop and wished he could see through it. He had a plan. If he was to attract Alastair's attention, the boy would enter and Stalk would hit him on the head – not too hard – with a frozen chicken. It would be in self-defence. But what if it was not Alastair but Mrs. Battlespoke or Colonel Midwitty? The idea was not a practical one. He trod lightly over to the store cupboard, his sight never leaving the door to the shop. He could walk through at any moment, a mad boy with a meat cleaver.

Florence pressed her nose to the butcher's shop window again.

'No amount of looking will make him be there,' remarked the policeman with a hint of annoyance. 'And as I told you, he said he was going to Mr. Stubb's house. He may have come back here but I'm sure he's not here now. Anyway, I'm going back to the station. I have other tasks, you know. Paperwork piling up; have a go at that typewriter again; warn the parish council of infestation.'

'I do realize this. But I've told you, I feel it in my bones; something is wrong.'

'If there was any trouble, I would handle it, Miss Dripping,' answered Constable Flute. He puffed out his chest and tugged at the lapels of his uniform.

'Of course you would,' replied Florence, unsure as to whether she truly believed that. 'Anyway, I'm going inside.'

'As you wish,' answered the policeman with a resigned sigh.

Stalk had been standing in front of the store cupboard still unsure of whether he was making the right decision but, upon hearing footsteps from the shop, he grasped the handle and pulled.

'Strange,' remarked Florence, 'perhaps it needed mending.' The brass doorbell lay on the mat. The still air was broken by a shout that came from the store room.

Constable Flute did not waste time. 'Quick,' he demanded of the villagers, 'follow me.' He held the door handle to the store room, twisted and pushed. The door remained firm. 'It's locked,' he muttered, almost indignantly.

'You,' shouted Stalk in the storeroom, 'do you know what you're doing?' The butcher backed away as Alastair advanced from the store cupboard with a firm grip on the handle of a boning knife. He chuckled and growled alternately, sounding like a dog worrying a beef bone, and with shoulders hunched, his eyes bright and twirling the knife blade in a circle, he quickened his pace towards Stalk.

They both ignored the raised voices and the sound of a heavy object crashing into the door which led to the shop. It shuddered but did not open.

Stalk wanted to speak but his words were lost suddenly when Alastair leapt at him and grabbed him by the throat. The butcher clutched frantically at the small hands which squeezed in a vice-like grip. His face seemed to swell and it became a repellent shade of red. For fear of toppling over, he staggered backwards as Alastair pushed upon his neck. His reversing was suddenly curtailed when he felt his back against the large walk-in refrigerator.

'Open it up,' demanded Alastair.

Stalk could not see the knife but knew it was held to his stomach. He felt it jab his flesh. He put a warted hand behind him and fumbled for the refrigerator handle and then, with some difficulty, pulled the door open. Icy fingers crawled from the interior onto his back.

'Unlock this door,' shouted Constable Flute from the shop, and another shoulder-ramming from him made the door quiver.

'Rat poison, Brood? Kill me? You should use it on rats you big oaf. Rats!' sputtered Alastair as flecks of saliva foamed at the corners of his mouth. Brood Stalk cried out as the thin point of the knife entered his stomach. A bright red spot grew in size to join those congealed on his apron. 'Not only that, but you wanted to lay your dirty paws on Eleanor. She is mine, do you hear?' His bellowing too deep for a boy, him pushing the whining butcher into the refrigerator. The white ice turned to black as Alastair heaved the door shut.

'No, no no, let me out, you!' Stalk screamed. He beat on the door with his fists and then thrashed about in blind dread but knocked his head on a large joint of beef which hung down in the darkness. He reeled forward and upon hitting his head again with a thud, slumped to the iced floor, cold and unconscious.

'Open up, I say,' shouted the constable for a second time. He threw his shoulder to the entrance again.

Alastair walked over and in a pause when the door was not being struck, he turned the key and held the handle down: thus upon the next strike to the door, it flung open without effort and the policeman was sent sprawling into the store room. He fell and skidded along the sawdusted floor on his front. He was stopped when his head hit the refrigerator. He lay still.

'Mr. Flute!' Florence Dripping cried out. She ran to him and gently turned the big man over. The three villagers followed briskly, concern on their faces and murmuring sympathies. The policeman groaned and rubbed his sore head. He pulled himself to his feet, aided by Florence and Sammy Solomon.

'You alright sir?' said the farmer's son. The policeman nodded and pulled out a handkerchief to dab his burning nose.

He winced when he touched his grazed face. Brushing himself down and thanking his helpers, he looked about the store room.

'Well, there isn't anyone here now. They've scarpered,' he said. 'If you come along with me, Sammy – you're a hefty lad – we'll have a look upstairs.'

Before they could move, Alastair leapt out from behind the door and gave a yelp. All eyes turned to him. He stood with both hands behind his back and his boyish features twisted into a veneer of hatred. He gazed at them. 'So sorry, best bacon is off today,' he sneered.

'Alastair, where is Mr. Stalk?' Florence said and she took a few paces towards him before being rooted to the spot: he produced the boning knife from behind his back and jabbed it threateningly towards her.

'No further, Florence,' was Alastair's harsh command.

'How dare you use my first name again,' Miss Dripping said. 'Alastair, what has got into you? Are you still feeling ill?'

'Bloody hypocrite,' Alastair screamed.

'Now really,' the policeman interjected, 'keep your foul mouth to yourself, youngster. Especially in front of a lady.'

'A lady? Our tittering maid a lady?'

Florence Dripping gasped and blushed. 'You don't realize what you are saying, Alastair.'

'Don't call me Alastair. This is Theodore you are speaking to.' The villagers threw glances to each other. 'Jumped into my bed, she did,' Alastair whispered coarsely. 'Made a regular habit of it.' He addressed the whole group. 'How do you think Abergail came into being? Why do you think she keeps the girl a prisoner? Young unmarried maid, pregnant? None of you knew she existed.'

'The boy has gone totally mad. He doesn't know what he's talking about,' moaned Florence Dripping imploringly to all.

How could he know of her past? When she was a maid in the Stubb household, even William Stubb would not have known such details. Even if he did, she knew that he was loathe to talk about times gone, let alone impart such intimate facts to his son.

The policeman was not looking at Florence, but instead kept a steady gaze on the boning knife. He had been edging towards the boy, inch by inch, but not slowly enough, for Alastair threw his head forward and his derision vanished. He stabbed with the knife.

'Don't you take a step nearer or I will cut you up for lamb cutlets,' he threatened and he backed out of the doorway into the shop.

Nobody moved until he had jerked the front door open and was running across the green, grinding insects into the snow with his boots.

'After him,' shouted PC Flute.

'But what about Mr. Stalk?' said Florence Dripping.

'It doesn't look as though he's here, does it?'

'But I heard his voice, I'm sure I did.'

'We'll look for Stalk later,' answered the policeman. 'Come on, let's catch the scoundrel boy.'

CHAPTER 44

The Chase

BROOD STALK THE butcher gained a vague, disembodied, frozen consciousness; enough to listen to his own last few heartbeats before the cold darkness about him departed and was replaced by a warmer, blacker nothingness. And, with a weak heart giving way, eyelids frozen open, and fingers white and set as though carved into claws, he died.

The landlord's spectators had dispersed to resume their drinking inside the public bar. Their excited discussion continued on the strange appearance of the insects, picking some wriggling from their jugs and pints of ale; watching them scurry over the plaster and crooked beams on the uneven walls.

Alastair awoke as though from escaping a dream. He found himself standing on the green by The Bulldog Fish Tavern, its snow-laden roof seemingly peppered with soot. 'What am I doing here?' he asked himself. His hands had numbed and felt to him as though he was wearing gloves. He looked down to them and upon seeing the long but thin boning knife which he held by the blade, he dropped it as if it was a scorching poker. The snow swallowed it. He was baffled by the sight of sore and bleeding cuts across his palm, then to the generous amounts of flies dotted about him, the furious buzzing while busy with their flying and nest building.

There were shouts and Alastair turned to look back across the green over to the length of small buildings which included the butcher shop and tea room shouldering each other.

Hazy, dark clouds of insects masked them, shifting this way and that.

Catching sight of the policeman and the other villagers paddling their way through the blooms of insects, Alastair began to jog casually towards them, expecting them to stop. When he saw that they kept on running, with angry and determined faces – one of them shouting, 'Come here you little devil' – he turned sharply to their right. With his energetic legs, he easily ran a half-circle about with a wide berth, to behind them, heading for the straight-through alley which was next to the wooden shuttering over the blacksmiths and the large spoked cart wheels of the wheelwright on the other side.

He went quickly through the alley and out onto the lumpy white track which led down past farmer Solomon's field. The land held the ghost of Thimriddy Fair and odd snow shapes, hiding rusted tractor wheels and other abandoned farming equipment.

With the help of a slight decline, Alastair accelerated his pace in an attempt to escape his pursuers. Several times he nearly tumbled to the ground when stumbling over dead vines and iced roots. Bushes tore at his clothes and he slipped and slid.

Ranks of bees flew from the trees, and a host of woodlice and weevils were swarming from holes in their wood. Earwigs in their thousands walked the same path.

Alastair held a strange elation that he could not explain. There was a feeling of achievement close by, as though an episode in his life was about to end. He stopped for a moment to catch his breath before looking back from where he had run.

Four figures jogged along the track, coming even closer, though he had gained a lot of ground in front of them with his younger limbs and lighter frame. Not that it mattered if they caught him, he knew; it was still a dream. He pinched his arm. Sure enough, he did not feel anything.

After a minute he found that the track levelled before starting a gentle incline. There was no mistaking the reason for Reverend Musty asking to abandon the church and for wanting another to be built on the scrubland surrounding the canal; Alastair was puffing and sweating from his armpits.

He lost all sense of time. When he reached the zenith of the hill, the church still a way onward, he stood panting for breath, moisture puffing from him as steam; and he gazed down to the village spread out below. The cool sky was clear and cloudless. The village green was grey with its insects, a patch of the muted quilt spread over the hills and slopes that formed the other side of the valley. The chattering brook wound its way down to the scrubland. A writhing mist played along the horizon. Isolated accumulations of insects rose from the scene before dispersing like steam or powder. The afternoon sun had become surprisingly warm for the season.

To the east, the smoking stacks of Grinding sent their dark vapours to the sky. He scanned the panorama again and his eye was caught by a bird wheeling and diving in the expansive sea of air. It floated for a while as though suspended on an invisible wire then pumped its wings and began to shrink until it was a speck of dust hanging over the side of the valley. He looked down to the track again and saw the four pursuers beginning the climb of the hill. They were no more than a minute away.

But what attracted his attention more was the abandoned family church alongside Dr. Snippet's manor house, there in the distance along Daisytrail Lane. A colossal dusty ball hung over it. All varieties of flying insects were hovering in position above its spire to form the perfect sphere. The shape made by their collaborative efforts flattened to oblate – becoming wider than the depth of it – only for the spheroid to morph into prolate, and then back again – flattening, then becoming taller again and thinning, flattening and thinning – as if the individual organic components making up the insect ball had become one breathing animal. But then, like a flock of birds or shoal of fish, wide curling strands emerged, depleting the sphere until it was no more, those strands weaving and flailing, curving and spiralling. New granulated black shapes were made fleetingly against the white of the sky; melancholic faces, oil lamps and candles.

Alastair stretched the muscles in his limbs and recovered from his exertion. He turned around, running back down another plain snowed track which came out into farmer Solomon's sheep field at the top of it. There was excitement within; he felt as though it was a game and that he was escaping from men with guns or crazed chimpanzees.

'There he is, we'll get him now,' called out one of the youths, and Alastair's pursuers pushed their way through undergrowth in a tree grove before coming out into the same field.

CHAPTER 45

The Church

A LASTAIR REACHED THE bottom of the white, blank
field and climbed over a wide gate into the quietness that
was Marshmallow Lane. He ran along a verge so as to
disguise his footprints. Not far down the tree-lined track was
Mrs. Wickling's ramshackle cottage sunken at the bottom of a
bank of wild snow-covered shrubbery, as though hiding. From
there, he jogged along to the end of the lane and turned right
into Daisytrail Lane. The manor house was ahead but before
it stood the flint wall surrounding the church. He ran the ten
yards or so, turned and skipped through the brick archway
of the derelict graveyard, brushing past the abundance of ivy
daubed with snow.

Row upon row of snow-crested tombstones stood at all
angles. Nature had overtaken: the alabaster figures strangled by
vines; the graves overgrown with weeds and nettles; all layered
with whiteness, flawless and clean. He took great pleasure from
being the first to impress the drifts with his footprints before
leap-frogging over tombstones and patting carved memorial
figures on their stone feet. He made his way up to the church and
glanced at epitaphs as he went. Such phrases on the monuments
for the dead were weather-worn, or snow and moss-covered,
though others, perhaps chiselled deeper into the stone, could
still be read: "Josiah Crookneck. May He Rest With the Angels
in Paradise" and "To our darling daughter Ermintrude Pole,
taken from us so early in life".

Alastair glanced to the left, over the wall to the back garden of the manor house. The marble statue there writhed with the countless insects upon it. The pair of angel wings fell from its shoulder blades into the mounds of pure snow about it.

The church stood with stained glass windows smashed and the stonework weathered and crumbling. Either side of the outer archway could once have boasted fine sculpture that was now marred and unrecognizable. A blackbird on the roof – still many insects there to be seen – let out a croak of a birdcall and flew into the writhing swirls. Alastair pulled on the large door, hanging by one hinge, and to his surprise it swung open wider without much effort.

He came into the nave of the church from the entry porch. A stench of decay and other musty odours emitted from within the interior. Suspensions of dust hung about, picked out by shafts of light that were thrown through the broken coloured windows and breaches in the roof. Pews were haphazardly scattered throughout, many upturned or laying on their backs, and carvings that had adorned them strewn about as though a giant hand had swept them all into confusion.

Alastair picked his way through the wreckage and stood as though in reverence before the bare altar. Cobwebs spanned arches and pillars, and weeds had pushed up through the mosaics and flagstones on the floor of the church. The pulpit lay on its side and was broken and splintered, covered with stone chips and fine powder. Though every step that Alastair took reverberated within the building, a deadness seemed to envelop all else, swallowing the few sounds which came from outside.

A shower of dust fell onto his head as there was a flurry of wings above him. Looking up he saw a group of pigeons swoop from their lofty perches in the vaulting before disappearing through a gap in the side of the nave. There, on the column capitals between each clerestory window, weird carvings of beasts and imaginary creatures jutted, all with jaws, mouths or jowls agape, their stone tongues hanging down.

Alastair decided he should hide. His nose began to run so he wiped it with his sleeve and as he did so he saw a door to his left, shielded behind a large pillar. The door was heavy and ornately carved. He went to its brass ring and turned it and pushed to open it. Beyond was another door and a landing with a flight of granite steps leading down. He opened this second door to find a small room lit by a subdued light coming from a half-boarded stained glass window set high into one wall. The place had been the vestry. Alastair kicked at the shards of glass and bricks and rubbish. He pulled open the drawers of an upturned writing desk and found that they were all empty save some sticks of chalk and pen nibs. He saw the many boxes of candles piled waist high at the end of the vestry, but disregarded them for he felt suddenly exhausted.

'You must get tired,' he muttered, 'even in a dream.' His head felt light. He rubbed his eyes with dusty hands. There was a familiar buzzing and then the fatherly voice, soft and soothing; and, not bothering to listen to the words, he drifted to some dark, quiet corner of his mind where he could be warm and safe and asleep.

Theodore, within the stolen spirit of his son Alastair, bent and picked up one of the candles from a torn carton. It was one of the smaller and thinner ones, and although he saw much larger and thicker candles in crates, he decided his choice would be adequate. He lit it with a match taken from his matchbox. He shielded the flame from a wayward draught and after spluttering and spitting wax and sending out a coil of black smoke, the candle settled and burned steadily. He walked through to the top of the steps then, waiting for a moment only, began to descend.

Constable Flute gasped for breath in Daisytrail Lane and surveyed the white graveyard before him. The muscles in his legs were so fatigued that they shook. He and the group of three youths stood for a full minute without speaking. They had been running the wrong way along Marshmallow Lane. Finally the policeman said, 'Right. If you three patrol the outer walls, I'll go inside the church to see if I can find the little scoundrel. Understood?'

The young men nodded and after a brief discussion as to who would take which side, all four walked through to the graveyard with determination. They began to disperse until the constable shouted out, 'Wait!' He looked to the ground and all followed suit. Winding its way before them about the gravestones and up to the outer porch of the church was a set of footprints in the snow. 'Quickly,' the policeman ordered. 'All inside.'

CHAPTER 46

Crypts

THEODORE – OR AT least some impression of his mind overtaking the now sleeping mind of Alastair – stood at the bottom of the steps, the mildew-covered walls brought to life by the shadow of a boy prancing across them, cast from the flickering candle.

Along the top edge of the stone corridor ahead, in between arches, were large and thick panes of glass set at ground level outside, allowing sunlight or strong moonlight to illuminate the corridor through them. Oil lamps at intervals were there also, hung on hooks down the length of the corridor, as well as a child's toys – clockwork amusements, dolls, playing cards, board games – laid neatly in a line.

The being within Alastair, that which was not Alastair, was not truly Theodore either. At least, it was not Theodore as he had been in life. It was a distillation of the man's inner self, his hopes and desires and ambitions, his evil and cunning. It was the embodiment of all of these characteristics and it was strong enough to live on and to steal another's corporeal self. But though an unusual type of consciousness existed for this version of Theodore to be aware of his final task, memories of the crypts and grey-shadowed corridors had left him. He was vaguely familiar with the place though he could not remember how and a feeling of unease began to grow.

He quickly reached the end of the first corridor under the church's length for it opened out to a small crypt, emptied of its tombs and religious artefacts. Upon walking its perimeter he saw that the place had been inhabited. The larger lights – those thick blocks of glass to allow light through, set in the stone ceiling – indicated that the crypt projected past the church, for even though the glasses were mostly snow-covered, light from the sun still managed to penetrate the gloom, sending feeble shafts underground. Sunlight even found its way through some of the airbricks set high up.

There was an abundance of straw on the ground and the smell of staleness and stagnation. He found a set of bowls, one with the remains of a meal soiling it, and then he came across three stoneware jars as well as piles of clothing, blankets, mugs and utensils in alcoves set in one end.

He coughed and the sound echoed about him and disappeared into the mysterious corners. Continuing the tour of the perimeter and trying not to touch the wet mossed walls, he discovered another corridor as he had expected, leading under the width of the church. It was wider than the first.

Coldness and dampness. The sound of dripping water from behind one of the walls. With an unexplainable sense of urgency pushing him along he began to walk briskly. The snow on the glass lights here must have been heavier, he thought. It was a short while after when the borrowed eyes became more accustomed to the darkness ahead and it was then he noticed the blackness seemed blacker still, richer and deeper in quality. The yellow light from the candle ate the darkness before him and he was confronted with a wall across his way: the corridor had taken a sharp turn to the left. This must be under the other longer side of the church, he decided. He followed it. Striding at a steady pace, he soon shrugged off the damp chill and felt warmer.

He discovered a small tunnel leading from one side. It had

slabs on its sides roughly hewn and was no more than four feet high. A cap which lay broken must have masked it at some time in the past. A priest's secret passage, he decided. He ignored it in preference to his arched corridor.

The corridor came to an end with a heavy wooden door barring his way. He tugged at the handle but it did not budge. Looking it over, only a trickle of memories seeped through to him. He shuddered at its sight though he did not know the reason. He quickened his pace away for he felt uneasy. He turned and inspected the candle. Already the cheap and poor quality wax had burned a quarter of its length.

A feeling of heaviness and oppression. Theodore wiped the back of the stolen neck and forehead with a hand. He sat down on a stone arch base to rest: he sensed the young body he inhabited was dangerously weary.

He stood and made his way back to the priest hole.

Taking hold of a side of the cold entrance and bending, he extended the other hand gripping the candle and entered. He shuffled along, kicking flints and stones, those rattling out of his path. He stopped after a few seconds only to rub an aching back which he was beginning to feel.

Further on, there had been a fall of dirt and rocks, narrowing the way still further. He went to his hands and knees and was forced to crawl along now.

With practice he found that by holding the candle from the ground with one hand, he could slide along over the piles of earth and boulders at a surprisingly fast rate on Alastair's remaining limbs. His trousers wore holes, and the knees and a hand bled. The pain was not his; the body of Alastair a borrowed convenience for Theodore's essence. He quickly learned how to transfer the pain to its rightful owner.

The spirit of Alastair, tucked away within his own persona,

wanted to shout in anger as his warm dream was turning into a cold nightmare. If he was tucked up in his bed asleep then why did his limbs seem tired and painful and why did they sting so and why was his back sore?

Theodore knew that the time was near. Because of the speed that he crawled, he did not see a large projection jutting down from above. He was not quick enough to avoid it; Alastair's forehead hit it and the agony that punched his brow caught him unawares. Theodore was roughly jolted back to his private purgatory and the essence of Alastair unfolded and bloomed to fill the whole of him once more from the dark corner of his being.

The ambushed passageway was plunged into darkness as the candle was dropped and extinguished. Alastair moaned and rubbed his head. His fingers felt warm and sticky. He groaned in terror: however wide he stretched his eyelids he could not see anything save for strange translucent amoeba shapes of purples, greens and blues that convulsed and floated past his vision. Upon a closer scrutiny they would vanish only to appear at the periphery of his sight. All this was on a backdrop of a dense, impenetrable darkness. He had gone blind, he was certain, in this tortuous nightmare; his cosy place of sleep had turned to something cold and hard. He whined in confusion and groped along the sides of his prison, an ultimate dread taking hold. His thighs shook and he collapsed onto his face as they gave way. He sobbed without measure.

It was then that something happened. He ceased his miserable weeping when, upon shifting what he thought was a small rock from under his outstretched leg, he discovered what felt to be a candle. Then as soon as his crying had ceased, another voice was heard at an indeterminable distance ahead. It was laughter, high and free of inhibition and echoing strangely.

The remainder of the candle was broken into two, he could feel. He sensed the unknown horrors of the darkness creep closer. Instinctively he felt in his pockets and, to his surprise, found a shape he knew to be a box of matches – previously placed in his pocket when under Theodore's influence. He ignored the deranged laughter and fumbled for a match. He struck it and shielded his eyes from the blinding flash. With his eyelids pressed to slits, he lit the candle. It was a few moments before he was used to the light from the flame and saw that the tunnel turned suddenly to the right.

Turning the corner, he looked with fascination and chuckled excitedly when he saw the dark stone tunnel, touching it to feel its texture; as he smelled the sulphur fumes of the match. He knew his nightmare had vanished and he was dreaming again, no matter how peculiar it seemed. He resumed the underground journey onward towards the steady glow lighting the exit, dragging his feet behind him.

⁂

'There's no sign of him, sir,' reported one young man as he scanned the church's dilapidated balcony.

'I suggest we all look harder then,' replied Constable Flute.

'I've discovered some steps and I reckon he's down there.'

'I think he's hopped it over the hills again,' someone else remarked. 'Could be on his way to Stillstone by now.'

The policeman ignored him. 'While you three make a more thorough search up here I'll go down those steps to see what I can find.' He puffed out his chest and feeling an irritating itch to his head, he put his hand up but found himself scratching his helmet.

'You'll need someone to help,' suggested Sammy Solomon.

Constable Flute was secretly relieved. 'Agreed. You will do nicely,' he decided, nodding his head towards him.

The constable was led to the stone steps, the other two men splitting off to search. PC Flute warned Sammy, 'Now, don't you say a word unless I speak to you.' With a flick of his thumb he switched on his police regulation torch.

CHAPTER 47

Finale

A LASTAIR GAPED AT the pulsing illumination ahead. He found that he could walk with his back stooped again and when finally out of the passageway, could stand upright. The laughter had ceased, the only sounds being his own panting breath.

He watched the large catacomb with suspicion. The glow he had seen came from thick candles which stood on tombs and sarcophagi, and encircling the pillars of stone and wooden posts, as well as being lit by more glass lights above from the church's floor letting in the diluted sun's rays. This sunlight threw stripes across the sculptures and carvings. Around each candle was a scarf of wax built up to strange and contorted shapes. A fetid smell; the straw that was scattered about was orange and black; a mass of cobwebs hung in dark corners. A rat scurried across a tomb and disappeared.

Alastair furtively went into the underground chamber and held his nose at the stench of the place. Life-size figures of stone lay broken on the floor between tombs. He crept forward and noticed that from one end of the left wall decorated with pilasters was the opening of a short corridor, the line of toys and juvenile amusements from it, flanked by candles and oil lamps, continuing across the icon-painted floor, to a stone archway. Whatever was beyond was shrouded in the darkness. Alastair went to the short corridor lit with candlelight and saw the heavy door which Theodore controlling

Alastair had found; a bar of wood across it had kept it from opening.

As Alastair was looking in his hazy dreamstate over the main crypt he felt weary and began to sway when heard the familiar voice. This time he tried to fight but he was too weak to combat it. Finally letting go of consciousness, he again slept in a small corner of his mind.

Eyelids flickered and now Theodore looked about. He walked along by the wall to the archway, kicking toys, and candles falling and rolling away, taking a step into this other part of the catacomb. He could make out vague impressions – ghost-like tombs set into the walls but nothing more. Going back to one of the candled tombs in the main part, he pulled a candle from its moorings and resumed his place before the archway and as the fingers of light groped along the walls, they showed a hazy shape. There was a muffled snigger. The shape became larger, gaining definition until it lost its fluidity and upon emerging from the darkness, took on human form.

Queenie – the mad Eleanor – corrugating her nose and looking bored, pointed downward. Theodore automatically followed the line of her finger and stared blankly at her big toe that wiggled through a hole in one of her green slippers. The spell was broken; he advanced towards her. The trickle of memories had grown to a stream.

'You sorceress, Eleanor!' he hollered with his voice echoing from the bricks and granite. 'You, more than all the others, must realize how you hurt me; and how much love I held for you.'

Queenie cocked her head to one side as if recognizing her name before taking exaggerated steps backwards. Theodore followed her under an arch which led to yet another foul-smelling and cobweb-tangled chamber. With him holding the candle threateningly as though a weapon, Queenie leapt backwards and from the few strands of light that escaped into this section of the catacomb, she was seen to leap about, pirouetting and jumping in a frenzied dance of madness. She pranced and gyrated, twirling her arms and crowed and shouted. Theodore stood waiting.

Suddenly, as if by some unseen cue, she ceased her insane ballet. She threw her head back in a snap and gripped her ears, emitting a high-pitched wail; a sickening monotone that made Theodore hold teeth together. He ignored the outburst and spoke gently but forcefully.

'Eleanor, this is Alastair. Your son, your offspring. Come here and stand before me.' His softened voice acted like a potion on her ill and tormented mind and she ceased her wailing and gave him a quizzical look. 'Yes, your child, your baby.'

He pointed to a spot a yard in front of him. As though in a hypnotic trance, the woman advanced, her arms outstretched and her eyes bulging as she stared to the ceiling, and she crooned, 'Bay–beeee…'

Theodore felt he must frighten her, perhaps even to shock her from her madness. All he would wish was for her to be frightened by flame, as he was frightened, and burned, in the attic fire thirteen years ago. He bent the knees of Alastair until he was low to the ground and leant as far forward as he was able without toppling. Then he extended an arm and touched the flame of the candle to the hem of Eleanor's nightdress. It was tattered and dry and set light without trouble. She looked down and saw the flames growing upon her and with a howl, leapt from left to right.

Once more she began her frenzied dance but this time trying to beat out the fire upon her with the palms of her hands. She cried out; the flames reached her middle and she shouted wordless sounds as it rasped her flesh. The old woollen cardigan over her dress began to singe. She flung herself to the ground and rolled and tumbled but the dry straw caught alight around her writhing body and the burning heat overwhelmed her, and a sickening scream filled the chambers and corridors but was cut short. Her hair caught fire and her arms flayed wildly about until, with a groan, she fell and was still, Eleanor's body engulfed by the blaze.

Theodore was shocked beyond measure. And then – from the light of her burning body – he caught sight of something which would have made his heart lurch had it been his own.

Through the odorous vapours of burning flesh and dense smoke he saw what he recognized as a massive chrysalis, as large as a cot. On closer inspection he found it was made of woven raffia, rope and thin branches. He looked down through the opening at the top; there within was the mummified remains of a rabbit dressed in the miniature clothes of a young child, half-covered with a silk blanket. And behind this strange construction were the remains of his own body on the stone tiles of the floor, the skull of it easily showing past dental work and missing teeth, with the ivory bones of the arms and legs spread-eagled from him, a hefty splinter of stone between two ribs, almost as long and sharp as found on a swordfish.

Theodore had been pinned like a butterfly.

A watch chain hung loosely from about the vertebrae and unusually shaped flints stood by the white bones of the feet.

Memories of the fateful day thirteen years before came to him in their scratching, terrible poignancy and he let out a howling echoed scream of revulsion.

Impressions from the past were a catalogue of insistent memories and they were presented as if flicking through index cards of himself; flashing before him, one after the other...

Thirteen years before, feigning death from arsenic poisoning; being carried up the stairs. Visiting Eleanor as she lay in her bedroom with labour pains then hiding after Dr. Snippet arrives to deliver the child. Moving the child to the spare room, dragging Eleanor's unconscious mind to wakefulness by slapping and shaking her to arousal; her immediate despair at losing her child again, tipping her more into maddened distress. Then Eleanor following to the insect collection in the attic, her mental state easy to persuade that her baby is safe there. Theodore listening as William returns and tries to find the body; mocking William as he considers he might be in the presence of a phantom; then chuckling upon William Stubb's anguish at the missing Eleanor. Returning to his attic to check on Eleanor's mental state, turning the key of the door and being pulled in, the door closed and locked; desperate features of a man condemned to die within the scorching embrace of a fire; the attic door opening again and Eleanor moving as if sleepwalking. Theodore escaping the flames and easily convincing Eleanor that the child is now in the church where her stillborn lay buried, knowing he must also leave the doomed house condemned by fire. Both coming down the staircases and Eleanor picking up the dead rabbit in the hall. Eleanor wrenching the entrance door open, now believing her child to be safe in her arms, naked but for strange fur, needing warmth and protection where she had prepared for Alastair's return; running to the abandoned church with her bewildered madness, Theodore following, insisting she return his watch, his prized possession.

The plumped moon sending silver light into the underground corridors, lighting their way until they reach the open wooden door to the catacomb. And there, before the eyes of the sculpted forms – shining as if alive – Eleanor placing the rabbit carcase into a handmade construction of raffia and branches; to her, the found child Alastair finally safe in his cot.

Theodore trying to calm her manic ways as she murmurs sweetness to what she saw as her baby but hissing to Theodore as he tried to intervene. Eleanor's piercing screams as Theodore pushes her out of the way, ready to pick up the dead animal to show her that that was all it was; Eleanor screaming more with her body quaking as Theodore pulls on the chain out from her pocket, Eleanor snatching the pocket watch back. A tug of war then, no less serious than the event at Thimriddy Fair, the chain snapping from the watch fob. She, snatching up a flint from the stone floor, battering tombs and granite ornaments in a maddened rage, until finally turning to Theodore. And with shock, Theodore seeing the flint raised high into the air, then down quickly to hit him sharply on the temple; sinking to the floor in shock and agony while Eleanor strikes him again and again...

The burned and battered body dragged to where it then lay with the strength of the insane, a large splinter of stone which had been knocked from a tomb puncturing and ripping his flesh as Eleanor hammers it with the flint into the chest of the deceiving cockroach; a total fragmentation of personality and normality for the already deranged Eleanor, gabbling and sobbing fitfully, now pulling tight the watch chain about Theodore's neck until the last of his life remaining left him.

Theodore felt his essence depart the place even then, perhaps to a denizen of the wicked undead or an unknown purgatory. Alastair's spirit blossomed and filled him, seeing through his own eyes once more; and he stared horror-stricken at the unidentified mass that burned on the ground, and to the bones of the long dead. He cried out and clutched his fists to his mouth, smoke stinging his startled eyes.

Choking, running blindly back into the main crypt and along the short corridor, finding the door there, drawing along the bar which held the door shut.

Pulling it open and seeing two misted silhouettes ahead, haloed with light. Running into a soft, warm mass, the last he knew as darkness descended; falling into a natural sleep.

'I've got him,' shouted Constable Flute and his voice echoed through the corridors of stone. 'He must have fainted.'

What's that burning? What a stench,' someone else remarked.

'Leave that for the moment, let's get him to the top.'

🙢

Alastair's sealed eyes opened as fast as any spring-loaded box lid and he looked up to the domed expanse above, sparse clouds rallying about the sun as they prepared to drag it over the horizon. A hint of the moon was beginning to gain definition. He greedily gulped the freshest of air to wash the smoke and dust from his dried throat and lungs.

He was uncertain of his whereabouts. Perhaps he was within his dreaming existence again – not that he cared.

A scarlet balloon was floating gracefully away, through the clear air, its basket holding two passengers, one of them seeming to glow with an effervescent light, the utmost love and affection emanating from her being.

Four misted shapes appeared in the firmament and as he looked with bleary eyesight, they became hazy plates which wore expressions of concern and sternness. He smiled generously, and then smiled the more for he found it an unusual but pleasant sensation.

'Hello,' he said, 'My name is Alastair Stubb,' and as he spoke, a shower of red admiral butterflies flew into the sky.

DAVID JOHN GRIFFIN is a writer, graphic designer and app designer, and lives in a small town by the Thames in Kent, UK with his wife Susan and two dogs called Bullseye and Jimbo. He is currently working on the first draft of a third novel as well as writing short stories for a novel-length collection.

His second novel, due for publication by Urbane in spring 2016, is a literary/psychological novel, entitled *Infinite Rooms*. He has independently-published a magical realism/paranormal novella called *Two Dogs At The One Dog Inn*. One of his short stories was shortlisted for The HG Wells Short Story competition 2012 and published in an anthology.

WWW.DAVIDJOHNGRIFFIN.COM

Urbane Publications is dedicated to
developing new author voices, and publishing
fiction and non-fiction that challenges, thrills and
fascinates.

From page-turning novels to innovative
reference books, our goal is to publish what
YOU want to read.

Find out more at
urbanepublications.com

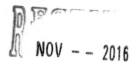